BLESS HIS CURSED SOUL

THE RIGHTE☠US SERIES

BLESS HIS CURSED SOUL

MEG COLLETT

CHAPTER 1

Fifteen hours before the events in the cemetery between the Skinned Man, Jeronimo, and Loey

"**W**HO DID YOU SAY YOU two were again? You're not with those damn Mormons, are you?"

"No, Grandmother Helene," Cross said patiently. "We're your grandkids. Cross and Dale. Darlene's kids."

Dale fought the urge to make a face. She sat with her legs crossed at the ankles, her hands cradling the cup of tea the nurse had poured for them. The assisted living apartment Grandmother Helene Rose lived in was expensive. Looked it too with its bespoke chaises and cherry wood fireplaces. But there wasn't enough money in the world to mask the stench of the elderly creeping toward their final sunset. The lights were low to keep from hurting Grandmother Helene's delicate eyes, though slips of sunshine slid through the drawn venetian blinds and cut across the gleaming wooden floors.

"That's right. The whore and the homo."

At the seventy-four-year-old woman's words, Dale spewed out the sip of tea she'd taken. Cross sputtered on his own spit beside her.

Their grandmother waved a papery-skinned hand. She presided over them from her wicker wheelchair with a Bible

1

in her lap. Her silver hair was coiled into tight curls, her skin appeared gray in the dim lighting, and cataracts clouded her blue eyes.

Grandmother Helene wagged her finger at Cross. "You know you'll burn in Hell for that."

Dale choked back her laughter. "Oh, he knows."

Cross shot Dale a glare. "Grandmother, we need you to sign some estate paperwork Mother sent with us, but I've left it out in the truck. I'm afraid the long drive from Righteous has left me scattered. I'll be right back."

Dale's smile fell off her face. "They're in your—"

"While I'm gone," he said to Grandmother Helene, "you two can talk about Dale here going off to rehab. That'll be nice, won't it?"

Cross stood in a flurry of tailored slacks and his Ralph Lauren dress shirt, pressed to within an inch of its life. As he breezed toward the front door, Dale snarled in a low-enough whisper so Grandmother Helene's hearing aid wouldn't pick it up, "Asshole."

The apartment door slammed shut, rattling the gilt mirror hanging beside it. Dale caught her reflection. Her golden curls were pulled back in a low bun, exposing the column of her pale neck and high cheekbones, hollowed with dark shadows. Her blue Gucci velvet tracksuit made the circles beneath her eyes look like bruises. She didn't dare stare too long, though, for fear of seeing *him*—her beautiful, broken mirror man.

Her heart panged with longing.

Longing and terror, because as much as seeing him scared her, she missed him when he wasn't there.

She tried to recall the first time she'd seen him. She couldn't, but only because he'd always been there.

She did, however, remember telling her mother about the mirror man for the first time. She'd been seventeen and terrified.

Upon hearing her daughter's tearful tale, Darlene Rose had taken Dale by the hand, looked her in the eye, and called her crazy. *"Don't you ever tell anyone about this, you hear me?"*

She'd twisted Dale's hand until her pinky broke.

To this day, her little finger stuck out at a funny angle. Mother had never taken her to the hospital. It served as a constant reminder that one's crazy was never to be spoken about, especially between mothers and daughters. Dale never told anyone else about the mirror man after that day. Her mirror man was her dark secret, her deepest insecurity.

Stop, she commanded herself. *You're crazy. He doesn't exist. And if he did, if he was real, he would never want you. No one wants you, so* stop.

"Did he say rehab?" Grandmother Helene asked, pulling Dale from her downward spiral. "Can't say I'm surprised. You always had the look of a boozer."

Dale put a smile on her face as she faced her grandmother. She hadn't been in the mood to put on a full face of makeup that morning after driving to South Carolina from Righteous through the night, but she regretted her decision. Makeup was armor, and she was going into battle defenseless.

"Actually," Dale said, "I prefer pills."

"Pills? There's nothing wrong with pills. Why do you need to go to rehab for medication?"

Dale reconsidered. Maybe the old bird wasn't so bad after all. "That's what I said."

Grandmother Helene waved a gnarled hand, gold rings flashing in the dim light. "Preposterous. You tell your mother I said so too. Ain't no reason someone can't take a few pills. Darlene always was too freethinking for her own good."

Dale held back the truth about taking more than a few pills. It wasn't the time to derail such pleasantries. However, she would admit she had an itty-bitty pill problem to anyone who asked. Luckily, this being the South and all, no one asked, though everyone in Righteous knew.

The situation was all so distasteful and messy, and Dale hated messy. Messy was for real addicts, the ones who broke into their parents' homes to hawk family heirlooms or lived in cardboard boxes and injected themselves with dirty needles beneath their fingernails.

Those people had real problems.

"My poison was always the drink. There wasn't nothing in this life that a good gin and tonic couldn't set right. With two limes." Grandmother Helene smacked her lips. Her red lipstick had bled into the fine lines around her lips. "Rose women have always loved our vices. It's one of the reasons most of us die so violently."

Dale sat up straighter on the pink linen couch. "How violent are we talking?"

"My sister drowned herself. Dreadful business. Much easier ways to go. My own mother was run over by a train. That was the booze again too, though. She'd wandered out onto the tracks. The carriage dragged her body clear to Asheville before anybody realized. Took them a while to collect all her pieces. And there was my aunt, who, rumor has it, liked to dress like a man. Got herself murdered by moonshiners up in the hills. Violence, you see, it's how we go. So mind yourself."

Dale was still feeling queasy over a woman's body being strewn from Righteous to Asheville, North Carolina as her grandmother continued.

"You're seein' him too. That's why Darlene is packing you out of Righteous. Same reason she sent me out here to die with these hicks. Payback for what I did to her in high school, I suppose. Vindictive bitch."

Dale had heard nothing else after that first sentence. It was too good for her to have heard correctly; she knew better than to trust seemingly good things. Regardless, her heart raced so fast she couldn't breathe. "Seeing him? Seeing ... *what?*"

"You heard me plain."

Dale sucked in her cheeks and held her breath. On its release, her question flowed out too. "You mean in the mirrors? The man? He's real? How can that be? Who is he and why is he in there?"

"Lock the door before that brother of yours gets back."

She did as her grandmother had instructed, moving quickly on numb feet. On her return, the only sound that filled the room was Grandmother Helene's wheezing.

"You can't let them hear you speak about the mirrors," Grandmother Helene said with sharp smacks of her lips. "They put you on the medicine that makes everything fuzzy so you can't see the shadows anymore to look for him. Not that I can see him this far from Righteous ..." She paused, perhaps wandering down a trail of misplaced memories. That wheezing had stopped, and Dale wondered if Grandmother also sometimes held her breath until she saw stars.

"Grandmother? Who is he? Why is he there?"

"Sometimes," Grandmother Helene continued as though she hadn't stopped, "they put you on the harder stuff. It takes away everything. Makes ... makes you forget about him." She patted her Bible. "But I try to remember what I can. I try."

Dale sat on the edge of the couch, close to tumbling off. Was her grandmother so senile? But how could they both be having the same visions?

"Please," she begged. "He's real? How can he—"

"Listen to me, girl," Grandmother Helene snarled. Dale nodded to show she was listening. "You do what I couldn't. What your mother wouldn't. Damn coward. Refused to acknowledge his presence. Put me in here for suggesting she was an ignorant cow for insisting she couldn't see him. She and her worthless sisters left him in there. I was so close after finding that book, but she wouldn't listen. Get him out, girl, and whatever you do, don't you dare get no help from a Keene."

Dale's insides went ice cold. She was transfixed and utterly numbed by the flood of information. Someone else knew her darkest secret; someone else had the answers.

"Why not?" she asked, breathless.

"They're the reason he's in there. It goes all the way back to Knox. Leave that no-good family out of this. Ellery put on like a saint. Everyone worshiped her, but she played God, she did. She damned him and she liked it. Ain't no good come from them Keenes."

Dale didn't mean to, but she thought about Loey and how weird she'd been acting. She thought about Jeronimo James and how everything changed after he'd strolled into town. Did Loey know about this too? Was she also connected to the mirror man?

Dale kept these thoughts to herself and said instead, "Yes, ma'am, but how do I help him? How do I get him out?"

"Let me show you something. It'll help you. Do this and you'll get him out, but you tell no one. That's the mistake I made, you hear me? Ellery found out what I was doing, and I confided in her. Then she and Darlene conspired to get me out of Righteous and far away from him. They'll do you like they did me. He can't leave Righteous, you see. That's why I can't help him no more."

Grandmother Helene grappled with the Bible in her lap, her hands fluttering like doves around the old black leather. She opened the good book. Thick black lines—curving and slashing—marred the scripture. Her grandmother tore through the pages until she found one in Revelations and ripped it free. She flapped it at Dale.

Dale took it with a shaking hand. The symbol scrawled

across the scripture was shaped like a *V* with two downward curling parallel lines.

"What's this?"

"Put it behind a private mirror only you use," Grandmother Helene said. "It'll open the door."

"What door?"

"The door that will take you to him. Now, shush."

The apartment doorknob jiggled. A second later, a knock sounded on the wood.

Dale's mouth fell open as she stared at her grandmother. The elderly woman nodded to the page in her granddaughter's hand. Dale stuffed the page into her purse. She had so many more questions—the main one being who the mirror man was, followed closely by what would happen if she put this symbol behind her mirror—but Cross knocked again. On baby deer shaking legs, she tottered to the door and opened it.

Cross saw her face, and his self-satisfied smirk dropped. "Are you okay? You look like you've seen a ghost."

Dale hadn't, not yet anyway, but she might if her grandmother's symbol worked. She swayed from the information. Cross's hand flashed out to catch her elbow.

"I'm sorry," he said in a rush. "Leaving like that was a dick move. Come on, let's get her to sign Mother's paperwork so we can get the hell out of here."

Dale managed a nod. Within minutes, Cross was walking Grandmother Helene through the estate paperwork while Dale sat on the pink sofa, watching a master at work. Her grandmother, who'd spoken to her so sharply, feigned senility as she asked Cross to repeat himself countless times. Dale wondered if the hearing aids were an act too since she'd heard Cross coming before he knocked.

Had her grandmother been trapped here, waiting years for another Rose woman crazy enough to free the man in her mirror? What if Dale had never come? Would Helene have taken the secret of this strange symbol to her grave, letting her descendants suffer in ignorance?

Cross finished up with the estate paperwork. With fake cheerfulness, he said, "It was good to see you, Grandmother Helene. Dale, are you ready?"

"Ah," she fumbled, stirring back to life, her skin freezing cold. She had a million thoughts, but she felt as trapped as the old woman clutching her Bible in her wicker chair. As Dale stared at her, Grandmother Helene subtly shook her head. "I—I'm ready."

Cross hugged their grandmother first, bending low over the wheelchair. Dale took her turn. The old woman's nails bit into Dale's back as she brought her mouth to Dale's ear.

"It's your task now." Her breath smelled like decay.

Dale couldn't speak. She stood upright, and the room spun.

Grandmother Helene waved them off. "Go on. It's time for my nap."

Dale followed Cross back through the building and past sweeping windows that overlooked courtyards full of flowers on their last bloom before fall. Beneath the vaulted ceilings, the walls were painted a timeless beige and adorned with white crown molding. The elderly wheeled around in their chairs or used canes to shuffle about, their chatter like birds flocking from tree to tree. Cross signed out and pretended to flirt with the nurses again for good measure. They turned their flowery goodbyes to her; Dale didn't respond.

Out in the parking lot, Cross started the truck. Dale paused at the open passenger door and stared up at her brother.

A frown creased his handsome face. Any other time, Dale would have warned him about getting wrinkles, but concern filled his eyes as they searched her face for the cause of her mood change. "What's wrong? What happened after I left?"

"We're going home."

His frown faded, though the concern lingered. She might be the older sibling, but Cross had always taken care of her. She knew that finding her on the urine-caked bathroom floor of a pill house in Little Cricket Trailer Park had messed with his head, but in true Rose family fashion, they hadn't spoken about it. It wasn't that they couldn't talk about their deep, personal issues; they had a lot of shit between them, and if they opened the floodgates, they would have to talk about how Cross was in love with her husband. And no one, especially Cross, was ready for that, so Dale would have to shoulder the burden of her disasters for a little longer.

"If Grandmother said something, you know it's the dementia. She didn't mean nothing by it, I'm sure. Besides, you need to do this for yourself. What happened last time wasn't okay. You need—"

"She didn't say anything." The page Grandmother Helene had given her burned like a freshly fired bullet in Dale's purse. "I'm not ready for rehab. I want to go home."

"I can't let you do that." He shook his head, and Dale wanted to punch his pretty-boy face.

"It's not your decision." Her hand tightened around the door handle. She considered slamming it shut and calling a taxi. She didn't need her brother's permission to go home.

Every minute she stood here arguing was another minute she wasn't putting this symbol behind her mirror.

"Come on," he pleaded. It hurt her more than she'd thought it would to hear him sound like that. "You can do this. You have to. I'm afraid I'll find you dead in that pill house next time."

His words stung more than his begging tone, but she shoved the pain down. "Oh, please, Cross. Don't be so dramatic. Take me home or I'm not getting in this truck."

"You're going."

"I'm not."

"What would Mother say?"

"Screw what she would say."

"She'll use this against you. Think of all the Thanksgivings and Easters. All those jabs she'll make about you not sticking with anything. Think about how horrible the Christmases will be with the entire family there to hear."

Dale almost shuddered. He had a point, but terrifying as it was, she wasn't wavering. She needed to get back to Righteous, back to her house and the mirror in her closet.

"Cross," she warned.

His shoulders slumped, but he tried one last time. "Please, for me, Dale. Do it for me."

She bit the inside of her cheek so hard it bled. She *could* go to rehab for thirty days for Cross and test the page after returning to Righteous. She could wait. She didn't need to know right away. The mirror man only came around now and then, but her brother had always been there for her. He was the only man she'd ever loved.

Cross waited. His blue eyes, so like hers, stared without blinking, not daring to break the spell.

It's your task now.

Metallic bitterness from biting her cheek to ribbons leaked down her throat. She was silly, crazy even, to think she had another option. She was choosing her mirror man over her own brother. It broke her heart, but her heart was used to it. Sometimes, she thought she thrived on pain.

Simply, to keep herself hidden, she said, "I'm sorry, Cross."

Twenty minutes before the events in the cemetery

Righteous was asleep by the time they drove down Main Street just before midnight. The exhaust from Cross's truck broke the night's silence with its rumbling growl, a beast prowling the streets.

The blinds were closed in Deadly Sin Roasters. Dale had thought about asking Loey to come over, but her grandmother's warning about the Keenes still rang in her ears. It wasn't that Dale didn't trust Loey—she'd *die* for her best friend—but the mirror man was Dale's darkest secret and the thought of sharing it terrified her.

More important than her fear of being truly crazy was protecting Loey at any cost. Dale would do anything to protect her best friend, and that meant keeping Loey well clear of her messy life.

Cross put his truck in park outside her dark house.

"Go on so I can make sure you get inside safe." Cross stifled yet another yawn. As a man and a proud Ford owner, he'd turned down every offer to let her drive back from South Carolina.

Dale popped a kiss on his cheek. After the long drive, she was frantic to get inside. Her hands were clammy with sweat. "Thanks, Cross. I love you."

She hopped out, her mind on the symbol in her purse, and tugged her suitcase free from the truck's backseat.

Before she could slam the door, he asked, "You sure you're okay?"

"Don't worry about me," she said with a jittery smile. "I'm fine. Next time, we'll try rehab."

His face shuttered with pain. "Next time. See you, sis."

Her throat too tight to respond, she shut the door softly. She hurried into her house and locked the front door behind her.

Travis clearly hadn't been home since his father's funeral on Friday. Their maid had come that morning, and the carpets showed no footprints. The smell of his cloying cologne, which she hated but Cross loved, didn't linger throughout the house.

Still, as a precaution, she called out, "Travis?"

Nothing.

She dropped her purse on the entry table, kicked off her Gucci slides, and pulled out the page with the *V*-shaped symbol. Her heart rate kicked up and sweat broke out across her skin. She felt high. A good high, too. Not the kind polluted by generic pills or pussied-down milligrams or bullshit time-released capsules. But the good high of a new pill on a low tolerance and empty stomach first thing in the morning, when nothing was ruined and everything was clean and bright and shiny.

She took the stairs two at a time, heaving her suitcase upstairs with her. The plush white carpet absorbed her hurried footfalls as she jogged down the hall to her sanctuary. Unlike the rest of the house's generic light colors, her bedroom was painted a moody navy. Above the bed, a Jackson Pollock print hung, its brutal slashes of red paint across the canvas reminding her of blood.

The closet was large enough to be a master bedroom unto itself. She deposited her suitcase next to her dressing bench and went straight to the floor-to-ceiling mirror that leaned against the back wall. The thing weighed a hundred pounds and had cost a fortune, but Dale took a specific sort of glee in spending her family's money. She'd paid for everything in this house, including the house itself, so why not have what she wanted? She'd enjoyed watching Travis go pale as he'd read the bill for the mirror.

Her hands shook as she stuck double-sided boob tape to the top of the symbol's page. Grunting and cursing, she eased the mirror off the wall and leaned it against her shoulder. A page was already stuck to the mirror's backing. Sticking her page between her teeth, she tore off the second page.

It was a symbol exactly like the one Grandmother Helene had given her, but it was clearly *A*-shaped.

Dale hesitated. She certainly hadn't put the foreign page back there. Someone else had been in her house without her knowledge. She had no clue where the page had come from or what it meant, but she was too impatient to consider the mystery any longer.

Juggling the pages, she crookedly adhered her grandmother's symbol onto the back of the mirror. She squinted into the darkness behind the mirror to make sure the *V* was right side up.

With the second page in hand, she settled the mirror back against the wall. Her reflection showed a young woman shaking with fear and excitement—and wild, boundless *hope*.

The closet's lights flashed, but they came back on so quickly it could have been a power surge. She returned her attention to the mirror.

The reflection was wrong.

She was staring at her reflection certainly enough, but behind mirror-Dale was a black, arid landscape covered in glittering ebony dust that twisted up into mini-tornadoes. Jagged black mountains rose in the distance. Lights like a billion fireflies flickered through the air, giving the setting a shifting quality of light. The wind blew hard enough to whip up mirror-Dale's hair, though she stared unblinkingly at closet-Dale.

Mirror-Dale cocked her head and studied closet-Dale. She lifted her hand to the mirror to touch closet-Dale's fingertips.

Mesmerized, closet-Dale settled her fingertips against her reflection's.

Mirror-Dale mouthed something short and repetitive.

"What?" closet-Dale asked. "I can't hear you."

Mirror-Dale kept repeating the word, her face growing more animated. Closet-Dale had never been good at reading lips, but it looked like her reflection was shouting, *"Hey!"*

Sirens whirred past closet-Dale's house. She glanced back. For a horrible moment, she thought the cops were coming for her. On her nightstand, the clock read a quarter past midnight. Based on the louder and softer whirring, she guessed the police were heading up Devil's Maw. A fraction of her mind not caught up in the sheer revelation of this moment worried that the police were heading to Loey's.

She forgot about her friend as soon as her focus returned to the mirror.

Everything had swapped. Closet-Dale wasn't in her closet anymore. She was mirror-Dale, staring at her reflection standing in her closet.

"Hey!" mirror-Dale shouted at her reflection. "Hey! Hey!"

"What?" closet-Dale asked, her droning voice taking forever to finish the word. "I can't hear you."

Mirror-Dale choked on her terror. What had her grandmother done? She grew frantic. "Hey! Hey! Please!"

The new closet-Dale looked over her shoulder, but her movements were in super slow motion like her voice had been. Mirror-Dale could read the clock on the nightstand over closet-Dale's shoulder: a quarter past midnight.

"Hey!" mirror-Dale kept shouting, but slow-motion-closet-Dale never turned back.

The air smelled different, reminding mirror-Dale of the time she'd burned her hair while curling it, too high to notice the smoke rising from the metal wand. The wind billowed high overhead. She didn't dare look up.

With closet-Dale still glancing over her shoulder toward the sound of the sirens, Dale slowly turned around, the dirt needling her bare feet.

The scenery was just as she'd seen from the closet side of the mirror. The wind gusted in spirals across a plain of black dust. To her right, a small hill swelled, concealing whatever was on the other side. To her left, the expanse stretched into nothing but darkness and shadows. In front of her, the mountains loomed like hulking mirrored giants, reflecting the surrounding world like a giant movie screen. All around, the strange twinkling lights lent a magical luminance that danced across the landscape. The flapping sounded again overhead.

The sky had no moon or clouds. Black silk stretched to the horizon and moved as if an invisible hand were shaking the dust from its delicate fabric. The light reflected off the mountains played across the fabric sky like a muted parody of the Northern Lights. Between its folds, a creature with bat-like wings and a long tail flew and released a cawing scream. An answering call echoed far into the mountains. The creature banked on those massive wings and headed toward the mountain peaks.

Beneath her feet, the ground *breathed*.

A scream lodged in her throat, Dale whirled around to launch herself at the mirror, but the mirror was gone.

She was trapped on the other side.

CHAPTER 2

The same time as the events in the cemetery

T HE GROUND EXPANDED AND CONTRACTED in long, slow pulls like she was walking across the belly of a slumbering beast. The grit was fine as glass and cut her feet with each hobbling step. Dale shivered in her tracksuit. The wind tore strands of hair free from her bun, but between gusts, she picked up hints of noise. She stopped to listen. The firefly lights danced around her.

Human screams, not the dinosaur kind, came from over the hill she walked beside.

She raced up the slope and the sound grew clearer. Definitely human screaming. Familiar and male, too.

She crested the hill and looked down into a valley. A ragged white rock bed twisted through the base like a dried-up salt river, and a wall of tumbling lights lit the entire black-dusted expanse. After the near-dark on the other side of the hill, these lights blazed as bright as sunlight. She shielded her eyes until they adjusted.

The light wall was a series of tightly spaced vertical streams, like the bars on a jail cell, but it wasn't the galaxy's scale that had caught her attention; it was the *hole* in it.

Most of the light streams were solid, their lights flicking up and down the string columns like cars on a highway, except the lights near the hole had ripped loose and were strobing in the wind. The hole felt *wrong* in Dale's core, like she was walking too close to a ledge above a sheer drop.

In the center of the tear, clusters of gray and green and a hazy silver circle came through from the other side of the wall.

Perhaps she was a dumb blonde like Cross often called her teasingly. It took her a moment of unattractive gaping to realize the silver circle was Earth's *moon*. Those gray bits were headstones; the green clusters were grass and trees. She recognized Blackmore Cemetery in a blinding rush of euphoria.

Through the lights, someone shouted, "Stop!"

It was Jeronimo. He was on the other side of the lights, barely visible on the ground as he crawled toward the gaping hole.

"Get out while you can," he kept shouting. "Barty!"

A second figure stumbled out of the lights. He grappled with what looked like a skinned eel with human legs and arms. The monster bit at his face, narrowly missing his throat. The tall man threw it away from the hole and into the white rocky riverbed. It screeched furiously as it grappled over the rocks.

The tall man looked up, panting heavily and shoulders heaving.

It was the mirror man.

"Oh," she breathed out. *"Oh."*

The lights at his back made his hair look like a halo atop his head, and his features were angelic enough that Dale wondered if she hadn't died and gone to Heaven. Another scream broke through her daydream.

"Get him! Loey, help him!"

Loey stood silhouetted in the lights. Her hands tied the flapping light streams together. The hole—the closest way to freedom Dale had—started to shrink.

The monster got to its feet in the riverbed. The mirror man, with his back turned to the creature, didn't notice.

"Watch out!" Dale shouted.

The monster leaped onto the tall man's back. Together, they collided into the wall of lights. Loey tied the threads faster, her hands pale flashes through the lights.

"Wait!" Dale shouted at her best friend. "Wait on me!"

The wind carried her voice away. The top of the hill felt safe, but it was too far away. Thinking only of escaping this world, she sprinted down the hill.

The mirror man wrapped his arm around the monster's neck and dragged it back from the lights step by step.

Dale couldn't run fast enough on her torn feet; she hadn't reached the rock bed yet, and Loey had nearly mended the hole in the lights. Only her face and neck were visible. Before she knotted the last of the loose streams, she nodded to the tall man. He nodded back, straining against the fighting monster.

"Loey!" Dale reached the dry riverbed. She leaped over the larger rocks, slashing her feet on the jagged dirt. "Wait! Loey! It's me!"

The mirror man's head jerked toward her. Panic flashed in his eyes. "No! Get back!"

"Wait!" Dale screamed at Loey, ignoring him.

Loey didn't hear. The hole was gone except for a few dim slivers of the dark cemetery beyond.

In his focus on her, the mirror man's hold on the monster slipped. It jerked free and blocked her path to the hole.

Dale slid to a stop in the riverbed, her blood turning the rocks slippery.

The monster's lipless mouth snarled over teeth yellowed with rot, gums black and oozing infection. It smelled like week-old roadkill—the dead bits even the crows wouldn't pick at anymore. Thick scars mutated the naked skin stretched across the monster's gnarled bones.

Its gnawed-off nose lifted, scenting her.

"Run!" her mirror man shouted and tore off after the monster.

The monster tore off after *her*.

He tackled the monster mere feet away from where she stood, frozen. They landed in a heap of twisted limbs, scarred ones and perfect ones.

Spurred into action, she skittered around them. Mirror man or not, she sprinted past him and straight for the teeny-tiny hole in the lights. One thing she knew for certain: she would never sacrifice herself for a man, attractive though he might be. She didn't glance back to make sure the monster hadn't bitten the man's head off.

She hit the light wall at full speed to see if she could run right through it. She couldn't. Of course it wouldn't be that easy.

The lights zapped against her like sparks of electricity. She crouched beside the nearest sliver, too small for her to stuff more than a few fingers through. She pressed her face to it instead.

Blackmore Cemetery stretched before her. The poplar at its heart rose toward the night sky, close enough to touch if she could have fit her arm through the rip.

"Loey?" she called into the night beyond the wall.

Something stirred on the ground on the other side. She peered down. Jeronimo lay on the ground. Blood streamed from his nose and coated the lower half of his face. His eyes fluttered open, his gaze focusing on her.

"Jer—"

The monster smashed her into the light wall.

With the full force of a massive body on her back, the lights seared into her skin, and she thought she heard the lights screaming. Or maybe she was screaming. She couldn't tell. The monster's breath, strong enough to make her eyes water, poured over her shoulder.

It bit her.

The pain was blinding, and she considered going limp and letting it rip her to shreds.

Screw that. She threw an elbow into the monster's gut to dislodge its teeth from the juncture of her neck and shoulder. They tumbled backward from the screaming wall. She thrashed with all she had, but its teeth only sank in deeper. A flash of hazel eyes filled her vision. The mirror man wrapped his hands around the monster's jaw and tore it off Dale. He flung the monster far enough away to buy them a few seconds of respite.

"Thank you." Her shoulder pulsed with a heartbeat of its own. "What the hell—"

The man heaved her over his shoulder, caveman style, and ran *away* from the wall. Away from her only way out.

"No, no!" She pummeled his muscular back, her head bouncing hard enough to make her see stars. "I have to get out!"

She craned her neck up. The monster had someone in its clutches back at the light wall, the body yanked halfway across the light wall through a tear far too small for his big body. The monster strained with every bit of strength its scarred body contained.

She slapped the mirror man's ass to get his attention. "Hey! That's Jeronimo!"

The mirror man dropped her and reeled around.

Dale barely managed to land on her cut-to-ribbons feet. "He won't fit through that," she said to herself because the mirror man was already gone.

He raced headlong for the wall. Dale hesitated. It would be stupid to run after him to help, but if Jeronimo's tight, round ass could squeeze through that hole, she could too.

Cursing under her breath, she sprinted after the mirror man.

He hurled himself at the monster. It dropped Jeronimo, who lay like a rag doll halfway across the wall, the lights

21

shrinking around him like they might cut him clean in half.

The mirror man pummeled the creature's face while it wrapped its hands around his throat. The monster kicked the mirror man off him and sent him flying into the light wall. He hit the ground in a stunned heap. The monster jerked Jeronimo again.

Jeronimo's body didn't move as easily as before, and as Dale limped the last few feet back across the river, she saw Loey on the other side, pulling on his leg.

The switch flipped in Dale. Without thinking, she let out a war cry and jumped onto the monster's back.

It snarled and spat, releasing its hold on Jeronimo, who surged back across the wall. The rip in the lights his body had stretched shrank back into a minuscule tear.

Dale pounded on the monster's back and neck in a blind rage. Its scarred skin felt gnarled beneath her fists. There was nothing remotely human about the creature; it felt wrong and evil. She wrapped her nails around a large knot of flesh at the back of its neck and *yanked*. Black sludge oozed out from beneath its skin. She peeled the flesh halfway down the creature's back, exposing the white ribcage and spine surrounded by seeping black blood and thick, viscous goo.

Howling, it ripped her off its back and threw her away. She scrambled backward. It snarled down at her, fists balled in rage, but tears welled in its eyes from the pain. Its fists shook like tree limbs in winter. Between snarls, it whimpered and hissed, spit pooling in its destroyed mouth.

Somehow, at some time, this thing had been a man.

Dale's heart wrenched over causing something, even a monster, such pain.

The monster could have killed her, but it left her on the ground. It tore off into the billowing black dust of the plains, a trail of cries left in its wake.

Dust and the monster's dripping insides covered Dale's skin and tracksuit. Her feet hurt so badly she didn't dare stand. She pushed her hair away from her eyes, smearing the monster's blood across her forehead.

The mirror man turned and stared down at her. She thought she couldn't possibly be any more shocked after getting herself stuck inside her mirror, but her mirror man spoke and proved her wrong.

"Dale," he said, stupefied, "what the hell are you doin' here?"

CHAPTER 3

Present Time

THE POLICE CRUISER ROLLED TO a stop in Loey's driveway.

Before she could reach for the car's door handle, Matt was out of the driver's seat and rushing around the hood of his cruiser. He opened the door and helped her out. Dewey barked inside the house, and Boltz paced in the living room's bay window.

"Thank you," she said, breathless and exhausted, her body a dull humming of pain. It turned out her ribs weren't broken, just badly bruised. It was nothing compared to the pain after her accident on Tempest, but it reminded her all too easily of that time.

"Let me help you inside."

"I need to check on the animals."

"I'll check on them. Lean on me and let's get you inside."

As he helped her to the back door, Loey glanced over her shoulder. Down the hill at the church, a light shone in the rectory. Farther away, toward the valley on the other side of town, the Sunday morning sun readied to spill its light across the town and wash Righteous clean of the night's sins.

Dewey greeted her with a slobber bath as Matt eased her inside.

25

He used his body to shield her from the big dog's more enthusiastic welcomes that might jostle her battered ribs. Boltz sauntered into the kitchen, his fried tail swishing.

Seeing the cat, Matt chuckled. "I wish we all had as many lives as that cat. Can't say he looks all the worse for wear, though."

"Did you call my cat ugly, Matt Everton?"

"No, ma'am. Here, sit down. Get back, Dew. Calm down, she's fine."

After getting her settled into a chair at the table and pushing the dog outside, he refilled the animals' food bowls and checked their water. Boltz slipped outside through the screen door.

"Can you check the water in the barn?" Loey hated feeling helpless. "And hay for Butters. Alfalfa pellets for the goats. The hens need—"

"Lo." Matt crouched in front of her so they were at eye level. He took her hands in his. His simple brown eyes and callused hands brought her back from all the things that had happened in the cemetery last night. Once she'd settled down, he continued. "I'll make you some tea and a sandwich. Then I'll take care of your animals. Sit here and rest."

Before she could thank him, he kissed her cheek. His lips lingered against her skin. He smelled of pine tree sap and burnt coffee, his milk-chocolate breath covered in cheap gas-station mints. His favorite candy had been Hershey's Kisses since high school, and she figured the mint was for her sake. Maybe he'd thought she would need more than an escort home.

He drew back to stare into her eyes. "I can still pretend you didn't tell me anything last night."

She leaned as far away from him as she could in her chair. "I lied, Matt. Folton is innocent."

"That bastard is *not* innocent. If I'd known what he was

26

doing to you, I would've killed him myself."

Loey's ribs contracted, and a breath wheezed from her lips. Eyes softening, Matt's hand slid up her arm. He squeezed her shoulder.

"It's eating me alive. I can't live like this anymore. Secrets aren't good for people. They'll tear you and your family apart."

"Did your grandparents know?"

She shook her head.

"Loey." His voice wrapped around her name like he'd spoken it since they were children, and he had. He was familiar with her on a level most people outside her family weren't. It was comfortable, and Loey leaned into his warmth.

"I want the lies to stop."

"He'll be released. You know that, right?"

She fought back a shiver. "I know."

"He won't come near you, not if he wants to keep breathing."

"Matt—"

He kissed her cheek again, closer to the scarred corner of her mouth, like he was daring her. He stood, and she figured she'd read the moment wrong.

"Where're your tea leaves again?"

"Can you please check on the animals first? I'm worried about Butters. You know he gets testy if he doesn't have his hay bag full."

"They're taken care of."

Jeronimo leaned against the doorframe like he'd been standing there for a while, watching them. Loey blushed. Her mind tumbled through everything he could've seen, like Matt holding her hands or kissing her so close to her mouth—the mouth Jeronimo had kissed only a few hours before.

"You shouldn't skulk around like that." Matt tried for an admonishing tone, but the effect dissolved beneath the way his voice quivered from the fright.

Loey took in Jeronimo's pale skin and blackest eyes. She thought he leaned so casually against the doorframe because he didn't have the strength to hold himself up too long.

"Or what?" Jeronimo challenged Matt, unsmiling. "You'll shoot me?"

Matt squared his shoulders so he stood taller. Even with the extra inch, he didn't come close to Jeronimo's wide-shouldered height, slumped as he was in Loey's doorway.

"The people in this town might have welcomed you, but I don't buy it." Matt kept his hand near his gun to prove his point. "I don't trust you, Mr. James."

Jeronimo straightened off the doorframe. Matt settled his hand against his gun. Warming to the game enough to find the energy to muster it, Jeronimo smiled.

It was the smile he'd given Loey the night she'd caught him in the church, right before she shot him. It didn't bode well.

With effort and a hiss of pain, she stood. "Both of you are acting like two old tom cats. It's embarrassing to watch."

Matt kept his eyes on Jeronimo. "Do you want him to leave?"

"He's fine, Matt. Thank you for the ride home."

"You're okay alone?"

He hadn't said it, but she heard the words just the same: *with him.*

Jeronimo chimed in. "She's fine. I'll keep an eye on her."

Jeronimo made the response sound like a promise of sexual misdeeds. He was half dead, and her ribs were mush, but he made Matt believe that something salacious would happen between them.

"Goodnight, Loey. I'll check on you tomorrow." To Jeronimo, he added, "I'm watching you."

He hit his shoulder against Jeronimo's as he exited through the back door. Jeronimo rocked back on his heels but kept from falling. Outside, the cruiser's door slammed, then the engine revved. Matt tore down the driveway, slinging gravel.

Loey carefully sank back into her chair, and Jeronimo stumbled over to the table, pulled out his own seat, and crashed into it.

"Did you actually feed the animals, or was that part of the pissing contest too?" she asked.

Jeronimo leaned his arms on the table. His lips were dry and cracked. It reminded her of another dry mouth, and she had to look away.

"I took care of them."

They sat in silence long enough that Jeronimo put his forehead against his forearms and possibly dozed off. Dewey came back in and ate his food, then eyed Boltz's bowl before the cat swaggered back inside and set the dog's wandering eye to rights with a smack of his paw.

"Your brother wasn't burned," Loey found the energy to say.

Without lifting his head, Jeronimo mumbled against his arms, "He wasn't."

"He was warning us the entire time. We couldn't see his features because of the shadows on his skin when he came through the tatter."

"He was."

"The Skinned Man is someone else. He was there with you two that night. He was the one you saw burning in the flames."

Jeronimo looked up. The slackness in his jaw proved he hadn't thought that through or simply hadn't had the energy to put it together.

"Three people were at the still during the storm," she went on. "You, Barty, and whoever you saw in the flames."

"Frankie was there too."

"But she was already well dead, right? She couldn't have made it to the still."

"No," Jeronimo said, his voice far, far away. "She couldn't've."

"The Skinned Man is the stronger thing across the Seam my grandparents warned you about. So, who was the third person at the still that night?"

"I …" He searched the knots in the table's wood for answers he couldn't find in himself. "I don't know."

"Think back to fifty-six. Did someone hate you or Barty? Someone's family member he killed? Or that revenuer? The one you said sent you up onto the ridge to hide."

"Who?" Jeronimo frowned, his brow creasing and his eyes squinting at her.

"The revenuer." She cast her thoughts back to the night he'd told her the story of the moonshine still's explosion, though she knew she was remembering correctly.

"There was no revenuer. I wasn't in hiding."

"You told me his snooping around town had sent you up into the woods."

"I never said that."

He'd slipped into a void without knowing it. A husk sat at her kitchen table. The man was gone. A chill cascaded down her spine.

"Whoever was there that night, we need to figure it out and soon," she added. "We need to seal up the Seam."

The words drew him back into himself. "I have to get Barty out of there first. You promised to help me."

"I remember and I will, but how are we going to do that? If being near a tatter made your nosebleed, you would've gotten sick right before the Skinned Man unleashed those snakes in the church. You didn't. It's your brother."

"I realize that now."

"How will you both survive on this side of the Seam?"

His jaw clenched with resolve. "It doesn't matter. I can't make him pay anymore for something he didn't do."

It didn't seem like the morning to push him, but he was

30

talking in circles and forgetting entire chunks of his history and it was *scaring* her.

"But he did kill Frankie. That's why you put him there." She paused. "Right?"

"It … it doesn't feel right anymore. I can't … remember the 'why' so easily after all this time." His lips trembled as though he could wither up right there at her table and blow away with the early morning light.

"Okay," she soothed. "What do we do about the Skinned Man? He nearly escaped. That can't happen again. If he gets loose in town …" She couldn't finish the thought. Thinking about everyone he could kill, could rip apart—Mr. Weebly, Ms. Ida May and her biddies, Mayor Goody and Riley, Martha Lee, Waylon, Emma Todd, Dale, Cross—terrified her to the bone.

"Your grandparents must have a book on Tending. Ruby had one to help me after the explosion in fifty-six. It might have the answers your grandparents were collecting about sealing the Seam."

"Why didn't you mention this sooner?" she spluttered.

He raked a hand over his day-old beard. "I thought we wouldn't need it."

"You mean *you* wouldn't need it because your only plan was to kill your brother and hightail it out of town. You were going to leave me with all the loose ends—literally."

He flinched as she delivered each word, but she didn't regret them. "I've taught you all I know about Tending. I'd hoped it would be enough, but yesterday proved it's not. We need help."

"You're a real jerk sometimes," she said without mustering the necessary bite.

"I'm sorry."

She was too exhausted, and too shattered from the fight, to dwell on her anger. "We find the book and solve who the Skinned Man is before he tries to escape again, all while figuring out if you and Barty can exist on the same side of the Seam."

"We don't need to know who the Skinned Man is to trap him."

"You would do that to a person? Trap them, nameless, across the Seam?"

Her words defeated him. He put his head in his hands, but he didn't take back the words. "Christ, I'm thirsty."

"Do you want some water?"

"Won't do no good."

She wished it didn't, but her heart ached for him. What would it be like to feel such exhaustion or thirst or desire and know it could never be sated? How demoralizing. How sad.

Dewey's peaceful snores filled the silence as the sun bathed the house with fresh daylight. Loey squinted against it.

"Lo," Jeronimo said.

She turned to him. "What?"

"I'm sorry."

He looked so cursed she couldn't hate him. She should hate him after all he'd done: ignoring her grandparents' calls for help and swooping into town like he could kill his brother and waltz right back out, leaving her with nothing but the knowledge of what her family had done for generations before her. She had many reasons to hate him, but they had too much to do, and after last night, it felt like they'd come too far.

Because there were no other words, she said, "I know you are."

"Are you tired?"

She nodded.

He dipped his chin. "Then let's sleep."

"But you can't."

"No." He reached across the table for her hand. "But I'll hold you while you do."

Taking it, he pulled her to her feet. They stood by her table, her hand in his hands. His thumb brushed across the soft skin between her thumb and forefinger, the flesh thin over the bones and nerves. Her nose tingled like the devil.

He was waiting for her to move first, or for her to tell him to leave. Before doubt could make her waver, she led him from the kitchen, down the hall, and to her bedroom.

He drew the room's blinds and curtains, sealing out the sunlight. He kicked off his boots and, stunning her completely, pulled off his shirt and belt. His jeans hung low on his hips beneath that patch of ash-blond hair below his belly button. The v-shaped muscles of his hips led up to a stack of muscular abs. Dots and slashing scars pocked his chest and ran over his shoulders onto his back, out of view.

He climbed into her bed and held back the covers for her.

She should've been too tired to get so flustered at the sight of him, but damn her hormones. She spun away from him, her cheeks hot.

Heavens, what now? Did she take off her pants? Her shoes, for sure. They were covered in dirt. She started there. They thudded beside the bed with two hollow thunks. Dewey, unperturbed as ever, settled onto his pillow with a soft grunt.

"I'm ..." She turned back to Jeronimo. He had his head propped on his hand as if he knew he might be waiting a while. "I'm going to wash up."

After snatching clean pajamas from her dresser, she rushed from the room. In the bathroom, she splashed cold water on her face, brushed her teeth and hair, and did whatever else she could think of to kill more time. She was too exhausted to shower. She peeled off her dirty, bloody clothes and stuffed them into the overflowing laundry bin. She would have to do the washing soon or she'd run out of clean clothes. Once she was dressed in her pj's and out of ways to stall, she stared at her reflection in the mirror.

The Skinned Man loomed behind her. He snapped his teeth at her. The fear crashed over her like a wave, and a scream rose in her throat—until she realized it wasn't the Skinned Man behind her, but a deep fold in her shower curtain casting a shadow.

She squeezed her eyes shut. The mirror was warded. Her home was safe. *She* was safe. The most dangerous thing she faced was the soulless man in her bed—and the far more dangerous fact that she *liked* him there.

She turned off the light and left the bathroom.

Back in her bedroom, she found the room smelled intensely of him. His clothes were heaped on her floor in the shadows. Dewey snored softly on his pillow, content to have everyone safely back home.

Careful with her ribs, she eased herself into bed, fractioning out her movements with tiny hisses. Jeronimo didn't move as she settled in, face to face with him. Once she'd delicately arranged her body, she laid her head on the pillow.

Jeronimo pulled the covers over them. His body gave off a kinetic heat that warmed her. Even in the daylight leaking through the closed blinds and curtains, he looked cast in moonlight, an ominous thing. He would've appeared predatory if he hadn't sagged into the bed like remembering to breathe took too much effort.

"You look tired," she told him.

"Thanks."

"What did the message mean, if it wasn't your brother?"

He didn't need to ask what message. She'd figured they were both thinking the same thing.

I'm back and I ain't forgotten.

"It could mean anything. Everyone who's ever died in this town had a vendetta against someone."

"If the Skinned Man can write that on Townsend Rose's

headstone, why can't he tell us who he is?"

"Maybe he didn't write the message."

She pieced together what his words meant, and her stomach turned oily with unease. "You're thinking it's the same person who left the symbol in Little Cricket?"

His eyes fluttered closed. For a while, he breathed through his nose, long and slow. In and out. In and out. Finally, he said, "I don't know anything. As soon as I think I've figured it out, something else comes along and fucks that up."

"Language, Pastor."

He opened his eyes and found her offering him a slight smile. He gave her a half-hearted one in return. "Sorry, ma'am."

"It's forgiven, but you do have church today. Ms. Ida May will be expecting her weekly dose of fire and brimstone."

"My sermons aren't that gloomy."

"They're depressing as heck. Speaking of, will you have the energy to give one in a few hours? I won't lie, I might have to skip this one."

"I'll make up a good excuse for you." His hand slid across the sheet between them. He hooked a strand of her hair and twined it around his finger. "How recently was the do-gooder cop in this bed?"

She tensed, and her ribs shot back their complaint. She grimaced. "A long time ago."

"You wear his sweatshirt."

She'd worn it once, but it seemed like a childish thing to point out. "I like how it smells."

"Why?"

"I don't know! It's comforting or something. Can we talk about something else?"

His gaze brightened with bad intentions. "What do you want to talk about?"

"I thought we were supposed to be sleeping," she grumbled.

"Do you want to be sleeping?"

"Do you answer everything with a question?"

"Are you stalling because you're nervous?"

"I *will* shoot you again."

That won her a laugh. Granted, it was a small chuff of a noise, but it stretched his smile and softened the hollows of his face.

"I know you would. You never let me forget."

He settled deeper into her bed, and she liked that more than she should. His finger kept twining in her hair. Her skin prickled at the soft pulling motion. A shiver settled deep in her lower back. Her stomach dipped in a dark and velvety warm place.

"Kiss me again, J."

He moved like the first breath of autumn air slipping down from the mountains. She didn't register the motion until he was upon her, easing her onto her back with one hand cupped behind her neck, his other arm bracing his weight above her. Careful, so careful with her ribs, he held her. His lips met hers, and all caution ceased.

He possessed her mouth like he had a right to her, like she'd always belonged to him. Perhaps a smarter woman would've held back a few pieces of herself, but Loey gave him all of her, all the hollowed-out dark spots. Like the time she'd looked at his obsidian threads that bound his nightmare together and thought him beautiful, he kissed her like Folton had never ruined her. He kissed her like her face was as perfect as Dale's. He kissed her like he could breathe for her if she ever needed the help.

With one last chaste brush against her lips with his own, he gazed down at her.

"Anything?" she asked him. "Even one drop of satisfaction?"

His lips quirked into a barely there smile, too sad to bring her any hope. "You were right the day you called me a hollow man, Lo. But you bring me the closest to life I've ever been."

"That's not true. You're alive." She traced his smile with her fingertips, trying to sculpt it into the real thing.

He caught her hand. He held her fingers to his mouth like he was sealing something inside him, but his eyes were as empty as Saturday night's sins.

"I could've loved you, Loey Grace Keene. I could've loved you."

CHAPTER 4

Present Time

"**D**ALE, WHAT THE HELL ARE you doin' here?"

"You know my name?" Dale asked, utterly dumbfounded.

"I know everything about you."

Her mirror man shook his head, and his grit-stiffened hair fell across his tall forehead. Not one wrinkle marred his face. His nose—razor sharp and hooked at the tip—would have looked perfectly villainous if it wasn't perched atop a cherubic mouth made for kissing. His only imperfection was a thin white scar that stretched almost all the way across his throat.

Even with the terrifying scar, he was more beautiful in person than from across the looking glass. Here, in this eerie aurora-brightened place, he was porcelain perfect and too stunning to touch.

Seeing him after all this time sent Dale around a funny little merry-go-round from Hell inside her head. If she let herself, she could stare at him with her mouth agape for hours, so she treated him like her mother had taught her to treat all boys and men: with disinterest, especially if she liked them. The same school of thought had taught her that if a boy hit her on the playground, it meant he liked her.

"My mirror trapped me. Can you help me up? My feet are killing me."

His hand wrapped around hers, and he easily pulled her to her feet. The motion tugged at the monster's bite. She grimaced. The mirror man didn't drop her hand but held it. Only a few inches separated her chest from his.

His eyes—a two-toned hazel shade that couldn't decide which color to be—swept over her features.

"You're the only one who looked back at me, and you finally came. You came for me," he said as if she had swooped down from Heaven to fly him home, like the Archangel Michael. His sense of awe made her forget that she was trapped in her mirror, forget about her feet, her shoulder, her fear. His marvel wrapped her up in a shroud of invincibility.

She *had* come for him. Her grandmother might have gotten her stuck in her mirror, but Dale was here. With him. That was more than any other Rose woman could say.

His slender fingers caressed her face, from her lips to her eyes to her nose to her hair and back again. He stepped closer, and Dale's skin prickled, but not in warning. With both hands, he held her face and stood over her such that his breath whooshed down from his tall height and rustled the fine hairs near her temples. She shivered.

No one had ever stared at her this way. There wasn't a mask thick enough or strong enough to keep him from seeing her. Dale had no armor to keep him out, not like a shield would have mattered. He'd already seen her best and worst through her mirrors. He'd seen it all, and he was still standing here in awe. It probably should've unnerved her that he'd seen so much of her, but it freed her more than scared her.

"Who are you?" she whispered.

"Barty James."

"A James?" Sunshine forgotten, her body flushed cold, and she pulled away from him. "As in Jeronimo James?"

"He's my brother."

"How …" Her thoughts scrambled around the implications. "But you've been in the mirrors for generations."

"Since 1956."

She held her breath until the only thought that remained in her head was, *Breathe.* She sucked in a lungful of air and asked, "How is he your brother? He would have to be nearly eighty for that to work."

Her beautiful mirror man frowned, looking so confused. "How are you here if you don't know? Did the Tender help you?"

"Who's the Tender? Know what?" There wasn't enough air in this miserable place to keep her vision from doubling the firefly lights around her.

"Your friend, Loey. She's the Tender. She's a Keene."

"A Keene …" Dale pushed away from him so she could breathe. Her grandmother had warned her about the Keenes. How much did her grandmother know about all this? Why in the world was Loey involved? "My grandmother—"

Light flashed in the corner of her eye. Too concentrated to be the firefly type, it came again, a single pulse of white light in the space between her and Barty. It seared her eyes, and she stumbled back.

"Oh, no."

Dale kept her focus trained on where the burst of light had disappeared. "'Oh, no,' what? What is that?"

"I don't think she likes you. She normally doesn't use up this much energy to materialize with light."

"Who doesn't?"

"Frankie." Barty stretched out his arm to shield her. His eyes glazed over as he stared at an invisible point a few feet in front of him. "You might want to get back."

"Who the hell is Frankie? *What is happening?*"

Typically, that tone snapped men to attention, but this

one ignored her. The light flashed again, and he spoke to it. "She's only visiting. Just passin' through. Don't get all twisted up, Frankie."

Light ballooned outward and hit Dale square in the chest. The blow hurled her through the air. She hit the black dirt ten feet away, bit her tongue, and rolled ass over kettle through the gritty dust. She came to a stop face down and spread-eagle.

Cursing like a devil, she pushed herself onto her elbows and hissed at the pain in her shoulder. She hawked up dust, feeling it deep down in her lungs like a fungus. Her chest burned down to her bones, and she was scared to inspect the damage, afraid she'd find her skin filleted off. Blowing her hair out of her face, she looked up.

Barty stood a few paces in front of her, hands raised in surrender toward a flashing, bobbing ball of light. He spoke too softly for Dale to catch the words.

Dale coughed again.

Without looking back at her, he said, "Don't move too fast. She's real mad."

"Tell your little friend I am too." Dale was proud that her voice didn't shake with fear, though on the inside, she was awash in it. Everything hurt, and it was high time she left this place.

She eased herself upright. Examining her injuries, she found her tracksuit jacket intact, not burned off her body like she'd pictured, but bruises swelled from shoulder to shoulder and neck to navel from the blast to her chest.

Dale had never been one to back down from another woman, and she wouldn't start now, especially if the woman in question was a ball of light trying to steal her man's attention.

"If she wants to come out of the dark and fight me like a real woman, she can. I'm not backing down."

"Dale," Barty warned.

The light flared, but Barty was faster. He darted in front of it. The blast hit him square in the nuts.

He fell to his knees, bowed over, his hands cupping himself. Dale cringed, but she kept her distance.

The light darted beneath his downturned head. Dale didn't speak Bitch Flashlight, but she assumed the thing—Frankie—was apologizing.

"Is she like the Tinkerbelle to your Peter Pan or what?" Dale called from what she hoped was a safe distance to shit talk.

Barty groaned in answer. He crumpled onto his side and landed in the fetal position.

The light hovered over Barty's shoulder. Dale assumed it was glaring at her like she was to blame for it hitting Barty in the nuts. Dale flipped it off.

The light ball flashed toward her. Dale had no time to react before it hit her. The impact was far harder this time, as if the thing had been holding back before Dale truly pissed it off.

Dale landed flat on her back, the wind knocked right out of her. She stared up into the blinding light that made her eyes stream water down her cheeks. She held up both hands in surrender.

But the light wasn't buying her weak attempt at peace. Hovering above her chest, the light began to vibrate. It concentrated into a thin beam that flashed straight into her shoulder. Into the bite. Beneath her skin. And it began to *suck*.

Dale screamed.

"Frankie!" Barty shouted beside her; she could see nothing but starbursts of pain across her vision. "Stop! That's not nice!"

Dale refused to let this bitch of a light kill her in this hellhole. The sucking deepened. It felt like the light was slurping up everything important inside her, and as it did, it bloomed and grew above her. Dale imagined she saw strands of hair floating through the light's particles at its center.

It stopped abruptly. Air flooded back into her lungs, and she gasped like a fish flopping on dry land. Slowly, her vision returned. She weakly tilted her chin up to see what had happened.

"Barty?"

Over her shoulder, she found him. He clutched a girl's arm, though she was more specter than girl. She screamed in a high-pitched peal that made Dale's ears ache. Barty dragged the girl to the light wall. She thrashed against him. He threw her into the lights.

She kept screaming from deep within the strands. Barty watched with his chest heaving and his fists shaking. Eventually, the screaming stopped. Between the strands of light, the girl disappeared.

"I'm sorry," Barty told the empty spot, "but you can't treat our guests like that. Your momma raised you better."

"Barty?" Dale tried again in a rough rasp that ended in a cough. Breathing was getting hard, and the thrill of finding her mirror man had worn off.

He returned to kneel beside her. He worked his arm beneath her neck and helped her sit up. "She shouldn'ta done that."

"What was that?" The effort to move left her breathless.

"Frankie." Barty probed her bite with his fingers. It seeped fresh blood down her arm. He brought his bloody, grit-covered fingers to his mouth and tasted them. "She was draining you. She's been doing that more often lately."

Dale tried to focus on Barty, but her chest felt like she'd swallowed a box of nails. "You have to tell me who Frankie is."

He paused to think. "Great-aunt, I think. Sometimes I lose track over here."

"My great-aunt?" Dale spluttered hard enough to make her body spasm. She winced. "Why the hell was she trying to kill me?"

"She wasn't tryin' to kill you. She wanted some of your life."

Her mirror man was awfully pretty, but she worried this side had sucked something out of him too. "That sounds like killing."

"You shouldn't stay here long." He ducked his head. "She'll hurt you if you stay. She's never liked me watching you."

Another cough racked her body, and her chest convulsed. She choked gritty, black oxygen back into her lungs. "You might be right. Can I fit through those holes?"

He looked toward the light wall and shook his head. A cold panic trickled through Dale's veins. "Those are too small, and you have to be very, very strong to tear threads in the Seam."

Her throat pinched closed. "I can't stay here."

"We'll get you home. You said you came through your mirror. Does that mean you took off the ward?"

"The ward? You mean that piece of paper? That was a ward? It's on my closet floor."

"Good. We can use that mirror."

"To go back through?" she asked hopefully.

"To wait for the Tender. She's the only one who can get you back out."

"But that could be days! I don't want to stay here that long." Dread sucked out what life she had left after Frankie's feast.

"Time moves differently here. Days have passed since you came through." He spoke so casually, but the words rocked Dale. She was too weak to interrupt him. "It's a walk to the mirrors from here, and we need to be ready. Can you stand?"

"I think so."

Like she was made of glass, he helped her stand. He kept his arm around her waist, his fingers splayed across her ribs, right beneath her arm, to hold her against him for support. His other hand reached across the front of her body and took her hand. She leaned against him as she took her first step. Pain, sharp as knives, stabbed the soles of her feet.

"I can't," she gasped. "My feet."

Barty stared at the blood seeping into the dirt beneath her feet. Without a word, he delicately scooped her into his arms. She folded against his chest, her knees hooked over his arm, his other arm supporting her back. She wrapped her arms around his neck and offered him the best smile she could muster.

"My hero," she told him.

He smiled back at her, wide and wonderful. It dimmed her fear a fraction. "No, Dale. You came for me. You're my hero. You saved me."

Something fell into place inside Dale. She was in too much pain to place the feeling as Barty started across the plain toward the mountains, dust devils whirling around them.

Whatever was happening inside Dale, it was important. She knew that much, like she knew she would do anything to save this man.

Her mirror man.

CHAPTER 5

APRIL 7, 1956

BARTHOLOMEW JAMES LIKED HIS MOONSHINE how he liked his women: fast enough to burn him on the way down and hell on the heart comin' back up.

And he didn't care none too much to work for neither.

Jeronimo worked the shine and Barty handled the talkin'. Barty was real good at talking. He rolled through Righteous, selling shine to the whores for the Saturday night rush or to the holy rollers for the Sunday sermon.

It was a good system.

'Course, Barty had never worked for anything so hard in his life as he'd worked to get Francis "Frankie" Rose.

She'd come around in the beginning, drawn by the pretty words he'd spun for her and the flowers he'd picked along the road to give her each evenin' before his shine runs. Back then, she'd taken the bees from his head, 'cept even her lovely smile and soft skin couldn't keep those bees from buzzing eventually. They wouldn't hush until he killed again.

The blood, well, it always set him to rights.

To feel it splatter on his face. To cut and feel like God. To watch as a bad man's life ebbed out of a world made cleaner for his death.

Frankie didn't like the killin' none too much, but she was a good woman and helped bury the bodies.

She'd loved Barty for a while, but that was a different story, and this wasn't about that. This was after she'd started hating him and fallin' for his brother, after everything had gone to Hell in a handbasket.

The handbasket was carried by a revenuer man from West Virginia with a funny-lookin' hat and a vest like he took himself too seriously. His boots were pointy and tipped in silver. He wore a watch from a dangle chain in his pocket, and he checked it as though he misplaced time like nickels. Thomas Wooten was his name, and the people in Righteous had taken to callin' him Agent Wooten in fear.

Wooten was poking his nose where it didn't belong, and folks were starting to ask questions better left alone.

After not coming around for a week, Frankie showed up on Barty's doorstep. "We've got to go get him, Barty. He has to take care of this."

Fear turned her voice into a shaky tremor, setting Barty's teeth on edge. 'Course she thought only his brother could fix this. She hadn't thought to ask Barty to make it right. "You don't think I can take care of that rev? I'll take care of 'im, all right."

"You're gonna kill a revenuer too?" She shouldered past him to collect the belongings she'd left scattered about and changed into her big, no-nonsense coat for hiking the deep woods and her boots. She took one of his hats and stuffed her golden locks beneath its folds so she'd look like a man. "Where we gonna bury him, Barty? We're runnin' out of spots, and they'll just send another one down from West Virginia. I'm getting your brother. He'll know what to do."

Barty was ashamed to admit he called her a bad name. Implied she'd slept with his brother and any other man who'd have her. He plied each of them words with venom. He hurt her as badly as taking his knife to her. It was plain as day across her face. Those brand-new denim-colored eyes he loved to stare into glared back at him with shock and hurt and resolve.

He drove her straight to his brother with those words, and she wouldn't be looking back no time soon.

For a second, and she saw it happen too, he thought about killing her, 'cause the thought of Jeronimo having her, having what was his, about sent him over the edge. She'd left quickly after that, without another word.

That had been this morning—hours ago—and she hadn't come back down from the ridge since, with or without his brother, the great and formidable Jeronimo James, whom Barty would never be and didn't wanna be no how.

The revenuer hadn't been seen around town none either. Barty sobered up later that afternoon, all those facts lying like blades on a table, but his head was fuzzy again. He was scared that this time the evil in him needed Frankie's blood.

A bad thought crept right up in his mind and dug its heels in: What if the revenuer had tracked Frankie up the ridge with the intent of locating the brothers' squirrel holes? Only Barty and Jeronimo knew the still's location, but to a revenuer, finding the squirrel holes full of illegal shine would be as good as finding the source that had brewed it.

Frankie was good at racing the black and whites, but she wasn't no good at watching her back. She kept her eyes resolutely forward, always on the road ahead, never behind her.

With the fuzziness in his head getting so bad he couldn't get his shaking hands to start the truck, he headed up Devil's Maw on foot.

He reached it as the sun was setting and a late spring chill crept down from the mountains, bringing with it a boomer boiling with fight. Lightning flashed far off, and the scent of rain made his eyes burn. The day had been unusually hot for

April, and the bent old men on Main Street had spat tobacco and promised a sinful storm was a-comin'.

Barty huddled deeper into his jacket and cursed. After pausing to drink from the flask at his hip, he started into the woods with a glance over his shoulder at the Keene homestead sitting in the clearing at the base of the ridge, its lights burning brightly, mourning candles still out for ol' man Knox.

The woods of Shiner's Ridge were like none Barty had ever been through. These woods were alive and spoke in whispered riddles and had shadows within shadows like the darkness had a beating heart. Barty only came up here to empty the squirrel holes of shine and scrawled notes from his brother. Otherwise, he never traversed these parts.

Higher up the ridge, an echo of a scream slipped between the trees.

It was a feminine scream, and part of him knew it was Frankie, though he'd never heard her scream, always too proud a woman to let him hear such weakness from her. His flesh crawled; part of him liked the way she sounded when she screamed.

He ran.

He ran until his heart thundered and his legs were foreign limbs beneath him that he could no longer feel. She didn't scream again, but the sound kept ringing in his ears, those bees madder than ever before inside his skull.

The buzzing was so loud it almost blocked out the sound of his name.

"Barty!"

Barty whirled toward the sound of the voice pinging off the pines. He swayed. His blood boiled in his veins, and his vision slanted.

"Who's there?" he slurred like a drunk, but the flask on his hip was mostly empty.

"Barty, it's me."

Barty spun around. A man with gray hair and honey eyes materialized through the fog of Barty's vision. He was bundled up like it was winter, a fur hat pulled low over his ears.

"Knox? But you're ..."

"There's no time for that." The old man grabbed Barty's arm and shook it hard for a dead man. "He killed her. Your brother killed her."

"Frankie?" Barty whispered. "He wouldn't."

"I saw him cut her at the head of the creek. She's dead, Barty. She's gone."

"But he loves her ... He wouldn't."

Knox slapped him, and though Barty hardly felt it, it made the bees right mad. Barty pictured killin' Knox right there, making him dead for good this time. The old man said, "You have to run. He's coming for you next. He's lost his mind to the madness. It came for his soul, and it won."

Barty blinked back at the man. "Jeronimo's coming for me? To kill me?"

"Go. While there's time."

"I can't ..."

Knox grabbed Barty's face and squeezed until Barty thought his bones would break. The man released him. Barty stumbled away. "All right. Meet me at the still. I'll take care of your brother. Don't go anywhere else, you hear? Straight to the still."

Barty nodded, wondering how the hell ol' man Knox knew their still's location.

Knox had to turn him in the right direction and push him forward for his aching legs to work. Barty followed the burbling creek up to the still.

The big metal moonshine still sat in the middle of the clearing. Its fire puffed thick smoke up into the night sky. The clouds rumbled with bad omens. The metal reflected the moon's face into the creek running beside it. Barty stared into the clear water at his reflection, and the branches overhead made the shadows dance behind him like there was something else in the reflection with him.

This was all his fault. He was the reason she'd gone up the ridge in search of help he couldn't provide. He hadn't been man enough or decent enough. She'd seen through him and found him lacking and needing his brother to take care of everything Barty couldn't. She was earnest and pure, innocent though he'd tried his damnedest to sully her. She'd died for his failures.

The James brothers were cursed men, bent on blood and death. If his brother hadn't killed Frankie, Barty knew in his heart he would've eventually. He was nothing but a killer, and the thing inside him craved Frankie's blood. It wouldn'ta stopped until it had her neither.

In a way, his brother had saved him the heartache of doing the deed himself. In a way, it was a relief to know his brother was as bad as him, as broken. In a way, it was easier. He had a reason to go. To follow after Frankie and beg her forgiveness in the afterlife.

Thunder boomed overhead, and in the quiet that followed, a knife's edge drew against leather. He turned.

Lightning flashed across the sky and cast his brother in firelight. *A god,* Barty thought, because Jeronimo had always been such to him. Still was, just maybe a dark god, an evil one, the kind their grandmother had always said lived up in these mountains. She'd taught Barty the symbols born of her mountain's magic—the magic Jeronimo had never had time for, calling it the hapless drawings of old women, but Barty had listened and learned, wanting to make his grandmother proud. By then, he'd been old enough to know Momma would never pay him no mind.

It began to rain. The water ran in rivulets down Jeronimo, who stood shaking across from Barty, his knife clutched in his hand. Her blood coated the blade and his shirt, which clung wetly to his sunken stomach. Knox was right; JJ looked soulless. His intentions were plain as day in his black-as-sin eyes.

The bees went quiet in his skull.

"You love her too," Barty shouted above the crash of rain.

Jeronimo didn't confirm what Barty already knew. They couldn't both love her, not in this lifetime.

"Oh God." Barty fell to the ground, the pain crashing through him in earnest now that the bees were quiet. "Oh God. She's really gone? Sh-she tried to tell me … She tried to stop … Oh God …"

He sobbed like a little boy and he was ashamed.

"I didn't listen. I couldn't stop, and she tried to stop me. Told me I wasn't doin' it for the right reasons no more. I tried, JJ. God, I fuckin' tried, ya know? I knew I shouldn'ta involved her. But the blood. It … it felt so good when it sprayed on me."

"You went too far, Barty."

Barty nodded.

"It shouldn'ta been her."

His brother was right. His brother had always been right.

Jeronimo walked over to stand behind Barty. This was it. It felt right.

He lifted his chin for his brother. To let the hand that had taken her take him too. After all he'd done, after all the wrong and no good, he craved this peace. The buzzing would finally stop for good. The need that kept him up at night would stop. No more would he taint the world by breathing in it.

"I won't stop if you don't stop me," he told his brother, and the knife nicked his bobbing throat. Warm blood trickled down his neck. "Thank you, brother."

A twig cracked in the woods. A flicker of gray dashed

between the trees. Lightning struck a tree beside him. The brothers didn't move as the massive trunk toppled onto the metal still.

"Watch the rev, brother. He's comin' after you," Barty said, but thunder boomed over his words, and his brother didn't hear his warning.

"I'm sorry, Barty."

It sounded like Jeronimo meant it too. He drew the knife across Barty's throat. At first, the cut was a tickle of pain, then it grew into a sensation so pure Barty could've cried if he hadn't been about to die.

But the world flew apart and drowned out everything Barty had ever thought was real.

The light receded, and Barty could see again. He'd been blown into the woods. A warm blanket of blood shrouded his body.

"JJ?" he called toward the clearing.

Someone screamed nearby, and Barty thought it was his brother, but everything was going in and out. Something was pulling at him, tugging on his shirttail. He glanced back and saw a world cast in shadows with a black satin sky. It swept over him and took everything he'd ever known.

"JJ!" Barty screamed. He'd never liked the dark, and the dark was all he could see.

If this was Hell, Barty deserved it, but he still wanted his brother to hold his hand like a brother ought to as they walked to greet the Devil, so he screamed for his brother again and again.

But Jeronimo never came.

CHAPTER 6

THERE WERE VERY FEW THINGS Loey hated more than folding laundry. It had been one of her chores since childhood, and she pointedly remembered Gran asking her as a child to fold the clothes while she watched her favorite cartoons on Saturday morning.

She couldn't recall *SpongeBob SquarePants* without thinking of folding endless towels. So Loey loathed doing laundry, but she was running out of clean clothes. Gran would've been ashamed of the way Loey piled her clean clothes on her bed like a mountain of forgotten good intentions and rooted through them for something to wear that Wednesday morning to the coffee shop.

She spotted her favorite pair of Wranglers. Today felt like the kind of day that required the comfort of her best jeans. The Skinned Man had nearly escaped the cemetery three days ago, and Loey had passed each day in a numb state of near mental paralysis.

She and Jeronimo had torn apart the entire house looking for her grandmother's Tending book. They'd searched late into the night and early the next morning. Maybe it had become a habit, or maybe he genuinely wanted to help her with her chores given her bruised ribs, but Jeronimo had all but moved in. He'd stayed over every night since returning from the church

Sunday with a bag of clothes, his research notes from Savannah, and a jar of moonshine that he sipped on in quiet moments between searching. He drank from the jar often, but Loey kept her mouth shut. Everyone had their demons. Mentioning it wouldn't be proper given how much he was helping.

The Skinned Man hadn't reappeared, and each day that passed without him testing the tatters tested Loey's fraying resolve. It didn't help that Jeronimo only spoke of getting Barty out and testing the theory of their ability to exist on the same side of the Seam with enough distance between them. Loey had kept him from testing his notions because he needed her to open the threads and she'd kept herself busy.

In the back of her thoughts, buried beneath the mountain of stress, she dwelled on Folton and the updates Matt had been giving her at the shop. The lawyers were meeting and drawing up deals. Loey had been to the station a few times to repeat her statement. Police had reached out to Dale to recant her story, but Loey's best friend was nowhere to be found.

Staring down at the jeans in her hands, Loey bit her lip to keep from crying. What if she went to jail? What would happen to the Seam and the tatters? Jeronimo couldn't keep it together; he knew little more than she did about Tending. Her stomach churned. If she let herself think on the things looming over her head for too long, she'd puke. Gran had always told her in times of worry to put one foot in front of the other and keep a smile on her face, that everything would work itself out as God intended. Loey didn't find God's intentions very reassuring, but she could keep moving. She might not have anywhere left in the house to search, but she could call Cross and harass him about Dale again. That was within her control.

As she went to put her pants on, she felt a bulge in the back pocket. Thinking it a handful of horse treats she'd let run through the wash again, she stuffed her hand inside and yanked out a small chunk of leather.

It took her a moment to recognize the book of wilted pages and crumbling leather. Her stomach dropped.

It was Obidiah's journal, the one she'd found beside the bank statements in Burl's house over a week and a half ago. The journal with Knox Keene's name scrawled in it.

"Shoot," she hissed.

She spun away from the laundry and strode to the bedroom window letting early morning sunlight slip in. She leaned into the scant bit of light. The damp book threatened to rip clean apart as she cracked it open.

Blue and black ink washed the words into useless smudges across the curling pages.

"Shoot."

She flipped through the pages as best she could, but most of them were ruined. Parts were legible if she squinted hard enough. She searched for the mention of her great-great-grandfather but found nothing.

She carried the diary into the kitchen and laid it on the windowsill, separating as many of the pages as she could to help them finish drying without falling apart.

How had she forgotten about the journal? It had strayed to the back of her mind and settled there. A hysterical laugh bubbled up her throat; she'd been looking for a book, after all, and she'd found one, but she'd destroyed it the same as she destroyed everything else.

She looked up at the ceiling like it was a bright blue sky and closed her eyes. Missing Gran and Pap made her heart ache from its deepest seams, the delicate muscular tissues working like magic to pump life through her. Something so important depended on something so fragile. She understood that burden, that weight, to keep pumping even though she felt so weak she could break right in half.

If she broke, however, the entire town and the people in it who meant so much to her would break with her. She was the Tender. This was her burden to bear, as it had been a Keene's burden since the beginning of the Seam. She could not fail.

One foot in front of the other.

Trouble came in threes, and the next two came for Loey later that Wednesday morning at the shop.

The second one happened after the morning rush, which consisted mostly of pumpkin spice lattes, apple crisps, and counter gossip. Loey checked her phone, and the text from Matt was enough to unnerve her.

Come to the station after work. It's ready.

It was time to face the consequences. Folton's deal had been finalized between the lawyers. He was days away from freedom, and her lie would be aired out for the entire town to see.

Loey felt sick until lunch. Cross came into the shop on his break from selling insurance at the Farm Bureau office down the street. A wave of nippy fall air trailed in after him.

"Hey," he said with a lift of his chin. His clothes weren't ironed, and his tie didn't match his suit—all bad signs.

Loey paused wiping down the counter. "What's wrong?"

Only old Kip Missions sat in a back booth, his knotted body huddled over a cup of Loey's strongest black coffee. He was a Vietnam veteran who pushed a baby stroller full of his belongings along the streets of Righteous. Most people in town did their best to help him out, but his random outbursts unsettled some people enough that they gave him a wide berth on his bad days. Loey didn't mind him, and Pap had always welcomed Kip in for free coffee, pastries, and war stories.

Cross waited until he was all the way at the counter before

speaking in a low voice. "It's Dale. I still haven't heard from her, and it's been four days."

"I told you she was missing yesterday, and you told me to wait. That you had it under control." Loey bunched the rag up in her hand. "Here we go again, Cross. Why didn't you make her go to rehab? She could be getting better instead of lying in some Little Cricket bathroom."

"I can't make her do anything she doesn't want to do. You know that."

"But she seemed so ready this time. What happened?"

Cross threw up his hands. From the back booth, Kip flinched, ducking his head lower over his coffee and muttering under his breath. "I don't know! I left her alone with Grandmother for five minutes. I came back, and she was freaked out."

None of it made sense. In all her low points, Dale had never disappeared this long. "Has Travis seen her?"

Cross's expression muted into one of cautious disinterest. "Travis hasn't been home much."

"Where has he been?"

"Not in my house, if that's what you're implying, though it would be rude if you were."

"Seems rude to have an affair with your sister's husband." Loey was in no mood to handle Cross with the kid gloves he required.

"Can you keep your voice down? We have a real problem here. Mother is getting fed up, and you know what happened last time Dale pissed her off real bad. They didn't speak for a year."

Loey felt ready to snap in half, and she didn't care to hear about Darlene Rose's mothering or lack thereof. "Do you want to drive to Little Cricket or do you want me to?"

"I already checked there."

Snap, she thought. There it was. Her world was slowly unraveling far too literally for comfort. "Where is she, Cross?"

"That's what I'm telling you. She's not in town. It's like she vanished."

"Do you think she … left?"

"I think"—Cross's hand balled up on the countertop—"she's not here, and I need your help finding her."

"Heck, Cross. You could've told me that to begin with." Loey yanked her apron ties loose and threw the cleaning rag into the laundry bin beneath the counter. "Hey, Kip, we're heading out. Can you lock up on your way out? Feel free to take more of them pecan scones for the road."

"Sure thing, Miss Loey. Have a nice day."

"You too, Kip."

She and Cross hurried out of the shop and cut down the alley along the side of the two-story building that had once been a soda factory, the white logo faded across the red bricks. The sky was too blue and perfect for this kind of day.

"Is it smart to let a crazy man hang out in your shop?"

Loey rolled her eyes at Cross, who, God love him, could be pretentious at times. "Why? Do you think he'll rub poop on the walls or something?"

Cross opened the driver's side door to her truck for her and held it back, squeaky hinges and all. "No," he snapped. "But he's *homeless*, Loey Grace."

"I doubt he'll move in." She climbed inside and fished for her keys in her purse. Cross remained at her door. "Are you getting in or what?"

"If we both run off looking for her, everyone will know something is up, and that won't look good."

Finding her keys, Loey slung her purse into the passenger seat with a bitter laugh. Cross slammed the door shut, and a wave of dust ballooned into the air. She rolled her window down. Her other hand stabbed the key into the ignition with more force than necessary.

"You're totally right. We should be worried about how this looks. I would hate for your missing sister to look bad."

She turned the engine to drown out Cross's response. He flipped her off.

"Son of a butthead," she muttered under her breath. She backed out onto the street.

She headed to Dale's house without paying one ounce of attention to the town's preparations for the Fall Festival that Friday. It was a big event, judging by the amount of traffic on the roads. To keep from dissolving into a fit of road rage, she called Dale's cell a few times, plus her home phone in case Travis was there. Loey didn't want to run into him; today wasn't the day for his special brand of douche. Both numbers went unanswered.

Dale's house wasn't in the richest part of Righteous. That was the historic district where her mother and father lived. Situated amongst an ungodly amount of magnolias, those antebellum houses were all nationally registered and part of a tour of Southern landmarks.

Dale's neighborhood sat on the outskirts of Righteous, near the head of the valley. Mostly upper-middle-class families with giant SUVs and pristine yards resided in the brand-new houses, a recent development from a fancy company in Knoxville. Most of the families weren't from Righteous; they'd moved in for the small-town experience and commuted to the big city every day.

She pulled into Dale's driveway and climbed out of her truck. Dale's house was nothing unique from the others on the street. It was a point-and-pick house built from a thick binder stocked full of trim choices, paint colors, and garage-door styles. The professional landscaping was well maintained, lest the neighbors complain of errant weeds. The entire neighborhood had methodically distinguished itself from all the other houses in Righteous. The disconnection had probably drawn Dale, but it also rooted a sense of dread deep in Loey's belly; her precious town might escape the clutches of the Skinned Man, only to be washed away by a wave of rich, white families who thought the simple life was for mentally slow hillbillies who sometimes misused their verb tenses and said "y'all" too much.

Dumbfounding Loey, Dale's front door was locked. Loey walked around to the back and found that door locked as well. She'd never had to use the spare key hidden under the potted climbing roses in the back garden. She unlocked the sliding glass door and entered through the kitchen.

All the lights were off, and wilted flowers sat in the middle of the kitchen island, their murky brown water smelling like rotted stems. Loey went through the entire house, top to bottom, searching every drawer, nook, and cranny. In Dale's bedroom, Loey went straight to the nightstand but stopped herself from opening the drawer. A woman's nightstand was sacred ground, and what she kept in there spoke about her secret self, her priorities, and her notions about the world. In Loey's drawer, her neon green vibrator shaped like an alien's penis lay beside her Bible. They shared the space with her gun, Chapstick, and hand cream. It felt like a blatant invasion of Dale's privacy to shuffle through her most intimate belongings.

But Dale had forfeited her right to privacy by disappearing without a trace. Loey opened the heavy drawer. Loey discovered one item.

A handheld mirror.

Closing the drawer, Loey turned away from the nightstand. A clammy feeling spread across her skin.

Dale had seen Barty in her mirrors—she'd confessed as much the night Loey and Cross found her in Little Cricket— but Loey had hoped her best friend's recent disappearance was a futile attempt to avoid her problems by dodging rehab. Loey hadn't wanted to consider the other option: that Dale was involved with mirrors like Burl had been. What if, like Burl and Pastor Briggs and Leigh Parker, Dale wouldn't come out the other side alive? Maybe she was already dead.

Loey's eyes settled on the walk-in closet. With a new urgency burning through her, she went to it and stepped into another dimension.

The closet was like a small house. It was certainly bigger than Loey's entire bedroom, closet, and bathroom combined. It was large enough to house a dressing bench in the center, a chandelier, a dressing mannequin in a Versace robe, and a huge floor-to-ceiling mirror that looked like an archway into a separate room. The closet smelled like Dale's custom perfume—bergamot and plums—and the thick carpet absorbed Loey's footfalls as she skirted the shelves and racks brimming with every color of top, pants, dress, jeans, skirt, and blouse possible. It was both grotesque and mesmerizing.

The closet was also perfectly organized and included a shelf of Dale's overnight bags, save for the one massive suitcase rolled into the center of the room beside the bench. It was as though she'd walked straight in from rehab, rolled her suitcase into the closet, and disappeared.

A shrill sound split the air.

CHAPTER 7

"**Y**OU'RE TELLING ME YOU'VE BEEN trapped here since 1956?"

The thin, long scar across Barty's neck seemed to glow neon in the firefly lights. Around her, as Barty carried her, the landscape was almost serene, save for the occasional scream and the ground breathing beneath them, but it did nothing to calm the rising panic causing Dale's heart to pound.

She didn't give Barty a chance to respond. "I have to get to Loey. She's attached to Jeronimo's hip. He could be killing her right now."

Barty's arms tightened around her. "We're almost there, and JJ isn't all bad. He just …"

"Killed an innocent woman? My great-aunt?"

"He really did love her."

"I'm *not* reassured. This isn't some twisted romantic comedy where you can hide these little tidbits beneath handsome jawlines and swoony kisses. This is *murder*, Barty."

Barty kept his eyes on the plains around them. The mountains were getting closer, the silken sky playing off their surface. "It sounds bad when you put it that way."

"No shit." But Dale couldn't keep talking about this, not if she wanted to keep her wits about her. Imagining Loey with that immortal monster terrified her, and she had to stay focused. "How did that explosion send you across the mirrors?"

Barty talked as he walked. "The mirrors are a bridge for the magic and work mostly one way. The explosion that night in fifty-six sent me across the Seam that divides this pocket world from Righteous. That fight you saw was the Skinned Man tryin' to tear the threads of the Seam to escape this world. Jeronimo and Loey stopped him, and 'cause she's a Tender, she tied the torn threads back together to keep him inside."

Dale stared at him with her mouth open. *Catching flies*, her mother would have admonished. "How can you know all this from watching the mirrors in town?"

"I have a lot of time on my hands, but my grandma taught me most of the magic when I was a boy. I had to learn the names this generation uses for the ancient aspects of our world that have been around since the beginning of time."

Dale laughed, a blunt sound that the vast surrounding plain ate up. "You're crazy."

Solemn-faced, Barty agreed. "It's 'cause I don't kill no more."

Her laughter faded. "That was true? You liked to kill?"

"I wouldn't lie to you, Dale. But I don't do that no more. There's no one here to kill anyway. Except for you." His eyes settled on her, seeing her too completely, and for the first time, Dale didn't feel comforted with him. "The urges are why I wanted my brother to kill me. The world was better off without me."

The sentences swept away all notions of discomfort and mistrust like a good rising tide on a beach. This was her mirror man, after all. She tightened her arms around his neck and snuggled closer. The world had broken him, was all, and he needed a good woman to fix him.

"I know that feeling," she told him.

A shriek cut across the dark world.

"That's him," Barty murmured.

"Who is he?"

"He was here after the storm too. When I woke up enough to notice what was going on around me, he was screaming and tearing at the threads, nearly killing himself trying to escape, though it's real hard to kill us for good over here. I tried to help him at first, and he 'bout killed me all the way a few times. He started murderin' innocent people with the magic my grandma taught me, and I knew he was a bad man, because he killed good people. Do you feel how the ground breathes beneath us?" Dale nodded, and Barty continued. "He lost the fight for his soul to the evil of this place. It's made him mad with sickness. It rots him and makes him crazier by the day. He's more animal than man."

"Is it Knox or the revenuer killing people? They were the only other people on the ridge that night besides Frankie, you, and your brother."

"The scars from the fire and his madness make it impossible to recognize him, and I can't talk to him without him tryin' to kill me. But this creature is too evil to be Knox. I knew Knox. He came to our house after Pa died at the sawmill and promised Momma he'd make it right by us. The Keenes always helped the folks of Righteous, especially those the Roses and the Jinkses hurt."

Dale grimaced. She imagined the Keenes had helped many people. "It was the revenuer?"

"Possibly. Or something monstrous this place created. It likes its monsters."

On cue, a caw descended from the mountains. The horrible sound would surely haunt her nightmares.

"What else lives here?"

"Mostly souls like Frankie's. Ghosts, you might call them, though most are nothing but faint shadows."

"How is Frankie so strong?"

Barty's mouth pressed into a thin line. His brows hooded his eyes and cast their hazel light in darkness. His grip on her tightened, uncomfortably so, but he didn't seem to notice.

"Barty?" she prompted, fear nipping at her again.

"You know how she fed on you?" he asked, his voice distant. "If she's mad enough or lonely enough or … hungry enough, she feeds on me. She takes bites, and it makes her stronger."

"That's *horrible*. You loved her once. You went up the ridge that night to save her, and she eats you?"

"At first I let her. I deserved it …" Barty twisted and turned through the sizeable rocks and boulders at the foot of the mountains, following a path only he knew, speaking the words to the rocks like they were old friends. "But she stopped asking, and it felt like she wasn't there anymore. Like the evil of this place had made her fade away. She began to take from me and wouldn't stop until I hurt her like I did earlier with the salt and the lights. Sometimes, I think she'll feed on me until she kills me. Sometimes, I think she would laugh as she did it. I can handle her most of the time, but the other souls are getting the same idea. They come in packs and chase after me every now and then. I spend more time running from them than I do the Skinned Man."

Dale put her hand on his face and forced him to look at her. He stopped walking. His heart pounded against her ribs. "She shouldn't do that. You don't deserve to have anything taken from you without your permission."

More pretty lies, Dale's mind whispered. How many things a day was nicked away from her without her permission? But wasn't that a woman's life here in the South? Or her life anywhere? Bits and pieces stolen with society's blessing. She'd never thought it could be a man's life too, but she reconsidered in the face of Barty's pain.

"I don't blame her," he whispered, worried Frankie might overhear his confession. "Early on, before she started taking without asking, she was the only thing that kept me sane. If it wasn't for her, I'd be mad like the Skinned Man. She saved me from that fate, but I'm not enough to save her. Again."

Dale's heart wrenched at his pain. Tears sprang in her eyes. He'd called her his hero, but she realized how true the words *needed* to be. Someone had to save him from this place before the evil beneath them took him away too. He needed her to save him, and he spoke to her like he already knew she would.

"We're here," he told her.

The opening of a sheltered cove emerged from the base of the mountains. Craggy cliffs and jutting rocks surrounded the cove on three sides, and a sloping slab of rock served as a tall ceiling that let in the firefly lights.

Barty carried her inside. The walls were smooth and shaped in places like wide benches or tall mirrors, all obviously hewn by hand from the rock. It must have taken him years to carve out his sanctuary in this brutal world. It was beautiful and horrible and broke Dale's heart.

"Do you like it?" He gently set her on her feet in the middle of the cavernous room.

"It's beautiful, Barty." She offered him a smile, and he took it with a satisfied grin, like her approval meant a good deal to him. "Where are the mirrors?"

"These mountains are every mirror and every reflective surface in Righteous. I built my home close to your mirrors. All it takes is a quick symbol to glimpse into your house."

"Holy shit." No wonder the rocks looked so reflective; they were mirrors. It was completely obvious now that she thought about it.

Barty helped her to a ledge carved out of the rock. The stone's coldness seeped through her velvet pants. He didn't release her hand, needing to touch her; she didn't mind.

"He tried to take this place from me once, but I fought him. It was the closest I came to killing him. He hasn't been back since. We'll be safe while we wait."

Dropping her hand at last, he moved to a slab of rock that stretched to the high ceiling. He sat on the ground in front of it and drew in the dirt. The rock began to change. Its surface churned. She stood on her cut feet and hobbled closer. Barty finished the last line of his symbol, and the magic of this world opened up before her.

He'd conjured her closet on the rock's surface. Her rolling suitcase waited by the bench. Through the open door, she could see her giant bed with satin sheets and her treasured bloody painting that now took on an entirely new meaning. Maybe, subconsciously, she'd been drawn to its darkness because of Barty. Because he liked blood too.

"That's my closet."

"It's the only mirror not warded in your house."

"Why can't we go to Loey's house? Wouldn't that be easier?"

"She's kept her mirrors warded ever since the Skinned Man tried to hurt her. He watches the rocks around her mirrors too closely. That's his territory, and it's far away from the cemetery's tatter."

"That was the wall of lights with the giant hole?" Barty dipped his chin in confirmation. "And the little lights all over?"

"They're threads in the Seam."

"But shouldn't a seam be a straight line? Those lights are dancing around all over the place."

She joined Barty on the ground in front of the mirror. He watched her move with care. She took his hand first, and his smile doubled in size.

"The Seam is everywhere. It's the threads between worlds."

"And Loey Tends to all of it?" Dale's heart ached for her

best friend. How much had Loey gone through alone? How long had she carried this secret? She had Jeronimo, but the thought hardly reassured Dale.

"The Seam in Righteous, she does. There're Tenders all over. Now, we sit and hope she comes by soon."

"She always does. Can I ask you another question?"

Barty grinned like he never wanted her to stop. "Shoot."

"Why do you watch Rose women? You've been with us for generations, driven some of us crazy too. Why not go to someone else to help you?"

He traced the back of her hand and didn't look at her as he said, "I never wanted help. I never thought of leaving until Frankie started …" He couldn't finish the sentence, and Dale wondered if he still had feelings for the ghost. "Then the Skinned Man started hurting more people, and Jeronimo came back into town. It feels like things are reaching a crescendo. Before, I was happy watching. And your family, especially the women, have always drawn me most."

Dale had asked the question, but she didn't relish the answer. She could easily picture him sitting here with another Rose, like her aunt or grandmother or, worse, her mother, and holding their hand. The thought made Dale's stomach hurt, but she pushed that down too and switched the conversation to safer ground. "Tell me about Frankie. How did you two meet?"

"She scared the hell out of me," he began, words full of wonder.

As he told the story, Dale lost herself in his words. Time moved strangely over here. She could sit here, wrapped up soft and warm in his words forever. She had no urge to move, no need to either. It was almost like being high.

After a while, Barty's story merged into ten others. A flicker from the rock's surface caught her attention. Pulling herself from her reverie was like surfacing from the bottom of a deep pool. Slowly, she turned her head toward the rock and blinked to clear her sight of the visions Barty's stories had conjured, like he'd conjured the mirror she stared at.

Dale jerked to her feet.

Loey stood near the nightstand, half of her body out of the closet's view.

"Loey!" She flung herself against the rock's surface and beat her fists against it as hard as she could.

Loey didn't react, and Dale remembered how she couldn't hear mirror-Dale while standing in her closet, on the other side of the mirror. Loey started walking almost out of sight, her movements in slow-motion.

"Barty! Help!"

Barty was already working. He drew quickly, his finger slashing through the dirt and dust at their feet.

In the reflection, Loey paused in front of the closet doorway. She should have seen Dale, but her best friend gazed straight through Dale. She walked deeper into the closet, and Dale's hopes soared.

"Loey!" Dale screamed, though she knew it was useless. "I'm right here! Look at me!"

Loey turned sharply away. Another noise had caught her attention. She started to leave.

"Barty!"

"I'm creating a disturbance, but it won't do much. It'll be more effective in getting her attention—"

A howl tore across the plains behind them. It bounced off the surrounding rocks. A chill spread across Dale's skin.

"What is that?" she whispered. Had her shouting brought the Skinned Man straight to them?

Barty rose from the ground, his symbol finished, but the look on his face scared Dale more than the thought of Loey leaving. "That's Frankie," he answered grimly. "She brought the other ghosts with her."

"They wouldn't happen to be the friendly sort, would they?"

"The friendly ones don't make that sound. I'll buy you some time." He pulled out a fistful of salt from his pants pocket. The thick grains tumbled through his clenched fingers. "The symbol will disrupt the threads on her side and hopefully get her attention."

Armed only with salt against a mob of ghosts, he strode to the cove's entrance and disappeared outside before Dale could object. Another howl ricocheted outside.

Dale spun back to the mirror and banged on the rock's surface with everything she had.

It was time to get the hell out of this place.

CHAPTER 8

L OEY CONSIDERED IGNORING THE PHONE ringing downstairs, but it might be Dale checking in. Loey needed to grab it before it stopped ringing. At the closet doorway, Loey heard a thump behind her.

Her skin prickled. She slowly turned around.

A neon pink clutch lay on the floor beside the mirror. Rows of purses lined the shelves around the closet ceiling. Dale treated her purses better than some people treated their children. She had Birkin bags up there that cost more than Loey's new barn roof. More importantly, Dale would never, ever risk putting a purse too close to the shelf's edge.

Loey crossed the closet as the phone fell silent downstairs. Distantly, she heard the answering machine turn on and a droning voice leave a message. She stopped beside the purse and looked up at the shelf, considering how it had fallen.

She was bending to pick it up when the rattling began. It came in a quick, sharp burst. She jerked upright. Nothing had moved to make that sound.

Then it came again. The mirror's heavy chrome corner shook against the wall.

"Oh, *fuck*."

Dale was trapped in her mirror.

Loey grabbed the chrome edge of the huge mirror. She

leaned it away from the wall, grunting from its weight, and scanned the back. Her eyes found the white piece of paper. She recognized the symbol, but this wasn't the symbol—or the paper—she'd used to ward Dale's mirrors. This symbol was inverted.

Upside down, it could trap a person in their mirror.

Hissing a breath, Loey ripped the page free and let the mirror slam none too delicately back against the wall. She crumpled up the page and threw it as far away as possible.

Eyes on Dale's expensive carpet, she trembled from the rush of adrenaline. She didn't know how long the symbol might last since right-side-up wards worked indefinitely. She couldn't afford to get herself trapped too, but she couldn't stare at Dale's carpet, nice as it was, for the rest of her life.

Loey cursed colorfully, using all the words and phrases she'd ever heard, then making up her own when she still hadn't gathered the courage to lift her gaze. She'd have to pray about all the swearing she'd done recently.

Another rattling sounded, louder this time and not from the mirror in front of her. The entire room shook. Accessories tumbled off the shelves and hit the floor all around Loey like a designer rainstorm. A leather duffel bag with fist-sized metal studs nearly hit her head.

"Okay!" she shouted at the empty closet. "Okay!"

The shaking stopped.

She drew her gaze up to the mirror. Her reflection stared back. After a minute passed and nothing horrible happened, she heaved out a breath.

To the mirror, she said, "I have to get some paper, but I'll be right back. Don't go anywhere."

A high-heeled stiletto flung itself from a shelf and crashed into the opposite wall.

Loey ducked, covering her head with her hands. Nothing

else took flight. She lowered her defensive shield and pointed her finger at the mirror. "This is your fault. You got yourself trapped in your mirror, so don't blame me."

She raced out of the bedroom and down the stairs. As she went, she pulled out her cellphone and called her house phone. While it rang, she ripped open drawers in Dale's kitchen, looking for paper and pens. Half the drawers were empty, and if they weren't empty, they contained white baking utensils in individual compartments evenly spaced apart. Loey couldn't find a piece of paper to save her life—or Dale's.

"Fuck!" she screamed right as Jeronimo answered the phone.

"Hello? Loey? What's happening? Did you *swear*?"

"Dale's stuck in her freaking mirror and throwing metal-studded murder weapons at me from her closet. I need a piece a paper, and this crazy girl is OCD enough to build custom drawer liners for her spatulas, but I can't find a notebook anywhere in this Martha Stewart hellhole!"

"What?"

"You heard me!" With her phone smashed between her ear and shoulder, she searched the drawers in the island.

"I'm coming over."

"No!" She dropped the phone from her ear in her panic. She picked it off the ground.

"… don't know it's her. It could be—"

"She threw a high heel at me. It's Dale. But you can't come over. Clearly, she's with Barty since I doubt Dale could cause a closet tremor of that scale on her own. You're too weak from the cemetery to be near him. Stay away. I'll deal with this."

"You're cursing, which means you're scared."

"I'm *worried*. My best friend has been stuck in her mirror for three days." She ripped into another drawer, found nothing, and slammed it shut with more anger than necessary. She flung open another. "Yes! Found it!"

She grabbed the notepad and pen and didn't bother closing the drawer, or half of the other ones she'd torn open, before racing back upstairs, taking the steps two at a time.

"Loey Grace," Jeronimo warned, "do not do anything without me. If the Skinned Man—"

"He won't," she said, rounding the corner into the closet. It was a disaster. Dale would have one heck of a mess to clean up. "Because," she added, talking to the mirror and her reflection, "Barty will keep him occupied while I look at the threads and find a place to get Dale out without causing a giant, gaping tatter in her house. Okay, Barty?"

"This is a bad idea," Jeronimo groaned.

Loey crouched in front of the mirror and set her page on the floor. She ripped open the pen's cap with her teeth and spat it aside.

"How did Dale learn the symbol to trap herself?" Jeronimo asked. "Did she replace the ward we put behind her mirror?"

"Yes, it was a different one. She got it from somewhere else."

"Someone else could have put the symbol there, knowing you would come to open the Seam. They could be waiting to attack you. Where the hell does your cat go? Can I leave him outside? Boltz!" The phone rustled and scratched, and somehow, the image of Jeronimo calling for her crispy cat comforted her.

"Don't come. I mean it."

The rustling stopped. "I can't bear the thought of you there alone."

"You're gonna have to deal with it." Loey drew thick black circles.

"Loey …"

"I've got to go."

She finished the last circle of the symbol.

"Wait! Don't—"

The call dropped the instant the Seam's lights bloomed to life in the closet. Loey tossed her phone aside. The threads were chaotic knots flashing all around her.

She hadn't expected to find a neon exit sign near the mirror, but she also hadn't expected the threads to look so impenetrable. There was no way she could untie all these knots and pull Dale through. She needed to locate a thinner spot in the Seam.

"Can you follow me? I need to look around the house for another spot. It's too thick here. Give me a sign."

The mirror clanged against the wall. Loey assumed it was an affirmative.

By the time she'd blindly felt her way to the closet door, the threads were fading. She ripped off a page in the notepad and drew another symbol. At the top of the stairs, the threads re-illuminated. She looked around for a frayed spot but found none.

Six redrawn symbols later, Loey found a frayed spot in the kitchen beside Dale's mint-colored Kitchen Aid stand mixer. She'd probably used the machine enough times to create a small tatter in the world's threads. Lord knew it was loud enough to do the damage; Loey had spent far too many evenings in this kitchen yelling over the sound of its relentless mixing.

She got to work on the knots. To the lights, she said, "Remember, Barty. You're on watch duty. No surprises."

Before she got most of the knots undone for a Dale-shaped doggie door through the Seam, Loey grabbed a can of salt out of a cabinet and dumped it in front of the tatter.

It wasn't the best insurance, but it was all she had.

Dale's house phone rang again. Loey made sure the salt line was straight before resuming untying the knots. The phone stopped ringing. The machine clicked on.

This time, as Loey untied knot after knot, she heard Dale's mother's voice on the answering machine.

"Dale Rose, if you do not pick up this phone and call me back within the next hour, I will cut off every single cent of your allowance. Do you hear me? Every cent. I know you're probably washing back every pill you own, but I don't care if you're two inches away from Heaven's gates, high as a kite, get your ass to your phone, young lady."

Loey undid a knot at face height. At first, she saw nothing but a black void, then a shadow-wrapped face with a few slices of sunbeam hair peeking through appeared right in front of her face.

"Loey!" Shadows spilled from Dale's mouth. "Get us out of here before this crazy bitch sucks the life out of me!"

"Who's sucking the life out of you?" Loey untied faster, moving on instinct alone.

The swirling shadows had cleared enough for Loey to read the fear spelled across Dale's expression. "My crazy-ass great-aunt!"

"Shit."

CHAPTER 9

"**H**URRY!" DALE SHOUTED.

Loey jolted back into action, her fingers flying from knot to knot. "Frankie's trying to kill you? I knew I was right about her grave not being salted in time."

"Not the time!" Dale screamed.

She wasn't holding it together very well. She threw another glance over her shoulder. Barty had disappeared to fight the mob of ghosts and still hadn't returned, nor had she heard any more howls. She didn't know whether that was a good sign

A knot fell loose and exposed a wide enough gap for Dale to stick her arm through, followed by her shoulder and head. Earth's air tasted crisper on her tongue than the stuff over here. Filaments of shadow wormed across the skin of her arm. She squeezed out as far as she could while Loey kept working, but the hole was too narrow.

"I need more room," Dale snarled. "Get me out of here before a pterodactyl eats me."

"There're pterodactyls in there?"

"Loey!"

Loey undid the last knot. Dale tumbled to the floor, awash in shadows. She swatted them off her.

"Are you okay? Dale, listen to me. Are you hurt?"

"I'm fine." Dale had raked most of the shadows off her

body. She used the kitchen island to pull herself to her feet. In front of Loey, she could see nothing but her countertops and cabinets.

Her heart stuttered in fear. What if she'd imagined it all—the fight, the monsters, the ghosts, the other world, *Barty*?

"Wait, where did it go?" She searched the kitchen, spinning in a circle, frantic. She could not be crazy. Not after so much hope.

She didn't know what Frankie or her gang was doing to him across the Seam, and it terrified her. An itchy desperation washed over her, like needing a fix.

"Only Tenders can see the Seam." Loey moved her hands through the lightless air, her fingers working, and Dale had to assume she was tying the lights back up.

"I saw it on the other side, but can you see Barty? Tell him to come on."

"Wait, what?"

"He was buying me time while I got your attention."

"I know he's over there, but he can't come out."

Loey was standing between Dale and her fix. Like any good pill whore, Dale blinked and her best friend was gone, replaced by someone to yell at, to rail against. She unleashed all that desperation on Loey.

"Why the hell can't he come out? Freeing him is the reason I went over there. He's *dying*, Loey Grace. Ghosts are trying to *kill* him. He can't stay in that hell a moment longer."

"He's the only thing keeping the Skinned Man from tearing into this world. Without Barty over there, Jeronimo and I won't have time to figure out how to seal the Seam for good."

As she spoke, Loey's fingers flew, tying up invisible threads of light. She remembered their brilliance. How their ends had blown loose near the rips, their flickering lights dying. How the lights had been like an aurora on the other side. They'd seemed horrible and dangerous, but she missed them. And Loey wouldn't stop her incessant tying. She wouldn't listen. The hole was getting too small for Barty.

"But he's—"

Loey's focus swung to Dale, and her expression was one Dale had never seen on her best friend's face before. Steely determination and damn the consequences. Actually, she had seen it before, but only once—the night of the graduation party at Little Cricket Creek, when Loey had agreed to frame Folton for Leigh's murder.

"Barty," she said, interrupting Dale, "has to stay over there for now. He's the only thing keeping Righteous safe from the Skinned Man. I need his help, and he knows that." She faced the empty air and continued to tie knots. To Barty, somewhere on the other side, she added, "If I could get you out, I would. You just have to keep him away from the tatters, whatever it takes. Use the mirrors to let us know if you need our help, but you know the problem. I have to figure out how to seal the Seam and how he can live with you over here too—"

"How who can live?" Dale ached to see Barty, but there was nothing but the endless white of her stupid kitchen. "Do you mean Jeronimo?"

"It's nothing," Loey said in such a hurry that Dale knew it was everything. "Don't worry. I'll figure everything out as soon as I find my grandmother's book."

Loey's mention of her grandmother's book pinged a thought in Dale's mind, but too much was happening around her to sift it out and figure out why it mattered. "Can you see Barty? Is he all right?"

"He's right here. He's fine." Loey paused. To the empty air, she asked, "Can you come here? She needs to see you. She's freaking out."

"I'm not freaking out," Dale argued on principle alone.

"You're freaking out."

Right in front of the cabinet that displayed all her favorite cake stands, a veiled shadow appeared. Dale screamed.

A sense of vertigo washed over her. She slapped her hand onto the island to catch herself. Loey spun around and grabbed Dale's arm to steady her.

"Calm down!" she said. "It's Barty. He's wrapped in shadows like you were."

Dale recognized him as she spoke. He brushed tendrils from his face so that his hazel eyes and swaths of his pale skin peered through. "I'm fine, Dale. Frankie and the others left after they saw you were gone. But Loey's right. I need to buy y'all more time over there."

Dale's hands swooped over his face, swatting away the darkness so she could see him. "I'm supposed to get you out. Frankie and her legion will snack on you until there's nothing left."

"I'll save a piece for you. How's that sound?"

He looked properly villainous with his devilish grin and mischievous eyes. Dale's belly tightened. No man had ever made her feel this way. Nothing had ever come close. And she'd only known Barty for ...

Still holding him so he wouldn't slip away, she asked Loey, "How long have I been gone?"

"Almost four days."

"Are you *serious*?"

"Your mother is not happy."

"Shit," Dale whispered and turned back to Barty. "That's not good."

Barty put his hand over hers on his face. "Don't you worry 'bout me. Frankie can be reasoned with and so can the others. Keep yourself safe. No more getting trapped in mirrors."

Acting on what her heart desired, she pulled him into a kiss.

He kissed her back like he was a man who knew what he was doing. She hated every woman he'd ever touched or considered touching. She gave him all she had to give, and nipping his lower lip, she pulled back. Another lesson from her mother: always leave men wanting more.

"That's not fair." Barty pouted, his lips glistening from her mouth.

"I'll be back soon," she promised.

No matter what, she would save him. She was meant to be his hero.

He winked like they hadn't just fought a monster and run from ghosts in a world that breathed with evil. He was pure and perfect and too bright a light for such a dark world, and she loathed watching him disappear back into it. The air in front of her cabinets became empty again.

Loey finished knotting the Seam. Her hands dropped back to her sides.

"Dale," she said. The word contained thousands of questions and statements and everything in between.

"I know. Trust me, I know."

Dale sagged against the island and sank to the floor. There was no strength left inside her to stand. She was drained, and not only from Frankie the Bitch Flashlight. Loey eased herself beside Dale, moving gingerly.

"Are *you* okay?" Dale asked.

"Bruised ribs." Loey noticed Dale's bloody shoulder and her Gucci jacket torn to oblivion. "Did something *bite* you?"

Dale released her breath before she started seeing stars. "We need to talk."

"A lot's happened."

"No shit."

"You *kissed* him." Loey opened and closed her mouth a few times, grappling with the words. She must've thought better of them because she said instead, "I need to call Jeronimo and tell him everything's fine. He'll be worried sick."

"Loey." Dale could say loads with a name too.

Loey had always looked so raw and innocent, but that was starting to change. Lately, her eyes held a certain knowing. She also looked like she hadn't slept in days. "What?"

"It's about Jeronimo."

Loey's tired eyes didn't blink. "What about him?"

"He killed Frankie."

"No, Barty did."

With their backs against the island, they were shoulder to shoulder. Beyond the kitchen's sliding glass door, the valley stretched past the reach of Dale's white picket fence threaded with climbing roses. The leaves on her maple were turning yellow at their edges. It was nice to see a real sky, even if the sun Dale was craving had begun to set.

Without preamble, Dale dove right in. "Knox Keene saw Jeronimo kill her in the creek before he found Barty at the moonshine still."

"Knox was dead before that night."

"Why would Barty lie?"

"Because he's been trapped across the Seam for decades and he hates his brother."

"He doesn't hate Jeronimo. Actually, he defends his brother a concerning amount, and that's coming from me, the expert in defending brothers."

Loey set her scarred mouth stubbornly. "I don't believe it. Barty must be crazy from all those years over there, and he's a killer. Did he tell you that? How he's killed countless people?"

Loey had called Barty crazy, but Dale was too beat up to voice her wrath. "He did."

Loey's determination slipped, and she looked scared and pale and too thin. "He told you everything?"

"Including how you warded my mirrors to keep him away from me. He told me about the Seam, you Tenders, the Skinned Man, a hell-bent revenuer hunting them all, and how the souls feed on the evil that breathes the entire world over there."

"I thought he was hurting you. That's why I warded your mirrors. Wait, did you say a revenuer?"

"His name was Thomas Wooten, and he might have followed Frankie up the ridge to see if she'd lead him to the squirrel holes. Barty thinks Wooten is the Skinned Man."

Loey chewed on that. Those deep thoughts pulled her far away from Dale's kitchen. It stung that she didn't share her thoughts with Dale, but she was too exhausted to pull them from her best friend.

"Barty is a good man," Dale said. "He can't stay over there paying for something Jeronimo did."

"You *like* him."

It sounded like an accusation on Loey's lips, and it chafed at Dale's insides, but she shoved the hurt aside. This was her best friend. Loey would never judge her for falling for the man in her mirror. "He's been with me a long time, Loey. I can't leave him over there."

Loey raked her fingers through her ponytail, ripping the tangles loose. "I need to find my grandmother's book. It's the only way we'll figure out how to seal the Seam in time. Without it, I can't help anyone."

That earlier thought came niggling back. Dale was forgetting something …

"I can help you," Dale said. "You can't trust Jeronimo. He's lying about what happened that night. You'll get Barty out before you seal the Seam?"

"I'll try."

Dale needed Loey to do a hell of a lot more than try, but her arguments tasted fuzzy on her tongue. The kitchen floor slanted beneath her. The past three days, nearly four, hit her all at once, and she swayed against Loey's shoulder.

"How long?" she murmured, her eyes drooping. "We have to hurry."

"You should be in rehab." It wasn't an answer, and it worried Dale. Or it would tomorrow, after she'd slept.

"I'm fine," she slurred. "Things are different. I'm going to save him, Lo. I have to 'cause I'm his hero."

Her best friend put her arm around Dale's shoulders and held her close. "That's what I was afraid of."

CHAPTER 10

NOVEMBER 19, 2012

DALE KNEW THREE IMPORTANT TRUTHS about how she would have to approach lying about Folton's abuse.

The first, she couldn't go to her mother right away. Darlene would want Dale to bury the secret in an unmarked grave inside Dale's mind and never return. That wasn't an option in her mission to obliterate Folton Terry Jr. from the face of the earth.

The second truth was that she needed Cross to punch her. People hated seeing something pretty get ruined. Burl would take her far more seriously if she had a huge shiner.

Thirdly, she couldn't go straight to Burl. She had to go to the next best thing. Men needed to be guided. Dale already knew this at the fresh age of eighteen. Her mother had preached this truth since Dale could bat her eyelashes. If Dale's story were to be believed—and it had to be, too much depended on it—she needed the men around her to tell the lie for her.

Dale left Loey's house and met with Cross. He dealt the blow. Dealt it well, too. He had to for it to start bruising right away. From the high school's parking lot, Dale called Travis. He picked her up, and she climbed into his lifted F-350 that his father couldn't afford, her hair covering her swelling, purpling skin.

Travis had driven into town before he noticed she hadn't spoken. His diatribe about the next UGA football game and the possibility he could start as quarterback trailed off. "Hey, you okay?"

She lifted her head and let her hair fall back completely.

Travis gaped. "What the hell happened to your eye?"

Tears welled on cue. "I can't say," she whispered like she'd practiced with Cross on the drive to Loey's after they'd executed the bulk of the mission at Folton's.

The truck slowed, its headlights illuminating a quiet Righteous, mostly tucked in for the night, except for the kids, like them, who liked to cruise the streets to be seen around town.

"Who hit you? Your mother?"

The sob tore from her throat, and it was a good one. Travis swung the truck onto the shoulder and shoved the gear shifter into park.

"Tell me." He shook all over with rage.

The emotion certainly wasn't for her but for *him*. People didn't speak well about the Jinkses in town. He, or his father's reelection campaign, could not afford the rumors that Travis hit his popular girlfriend, especially since she was an untouchable Rose. His fear-rooted rage was exactly why she could count on him to take her straight to his father with a fire in his belly for justice.

After she'd told him the tear-choked lie of Folton's abuse, he sped his truck straight to the police station. She had to hide her smile.

The kids in school took her for a slut—a dumb but pretty one. The role suited her well. It came with a protective cloak she hid behind. People didn't love Dale Rose because she was interested in baking cakes, loved Chris Cornell like he was a sexy Jesus, and thought her best friend was the strongest woman she knew. No, they loved her for her nice face and bouncy tits. Not to mention, if she was the slut they all proclaimed her to be, she might very well sleep with them.

She'd been a virgin before Folton invited her into his home. She wasn't walking out.

Cross had hit her earlier that night to leave the bruise that would seal the mission, and the impact of his fist had sung from her cheekbone, through her chest and her belly, and deeper to an ache she worried would never ease.

The bruise had done the trick, though. Travis barreled through Burl's office door in front of Dale. His father slapped at his computer keyboard to exit whatever porn website he'd been on. Quietly, Dale closed the door behind them and took her position in the corner.

"What's the matter?" Burl half rose from his desk chair, his eyes roving from Travis to Dale to her bruise. "What the hell? Who did that?"

His eyes snapped back to his son, his precious son, and the red-cheeked rage that bloomed across his face terrified Dale. The instant reaction meant he believed his son was capable of the strike that had bruised her.

Burl opened his mouth to yell, but Travis cut him off. "It was that new teacher. The queer. Folton Terry whatever. He forced himself on Dale tonight, and he's done it a lot too. She didn't ask for it neither."

Dale's heart stuttered at the last sentence he'd rushed to add—to clarify because he figured it was needed. He didn't touch her or hold her hand as he spoke. She hated to admit it, but part of her wavered. She'd been untouchable before this, a Rose put on a pedestal that her last name had bought her. After this, she'd be untouchable for an entirely different reason.

If she could cut that doubt right out of her heart, she would. It had no business in this mission.

Burl walked around his desk, put his arm around her shoulder, and guided her into the chair in front of his desk. She winced as she sat down, a detail that was fractionally an act. But both men noticed. They flocked closer to her, the broken female they needed to save.

They didn't know Dale was already the hero in tonight's story.

The thought threatened to make her smile and ruin everything. She focused on being what they needed to see. Even at eighteen, she could morph herself between one breath and the next. She began to tremble.

"You're okay, honey," Burl said softly in his big-bear voice. For some reason, Dale had always liked him. Much more than his son. "Is that true? Did Mr. Terry hurt you?"

Dale nodded behind a curtain of hair that still smelled of Folton's sweat. She hadn't had time for a shower before visiting Loey to explain what had happened in case the police came by, and now she ached for one more than she'd ever wanted anything in her entire life.

"He used to do it at school," she mumbled, "but he took me to his house this time." She lifted her battered face and teary eyes to Burl, who so desperately needed to be a real man. Burl, who so desperately needed the people of this town to need him again. To seal the deal, she begged him, "Please make it stop."

Resolve filled in the cracks in Burl's confidence that Leigh's murder had left. His newfound resolve in the face of her brokenness would put Folton behind bars for a long, long time, and Loey would be safe. Other girls at school would be safe. And the town would get the monster it craved so badly.

The only price Dale had to pay to be the hero was everything.

"You're safe," Burl told her. "Tell me what happened. Take your time. It doesn't matter how long it takes. I have all the time in the world to listen."

"We should go there right now and get 'im." Travis paced his father's office behind them.

Burl's fingers tightened on Dale's shoulder. "Get out," he ordered his son, all gentleness gone.

Travis's pacing stopped. That was a tone a son did not ignore from his father. "Yes, sir."

He didn't check with her before he scampered out of the office. That was fine. She didn't need him. His role in her mission was over.

Burl listened to her spider-web-spun story. *She* was the spider, and Folton was her prey, wrapped up tight in her web. After, Burl called her mother, and it was too late for Darlene to bury the secret; Burl had already sent deputies to Folton's house. There, they would find all the clues the sheriff desperately needed to nail a suspect in Leigh's murder.

It was a bad night, but Dale believed she could put it behind her as Burl walked her out to her mother's car. After a few murmured words between Burl and her mother, Dale climbed inside the Lincoln Navigator, which still smelled new and perfect, and closed the door.

Sitting across from her mother in the dark SUV, Dale found the one flaw she hadn't accounted for in her hero's mission: no one would save her from Darlene Rose.

CHAPTER 11

LOEY DIDN'T BELIEVE BARTY'S STORY about the night the moonshine still exploded in fifty-six—or she didn't completely believe him.

She couldn't argue that his information on the revenuer following Frankie that night wasn't useful. It meant the revenuer could have been on the ridge. He could be their Skinned Man like Barty thought. Loey knew Jeronimo hadn't killed Frankie, and Dale was convinced Barty hadn't either. It only left the revenuer. Or Knox Keene, if Barty's version of the truth could be believed.

Loey's stomach churned. If her great-great-grandfather had been on the ridge that night, she had to add him to her list of suspects regarding the Skinned Man's identity.

Sitting in her dark truck while the young families in Dale's neighborhood ate their dinners, she had called Jeronimo. She'd spent too long with Dale, listening to her sleepily hash out every detail from her time across the Seam. Loey had helped Dale stumble to her couch before leaving. A better friend without bruised ribs would've seen Dale showered, her injuries cleaned, and tucked safely into bed. One day, Dale would wake up and realize she could do better than Loey.

Jeronimo had answered her house phone right away. He'd been frantic in her ear, his worry almost comforting. Loey had meant to tell him everything while it was fresh in her mind, but she'd held back. Now that she was driving home to him, it felt like a mistake. Like she didn't completely trust him. Barty's story had gotten in her head, its tiny roots seeking purchase in her fear.

Remembering she still had one more task to complete tonight, she called Cross.

He answered on the first ring. "Did you find her?"

"She came home while I was at her house."

Cross swore. "Where the hell was she?"

She forced herself to say the words that would make him buy the story of Dale's disappearance without asking too many questions. "Little Cricket."

"But I checked there! I told her she needed to go to rehab. I *told* her."

"I know you did, but she was fine when I left. You did all you could."

Cross fell silent long enough that Loey was driving up Devil's Maw by the time he spoke again. "You were right."

Loey put the phone between her shoulder and ear so she could navigate the switchbacks and clutch with both hands. "About what?"

"Hiding her problem. We've said 'she's fine' too many times. It's time for some tough love."

Loey shifted into a lower gear and cranked the wheel. Her headlights swung around the turn, lighting patches of bent guardrail, white crosses, and scraggly pines in flashes of white light. "Give her some time, Cross. Let her catch her breath. A lot's happened here lately with Pastor Briggs and Burl, and I haven't helped matters by telling the truth about Folton. She needs our support. She needs to know we love her."

"Loving her and supporting her hasn't worked yet. It's time to rip off the Band-Aide. She needs some tough love. I can't do this anymore."

This conversation wasn't having the effect Loey had intended. If anything, it was ticking her off. She wanted to snap back at Cross that it wasn't fair for him to say he couldn't stand by Dale anymore, even though she'd stood by him for years while he slept with her husband. She held those fighting words inside. There was already too much strife in the air; she couldn't bear to add to it, not with Cross, who'd only ever wanted the best for Dale. His harsh words came from the same place of fear as her mistrust toward Jeronimo. She shifted gears and accelerated, her tires bouncing over potholes and ruts.

"Talk to her first, okay? Check on her tomorrow. When I left, she was ready to crash."

Cross cursed colorfully. Loey left him to it as she drove. The lights were on in her house. Jeronimo was likely still searching for her grandmother's book that was nowhere to be found. Blackmore Baptist had its front porch light on, and the cemetery's path lights glowed warmly in the evening's growing darkness. Jeronimo had also left on some lights in the rectory. The base of the ridge glowed to guide her home.

Why hadn't she told him everything while parked in Dale's driveway? Why had she let that seed of doubt have any room to prosper? But she couldn't help it. As she drove, she slowed the truck, her eyes on the rectory tucked in the field behind the church.

"I'll head over tomorrow and let you know how it goes," Cross said.

Loey had almost forgotten she was talking to him. A thought was forming, and she distractedly said, "Yeah, okay good. Thank you, Cross."

"Thanks, Loey. Night."

"Night."

She hung up.

The truck rounded the last curve, and the road leading to

the church came into view. Her eyes traveled farther up the ridge to her house.

To know who the Skinned Man was, she needed to know the truth about that night. If she couldn't trust the stories the men around her were telling, she would have to figure it out for herself.

She grimaced at the implications.

She switched off the truck's headlights and turned into the church's gravel drive, navigating by memory and moonlight. She said a quick prayer that Jeronimo wasn't looking out her windows to catch the glint of the truck moving along the church road. She parked alongside the church to hide the truck from view.

She opened the door and carefully closed it in case Jeronimo heard the door slam from inside her house, all the way up the road. She crept around the church and through the cemetery. Using the trees as cover, she headed toward the rectory.

She reached the sagging cottage and skulked around the side to the back door that led into the laundry room. The door tended to stick on the back porch's wooden planks, the foundation having shifted overtime, which meant the door never shut properly. It scraped horribly over the wood as she wrenched it open.

She paused before crossing the threshold. There would be no turning back once she trespassed. Out here, she could pretend she hadn't thought it necessary to search Jeronimo's home.

What did she know about him? She trusted him, for the most part, or she had before tonight. She'd kissed him twice and wanted to again, but what did she *know* about him? She'd only known the man for barely over two weeks—not enough time to be so convinced of someone's morals, especially the morals of a man prone to questionable decisions.

Before she could keep second-guessing herself, she charged inside, leaving the door open behind her.

The laundry room held the washer, dryer, and water heater, plus a large farmhouse sink stacked with cleaning supplies. Jeronimo's boots sat beside the door, and his cattleman hat hung on the hook alongside his brown leather jacket. The laundry room led into the galley kitchen, empty as she'd expected, but in the living room, she stopped cold.

"What the ..."

Books were heaped in crooked towers along the walls. They bowed the dining room table beneath their weight. Wide-mouthed mason jars full of clear liquid dotted the spaces between the books. Pages with various black symbols were strewn about as if tossed in the air in anger and left to fall like autumn leaves. Teacups, a sandwich, a batch of glass tubes like a science experiment, and a pair of reading glasses Loey had never seen Jeronimo wear marked the room like fingerprints. She couldn't comprehend how he'd gotten so much stuff here on his motorcycle, nor could she rationalize its sudden appearance. She'd seen this place cleaned out of everything aside from cleaning and cooking supplies, meaning all of this, every scrap of paper, belonged to Jeronimo.

A path through the space revealed he lived in this mess. She imagined him spending every sleepless night in this place, turning page after page in these ancient books and sipping cup after cup of tea that would never satiate his thirst.

Her first thought was *how sad*. How lonely. How ... empty.

Why hadn't he brought this stuff to her house days ago? Did he also have a seed of doubt inside him? Did he trust her? Did he wonder how she spent her late-night hours?

She picked up a full glass jar on the dining room table. She uncapped the zinc lid and sniffed. The liquid was odorless. She took a gentle sip.

The moonshine spewed from her mouth. She coughed until she saw stars.

Shakily, she screwed the cap back on and set the jar back.

She crossed to the side table beside the sofa, worn from hours of sitting. She crouched beside a wobbling stack of books. She hated the sneaking thought that surfaced as she ran her finger along the worn spines: What if Jeronimo had already found her grandmother's Tending book and he was hiding it here for his own uses? But he needed her, the Tender. He couldn't see the Seam without her.

She opened the top book—an old Bible with a family tree beautifully drawn on the first page. The trunk, limbs, and leaves were gilded. Black ink marked each branch. It was the Keene family tree, too old to include her mother's name. "Ellery" was written on one of the lowest branches. No one had filled in her death year beside her birth year, 1947. Above Loey's grandmother's name, on four separate branches, were Knox's children. Ruby Keene, Ellery's mother, had the years 1929–1961 marked on a line beneath her name. Two other branches were marked with faint names: Thomas and Penelope. The last branch from the generation was labeled "Unnamed." The death year belonging to that branch, that life, was the same death year as Knox's wife, Reba. Loey had heard she'd died in childbirth. She traced the space between the two branches. So much history on one page. So much life and death and struggle. All these names represented people with so much knowledge about Tending, knowledge Loey might never know. Her ignorance might be the end of this line of Tenders.

Where is your book, Gran? she pleaded to the page, hoping those carefully written names could answer.

"If you're looking for a dead body, it's not in there."

Dropping the book, Loey leaped up, crashed into a side table holding a lamp, and screamed. The lamp toppled onto the floor and broke in half. Jagged porcelain shards sprang across the floor.

Jeronimo stood behind her, blocking the path to the back and front doors, her only two exits.

She laughed, but sweat coated her hands. "I wasn't looking for a body."

"What are you doing, Loey?"

She was being an idiot, that's what she was doing, but she couldn't stop.

Everything she hadn't said in Dale's driveway came tumbling out. "Your brother told Dale an interesting story while she was across the Seam."

Jeronimo's jaw clenched, but he didn't take the bait. She wished she could do that: stare without blinking, mouth pursed tightly, eyes deadened of interest, not caring enough to ask the question that would be choking her if their roles had been reversed.

Loey tried to hold out for as long as she could, but in the end, they only stood there staring at each other for thirty seconds before she caved.

"He says he didn't kill Frankie."

Jeronimo didn't flinch or blink or breathe.

She really didn't like that about him.

"He said he saw Knox Keene on the ridge that night. He said Knox watched you kill Frankie in the creek. In Barty's story, your knife was already covered in blood before you put it to his throat."

"And you're looking for the knife like a good little Nancy Drew?"

His words were more challenge than question, but she answered him anyway. "I don't believe him, not completely, but you can't deny you don't have all the answers about that night. I know you said a revenuer from West Virginia sent you into hiding. Barty thinks he followed Frankie up the ridge before the storm. We need to know what happened to figure out who the Skinned Man is."

"We don't need to know who he is to seal the Seam."

"I'm not damning a man to hell without knowing his name."

"What difference does it make?"

"It makes a darn big difference," she fired back. "Was Knox Keene on the ridge that night?"

"He was dead," Jeronimo growled. "You know this."

"Then why did your brother say he was there?"

"My brother killed more men than the dirt on this ridge could hold. He lies. He cheats. And he manipulates. He's been on the other side for over sixty years. I left him there with Frankie's ghost and a monster. It's my fault he's the way he is and lying the way he is, so drop it."

She wouldn't. "Did you kill Frankie?"

Jeronimo stalked toward her. If there had been room around her to retreat, she would have. As it was, she had to hold her ground. She lifted her chin as he stopped a few steps away from her, close enough that she could touch his chest if she wanted to. She didn't.

"Why would I try to kill my brother if I killed her? Do you think I'm so horrible?"

"I don't know what to think."

"You said you didn't think I'd done it. Now you don't know what to think?"

"J," she whispered, "what happened that night?"

His midnight irises lightened to smoky gray, but he blinked and they were black again, the moment gone. "I've told you once, and I won't tell you again. Get out of my house."

"But—"

"*Now.*"

110

She stood there for a breath, hoping he'd change his mind, ask her to stay and talk it out, but he glared at the Bible she'd dropped and the lamp she'd broken. Anywhere but her.

Giving up, she brushed by him and hightailed it to the front door. She tumbled into the night air, her breath in her throat and her heart pounding. She slammed the door shut and ran.

At the cemetery's gates, she leaned against the metal to catch her breath, her aching ribs making it nearly impossible. The rectory's lights were all off, the cottage cast in darkness, merely a shadow in the night. It would've been lost to the tree line if Loey hadn't known where to look. She walked back through the cemetery with her arms wrapped around her waist and her shoulders hunched to her ears.

In the heart of the graveyard, she paused at Townsend Rose's grave. She'd long ago scrubbed away the message that had been scrawled on the weather-worn rock the night Briggs died.

I'm back and I ain't forgotten.

A message of vengeance, perhaps written by the Skinned Man or someone who liked inviting evil into their lives. Who that someone could be was an entirely different tangle in the web of lies ensnaring Loey.

Alongside Townsend's grave were the graves of the other men who'd ruled Righteous. One from his Tender throne. Another with his iron crown. A trio of power. Knox Keene's headstone carried the death date of March 3, 1956, like the Bible in Jeronimo's house had listed. The date was over a month before the moonshine still's explosion. Why would Knox fake his death? And was it connected to the land on Shiner's Ridge he'd willed to Townsend Keene? If so, could Loey have found the answers in Obidiah Jinks's journal? The one she'd all but destroyed?

If Knox had been alive a month after he was buried, damning Thomas Wooten as the Skinned Man wasn't so clear cut, even if the bloody message left on Townsend's grave made more sense coming from a revenuer bent on justice decades later. Considering Knox as a suspect, that her family could harbor a monster made evil by fire and a pocket world, was too much after such a long day.

Her gaze drifted down from Knox's headstone to the packed earth before it.

Blasphemous and horrible—her grandmother would be ashamed of Loey for thinking it.

But Loey knew of one way to know for certain if Knox had been alive that night in April, and it involved shovels.

CHAPTER 12

DALE WOKE UP ON HER couch to sunlight cutting across her eyelids.

Shielding her face with a hiss, she dragged a blanket over her head, but the minuscule movements sent nauseating pain rolling from her chest to her shoulder and into her head, where a raging migraine built. Even her eyelashes hurt.

And she *smelled*.

She eased back the blanket to see the destruction. Her velvet tracksuit was ruined with black dirt and dried blood. The same dirt and blood coated her cream sofa, which had cost more than a month's mortgage payment.

Ruined. All ruined.

She knew what would make it better: a Valium. A few of those little magical unicorn pills and she wouldn't care about the damn sofa.

But she couldn't get high; she had important things to focus on today. Too much was at stake. She was on a mission, again, and she could not fail.

Her first order of business was getting off the couch. Simply considering the act felt like more than she could manage, but picturing Barty was enough to get her moving. With one leg sliding off the couch then the other, she slowly sat up. The room spun. Her mouth watered with the impending threat of puking up every last bit of her insides. She swallowed it down and dragged herself upstairs. The only sound in the entire house were her footsteps shuffling across the carpet, down the hall, and to her bedroom.

She undressed as she limped to the bathroom on her swollen feet. Naked, she cranked the claw-foot bathtub's hot knob all the way open. The water jetted out, splashing across the pristine porcelain to fill the tub.

Knowing better than to sink her bloody, dirty body into the clean water, she went to the shower. She stood beneath the icy stream as her shivers worsened. The water battered the raw bite on her shoulder. She bore the pain until, eventually, the water ran clear and the punctures on her shoulder were clean. She stepped out, dripping onto the bathmat and across the bathroom tiles as she limped to the bath, and gingerly eased herself into the steaming tub, one foot after the other. Her skin prickled and turned numb at the drastic change from cold to hot. It was her favorite way to feel. Only then did she examine the damage Frankie had dealt her.

Dale's chest was a Fuck You Hallmark card of purple, black, and yellow bruises spread across her torso. Rose women could land a solid blow, that was for certain. Dale sank deeper into the water so she wouldn't have to see her battered body.

Her skin pruney, Dale climbed out. She toweled off, scrubbing until she was pink and raw but clean, as clean as she'd ever been. She rubbed antibiotic ointment into her shoulder and bandaged the deeper punctures. Her feet were another matter. She settled for coating them in a salve and wrapping them in mounds of gauze so she could bear to walk.

A tightness constricted her lungs. She coughed until her mouth filled with thick mucus lined in grit.

She spat a black lump into her sink, turned on the water, and watched it swirl down the drain. It should probably worry her more than it did—for all she knew, the pocket world could have given her cancer—but she'd always had a knack for focusing on the issues at hand.

The biggest one being Barty.

Naked and dripping the last few droplets of water from her skin, she regarded the mirror before her, ignoring the woman in it. She gripped its edges and lifted it off the hooks. It was heavy, and the muscles in her chest and shoulders screamed with pain, but she got the mirror off and sat it down on the vanity. Sure enough, on the back, she found another page like the one behind her closet mirror.

A ward with an *A* shape.

She ripped it off.

It fluttered to the bathroom floor. Ignoring the pain, she sat the mirror back in its spot; things out of place bothered her in the raw spot of her stomach that liked to burn and hiss and spit.

A rattle came so softly she thought she imagined it. She held her breath, waiting, her eyes trained on the mirror. Nothing else happened.

"Barty?" she whispered to her reflection. "Is that—"

The bathroom door banged open, and Travis barged in, stumbling and swaying to a stop at the sight of her naked in front of her mirror.

"Hey!" Dale clapped her arms over her chest. "Get out of here!"

His eyes roamed her naked, battered body in the least sexual way possible. "Holy shit. What happened to you?"

He smelled like a barroom floor and looked as bad as one. "Are you drunk at nine in the morning?"

"That wouldn't be very Christian of me, would it? No, I'm still drunk from last night."

"That's so much better."

He stabbed a finger at her, but the effort nearly made him

fall forward. She scooted a couple of inches away. "You can't say nothin'. Where you've been, huh? Little Cricket? That why you need a bath? 'Cause you had to roll some inbred hick for a few pills? Gotta clean out your—"

She lunged. Travis skittered back toward the door and snarled at her like a cornered fox.

"You don't speak to me like that." She dropped her arms from her breasts, baring herself before her husband. He only cowered farther away from her naked form.

Back in high school, he had touched her sometimes, his fingers uncertain. She had the impression he'd hated it, but occasionally, he would try to convince himself he couldn't be gay if he enjoyed his girlfriend's youthful, bouncy body, though it never went further than a hand under her skirt.

That was before Folton. After the details—the *lies*—she'd told Burl came out, Travis stopped trying to convince himself with her body.

She reckoned he found other women for that. She was stained. He didn't say it out loud, but she knew.

"Or what?" He clutched at the last few scraps of his dignity.

She stepped toward him and he moved back, toward the door and safety. "Why are you drinking so much that you're still drunk the morning after?"

"We all have our vices in this family."

"This," she snapped, motioning between the two of them, "is *not* a family, and you better be careful. Keep this up and people will see you for what you are."

"They can't tell I'm gay from the way I drink."

"No, Travis." She shook her head, her anger dimming. It felt wrong to rage against such a broken man. "They won't know you're gay. They'll know you're just like your father—a drunk who hated himself. That's what they'll see."

"Pill whore."

"Nice. Very mature. Now leave."

She grabbed her robe from the back of the shower. It engulfed her like a giant fleece of safety.

Travis lingered by the door. He looked like hell. Wrinkles had appeared on his once handsome face overnight, his eyes were bloodshot, and his hair hung in greasy clumps. His clothes reeked of sticky bar tops and cigarette smoke.

"Travis," she tried again. He had always been her weak spot. She'd once believed he'd needed her to save him, and perhaps he had, but they'd forgotten that along the way. He looked like he could use a savior, though. "Are you okay?"

He sniffed. His eyes skittered around the bathroom but never met hers. "What do you think? My father killed himself."

"I am sorry. I know he was hard on you, but he was your dad."

"What if I'm next?"

Dale flinched. "You're not."

"We're blood. That weakness runs in the family."

"It's not a weakness to be hopeless, Travis. He couldn't see his way out of it, but you're too stubborn to go the same way."

His roving eyes landed on her. It had been longer than she could recall since they'd looked at each other. Normally, they were ships at sea, passing each other with distant hails but nothing more, never too close, the current and trade winds ensuring their lives remained distant.

"Thank you," he whispered.

"Should I call Cross?"

"I'm going to bed." He hesitated. "Are you … okay?"

"I'm fine, Travis. Be careful. You might redeem yourself from calling me a pill whore."

His lips fluttered toward a smirk. "You would never—"

Someone banged on the front door. A squeak of fright slipped from Dale's mouth before she could clutch it back inside.

Travis grimaced. "That must be your mother. I texted her after I saw you were home."

"Wow. Thanks."

"Sorry, sweetie."

She flipped him off.

"Let me know if you need backup. I'll be in my room."

Dale checked her reflection. The shower and bath had rid her body of evidence from the pocket world, but the experience showed in her sunken eyes and the bruises beneath them. It looked like a pigeon had roosted in her air-drying curls.

Her mother had taught her that unruly curls were for ugly girls. Dale had learned to blow out and straighten her locks to within an inch of their life since middle school.

The banging came again. Dale didn't even have time for mascara.

She went downstairs to face her fate.

Darlene Rose had used her emergency house key to let herself in. She stood in the center of the living room, wearing a black suit with a white shirt unbuttoned right above her décolletage. Black because she was in mourning, and the risqué show of skin because she'd had her tits redone and was proud. But not too proud. She was a married woman, after all, though only a musty piece of paper filed away in the courthouse bound her marriage.

Her mother gawked at the sight of Dale descending the stairs. "Heavens above, what in His good name happened to your hair?" She made a face as she inspected the disgrace that had shuttled from her vagina. "And what happened to your *face*? Couldn't you have put on a dab of concealer?"

"Good to see you too, Mother."

Dale stopped in front of her mother, and Darlene scrutinized her, steps away from the ruined couch she had no doubt already noticed. Her perfectly sculpted brow lifted, a feat given the amount of Botox in the woman's forehead. "Shouldn't you be in rehab?"

Dale lifted a shoulder. "Decided to pass."

"You always were *so* smart."

"Got it from you."

"If you think you're not paying me back for that resort, you're wrong. Gracious, Dale, it was a glorified vacation and you couldn't do that much."

"Sorry my addiction is affecting your schedule."

"If you'd exercise some self-control, we wouldn't have this problem."

"What problem is that?"

Darlene's cobalt eyes turned arctic. Dale knew that look. She swayed, and her mother noticed how she had to grab onto the couch cushions. Darlene sniffed, the sound self-righteous, assuming her daughter was already high this morning.

"About Folton Terry Junior. Ring any bells?"

The breath gusted out of Dale. Things would be so much better, so much duller, if she'd taken a few pills. Her heart panged with desire for the powdery residue on her tongue, the feeling of swallowing that hard promise down her throat.

"Oh," she managed.

"Your friend thought it a good idea to tell everyone it was all one big lie. Apparently, he was diddling her all along. Imagine my surprise to hear this from Matt Everton of all people. Do you understand how much money this will take?"

Dale rubbed her aching temples. She felt, with every fiber of her being and deep into the gross stuff in the middle of her bones, exhausted.

"Don't you *dare* ignore me."

Dale looked up at her mother. "Why does it need to take any money?"

"To make it go away."

"I don't think this can go away."

To Darlene Rose, suggesting such a thing implied incompetence or a lack of available resources, and such a slight would not go unpunished. Dale watched her mother store away her daughter's careless words into her mental filing cabinet of punishments to be doled out at a better date. The only outward sign that Dale had royally pissed her mother off was a slight flaring of her nostrils.

"Keep close to Travis, stop going to that coffee shop so much, and start volunteering at a homeless shelter."

"Whatever you say."

Her mother moved far faster than any woman had a right to in stilettos, and Dale's cheek bloomed with spiking heat, her head cracking to the side beneath the blow. She hadn't seen her mother raise her hand, so fast was the strike. The heat spread across her cheek to her eyes.

"Don't you take that tone with me, young lady. Don't forget who you are in this town."

"How could I? You always remind me."

Darlene trembled at Dale's words. Her rage crashed over her like a full-body immersion in a cold creek. Dale sensed her mother's desperation to hit her again, saw it in the shaking of her hand, still red from the first blow.

"Your last name is all you've got." Darlene clenched her hands to hold back their shaking. "But that can go away too. Your father and I can step away from you, and you'll have no one. You'll be alone to burn like the sinner you are."

Her mother spun on this season's Prada heels and clacked out of Dale's house. The front door didn't slam. Her mother likely already wore a smile, her red hand discreetly folded against her purse. She'd nod hello to any of Dale's neighbors on the street, painting a vision of togetherness and fortitude. A shining example of a good Christian, Southern woman. A Rose through and through.

"Good pep talk, Mother," Dale murmured to her quiet house. "Real encouraging."

She sank onto her ruined couch in her clean robe. All her previous gumption toward the day dwindled away.

On top of everything else, Loey had unearthed the dirty lie about Folton. They should've kept it buried. In areas concerning Folton, Loey was blind. That was okay—it always had been. That was why she had Dale to protect her, but sometimes, Dale got tired. She wanted to shake Loey and tell her to let it go, to move on and stop letting this man drag them into these dark places where Dale couldn't breathe and couldn't see and couldn't find her way.

Look, Loey, Dale wanted to scream. *Look at everything I have to keep you from. Look at everything that is so* not *okay, no matter how honest you are.*

Dale wasn't okay.

And she wouldn't be until Barty was free.

CHAPTER 13

NOVEMBER 19, 2012

THE PASSING HEADLIGHTS ON THE highway burned Dale's eyes. She sank down in the seat of her mother's SUV, her knees drawn up beneath her chin and her arms wrapped around her shins.

She was exhausted and she hurt deep inside and she smelled like the stale air of the small room she'd sat in for hours, telling her story over and over again. Her stomach growled, but she didn't dare ask her mother to pull over at a McDonald's, because Darlene Rose was very, very unhappy with her daughter.

Her tirade had started as soon as they'd pulled away from the station, ensconced in the soundproof barrier of her Lincoln. They were halfway to Knoxville, and it hadn't stopped.

"… can't believe you would do this. What were you thinking? Why didn't you come to me first? We could have handled this discreetly. My God, Dale, it's going to be in the paper."

"It's called rape, Mother."

Darlene made a noise in the back of her throat. Perched on the edge of her seat, she gripped the steering wheel like it was the only thing tethering her to Earth.

"Oh, hush. That's such a nasty word."

"But he did." Dale hated how pouty she sounded. She sank deeper into her cocoon. They hadn't called her father yet. She wondered if they would, or if her mother was taking her to his office in Knoxville.

"Let me guess, you had nothing to do with it?"

"Mom!" Dale had had something to do with it today. She had lured the snake, but that wasn't the point. Loey hadn't, and for her, Dale would fight for both their honors. "Hell no."

"Don't you dare swear, missy."

Her mother didn't speak for a long time after that. They took an exit into a town called Maryville outside of Knoxville, and Dale breathed a sigh of relief. They weren't going to her dad's office.

"What are we doing here?"

Her mother drove into the parking lot of a CVS. She put the car in park but left it running. She didn't take off her seatbelt.

"You're going into that store," she said, "and you're asking them for Plan B. If they ask how old you are, call me and hand them your phone."

Dale sat up straight in her seat. "Isn't that the stuff you take after sex to not get pregnant?"

"Yes." Her mother pulled out a few crisp bills from the wallet she kept in the console. She held them out to Dale.

Dale did not take the money. "You drove to Maryville to buy Plan B? Why?"

Her mother snapped the bills at Dale, who finally took them. Her hand shook with fear. She'd executed her mission flawlessly. She'd moved adult men around her chess board like pawns, all to protect the queen. But Dale faltered.

"Mom?" she asked, her voice cracking. "Why are we buying that stuff?"

Her mother stared forward, her spine achingly straight. "The one thing that would make this distasteful situation worse is if you fell pregnant with his bastard."

Dale tightened her fist around the money in her hand. Could she get pregnant? She hadn't considered it. Her mission hadn't ventured into the realms of what might happen *after*.

"Hurry up. I don't want to be out all night."

"You ... you won't go in with me?"

"Of course not," her mother snapped.

Silly, but Dale was scared to go in the store alone. She'd stared a monster in the eye as she'd lain in his bed and he ... It was silly because, of all the things she'd done today, this coldness from her mother as she stared straight ahead and refused to look at her daughter scared Dale most of all.

"Of course you won't. Someone might recognize you."

"Don't take that tone with me, young lady," her mother said, whipping her glare toward Dale, and Dale thought she'd won, but her mother gazed off over Dale's shoulder. She hadn't won at all. Maybe she'd lost more than she'd thought today.

She stepped out into the brisk winter air. She didn't have a jacket. The wind stirred up his scent beneath her nose. Dale wanted to throw up.

"Don't dally and no sweets, either," her mother called from the car. "I expect change—"

Dale slammed the door on her mother's words.

Inside, the clerk at the front register said, "Good evening! Let me know if you need anything."

Dale walked straight to the back of the store, to the blue and white restroom symbol atop an archway into a low-ceilinged hall. She went into the women's bathroom and locked the door behind her.

The floor was dirty, wet in spots, and littered with used paper towels. She gripped the sink's sides hard enough that her arms shook. She stared at her reflection. It would've been nice, this once, to see him. He would've given her the courage to walk out and ask the clerk for baby-killer medicine with her head held high, her hero's armor protecting her heart.

But he wasn't there. She was alone.

It's okay, she told herself. *Things will be better now.*

It didn't work, so she spoke aloud.

"You are okay. You are not sad. You are not scared. You have to be okay. Do you hear me? Do you hear me, young lady?" With each word her voice rose. Her breathing came in shallower. The room swirled and she couldn't breathe and nothing was okay and nothing might ever be okay again and her mother hated her and her father would never come home for sure anymore.

She was not okay, and no one cared. Not her mother or her father or Travis or Cross or Sheriff Jinks or, worst of all, Loey.

Not even Loey, because Dale had taken care of the monster. She'd only ever wanted to protect Loey, so she did not blame her best friend.

She opened her mouth to tell herself she was a hero, but the words came out all wrong.

They were a single, long scream. She screamed and didn't stop until fists banged on the door and someone kicked it open and her mother pushed the store clerks aside and said her daughter had mental problems and no, they didn't need to call the police, they were fine.

They had to stop at another store for Plan B.

Her mother was very, very unhappy with her daughter.

CHAPTER 14

LOEY'S CUSTOMERS HAD STARTED ASKING about the lack of Dale's baked goods. The roll-top counter sat empty of blueberry scones, puff pastries with cream, breakfast sandwiches, and all the other temptations Dale provided the shop daily. The customers wondered about Loey's stiff excuses, and in their eyes, she saw their assumptions.

Fallen off the wagon again, they would murmur just out of reach of Loey's hearing.

As if she was ever on it.

Have you heard …

Nasty business, all of it.

Loey slammed down a mug on the counter. The handle broke off, but Mrs. Herbert's gossip cut right off. The woman flushed up the back of her neck as she and her fellow crones scampered to the back of Loey's shop. They would continue to wag loose tongues about Dale, but Loey wouldn't have to hear it, though it was bad enough that they had the nerve to speak the words in her shop.

Toward the end of the lunch rush, the crowd had dwindled. The bell above the door chimed.

Loey looked up and said on reflex, "Afternoon. How can I help you?"

She recognized the person gliding up to her counter

131

wearing a cat-with-a-mouse grin.

Tabitha Richart, editor-in-chief of *The Righteous Daily*, was no sweet housecat. More like a panther. She was in her late thirties and had a whip-lean runner's body, with black skin and green eyes that could spook a grown man, which was why people liked to joke about her spinster ways and collection of cats.

Like most people who dared to be different in a small town, the gossip kept Tabitha contained in a safe box of stereotypes.

In truth, she had birds, not cats. An aviary took up her entire backyard. A hodge-podge of salvaged windows and doors framed out the aviary's dome that stuck up between the hickories down on Charlatan Lane, the bird calls like a forest unto itself. The neighbors would have bickered about the noise, or perhaps for a more buried reason like Tabitha's skin color— Tabitha being one of the few women of color in town—but the beauty and sound of the aviary, and the fact Tabitha let anyone come visit her birds, kept her neighbors quiet.

She'd been a war journalist in Afghanistan, Iran, and Syria. Rumor had it she'd been fired for publicly protesting her magazine's stance on the refugee crisis. She'd written an exposé about the capital-funding company, which owned the magazine, loaning money to companies that employed refugees in sweatshops for pennies on the dollar and the unfulfilled promises of work VISAS in countries where their families wouldn't be blown apart in the streets.

The magazine had sued Tabitha. The case had been ugly. She'd won in the way the mattered, but in all the ways that mattered more, Loey guessed the woman hadn't since she'd ended up in Righteous, writing pieces on the town's current events, like the Fall Festival.

When she strode into Deadly Sin Roasters, Loey's stomach cramped.

"Good afternoon, Loey Grace. Nice day, yeah?" She flopped her massive leather satchel onto the counter. The stack of bangles jangled on her thin wrists.

"Yeah, sure. Great weather." Loey laughed nervously. "What can I get you, Tabitha?"

The woman exuded a viscous presence that dripped like warm honey over anyone brave enough to bask in her glow. Today she wore black jeans and a faded denim shirt with an embroidered leather jacket tossed over her shoulders. Giant silver hoops danced through her careless curls.

"Call me Tabi. We haven't actually talked before, have we?"

"You don't come in very often. Or at all."

"Why buy coffee if the paper has a perfectly good machine in the break room?"

Loey wrinkled her nose. "That's not coffee. That's a massacre."

"I've seen massacres." Loey noticed the slightest gap between her two front teeth as her lips peeled back around the words. "Coffee does not equate. But I didn't come here to correct your privilege."

"Oh. Oh, no. I meant …" Loey's thoughts scrambled. Everything she could say might be taken the wrong way, leaving nothing but gibberish and apologies. "I didn't mean that literally. Tabitha—"

"It's Tabi, and before you start, you should know I'm here for the story."

That took Loey's attention off her blunder. She knew exactly the story Tabitha wanted. Her gut burbled sourly. She should've known this would happen. The townspeople were already murmuring about the drama brewing down at the police station. "How did you find out?"

"Mrs. Rose's small army of attorneys piqued my interest."

Loey wiped her hands down her apron, leaving behind a

gritty streak of coffee grounds. "I don't know if there's a story after all this time."

"There's a story. Trust me."

"I don't."

Her smirk fell away in favor of surprise that Loey could bite back. "That's fair. I get that."

Loey put her hands on her hips to feel bigger, taking up space behind her counter, in her shop, in her town. "I'm assuming you're publishing a story with or without me."

"I am."

Tears sprung in her eyes, and Loey glared at the wooden floor. So much for feeling big. She was shrinking by the second.

"But," Tabi continued, "I'm not trying to capitalize on your pain—"

"Get off your high horse," Loey snapped, surprising them both. "You are. Don't call it anything else."

Tabi held up her hands in surrender, but her eyes shone too brightly. "I want *your* story. The real one. This isn't a news article for the paper. I'm not reporting on who won the cake walk at the Fall Festival. I want a thought-provoking editorial that'll give people the gray truth behind the black and white facts."

"You want a viral sensation."

"That too."

Loey's heart sank. She'd only wanted the lies to stop. To have control over one truth in her life. She hadn't anticipated this, though. She couldn't remember why telling the truth had been paramount in the wake of so many other things to worry about.

"Maybe we can work out some sort deal ..." Tabi said, her words dripping honey. She wanted to catch Loey in her trap, but if Loey saw the trap coming, that wouldn't make her a fool, right?

"What kind of deal?" she asked carefully.

Tabi reclined against the countertop like she was modeling, her eyes slanted up at Loey with a mischievous glint. "Name something."

Loey opened her mouth to refuse, then recalled the diary drying on her windowsill.

Given how this conversation was going, she had two options: she could put a supremely capable and ruthless journalist on the scent of the diary and the timber deal between Righteous's three founding families, or she could turn Tabi onto the missing revenuer. The second option felt too close for comfort, and if Tabi sniffed too closely, she might unearth something.

Loey made her decision, even though she knew it had been made for her long before Tabi decided to give her the courtesy of pretending she wielded any power in this scenario. If Loey was going to lose, she could at least get something from the exchange.

"There is something," Loey began. "Do you know about the deal between Townsend Rose and Obidiah Jinks? The timber reserve that fueled the Jinkses' smelteries?"

"I know the Roses pulled the deal because of some slight way back when, and it ruined the Jinks family."

"A slight? I hadn't heard that." Or had she? Keeping track of all the small-town grudges was impossible.

"What does this have to do with Folton Terry Jr.?"

Loey tucked away the nugget of information about a slight and reminded herself to ask Jeronimo about it—if he ever spoke to her again.

"This has nothing to do with him," she said. "This deal is connected to my family. Knox Keene willed the land in that deal to Townsend Rose, but I have a diary from Obidiah Jinks."

Tabi's interest honed. "How did you get it?"

"Ah … I found it."

"You stole it."

"No!"

"Loey," Tabi said, "in this business, finding means stealing, but I'll pretend I didn't hear how you 'found' this journal. Keep talking."

"I accidentally ran it through the wash—"

Tabi laughed. The sound filled the coffee shop, spilling into the corners and up the walls. Loey might have smiled if she hadn't been up to her eyeballs in stress about her grandmother's book, the Skinned Man's identity, and a man she couldn't trust but whose lips she craved.

"The ink is all muddled together. I don't have time to sort through it, but it could shed some light on that deal."

"Why does the deal matter?"

How could Loey explain that her family might have produced the worst monster the town had ever seen? How could she tell enough of the truth to spark Tabi's interest without telling her everything? Tabi wouldn't follow the scent based on a hunch alone. She needed to sink her teeth into some meat first.

"I have reason to believe," Loey said slowly to give herself time to change her mind, "that Knox Keene was a bad man."

Tabi angled her head in silent question, not interrupting but prompting Loey to continue.

"My grandparents raised me, and they never spoke of him much, but when they did, it sounded like he'd done something bad." A small truth bundled in lies. "That diary mentioned Knox, but I ran it through the wash and now I can't read most of it. With Folton and all ..." Loey paused for effect. She'd been around Dale enough to know how to play people. "I don't have time to decipher it."

Tabi wasn't one to be played. Those green eyes shone. "Or it might be that new preacher taking up all your time."

"We're friends," Loey said through clenched teeth.

"Sure. You got this diary with you?"

"It's at my house."

"Good. You can bring it to our next meeting. I'll call you." Tabi slung her bag onto her arm.

Her long legs had carried her to the shop's door by the time Loey called out, "You don't have my cell number."

Tabi paused, her hand on the door handle, and tossed back a grin. "I have my ways, remember?"

The door opened before she could leave, and Matt Everton walked in. With a smile and nod that only looked slightly mocking, Tabi stepped back to let him pass. Loey was starting to understand why most people in town didn't think too highly of the paper's editor. It might have been the pull for the underdog, but Loey didn't mind her, not yet anyhow.

"Afternoon, Sheriff," Tabi crooned.

"Tabitha."

"Talk soon, Loey!" Tabi waved and left.

While he watched Tabi stroll down the street, Loey returned to her cleaning. Finally, he walked away from the door, scratching his head, his cop face in place. "What was Tabitha doing here?"

"She likes to go by Tabi."

"I don't care what she likes to go by. Why was she in here?"

Loey paused in the middle of stacking clean mugs beneath the counter. She straightened and studied Matt. "Are you going to question me about every customer who comes in? Should I have sign-in sheets at the door so you can double-check alibis?"

"Loey," he sighed like she was the ridiculous one. "She only came in here for one thing—"

"I know what she's after. You don't have to speak down to me just because you've seen me naked."

Color flooded his cheeks. He darted glances around the

mostly empty shop to make sure the dust bunnies beneath the bookshelves hadn't overheard.

"That is not why. Why are you acting like this?" he asked under his breath. "I care about you, is all, and I don't want that woman's stories hurting you. She was fired from her last job 'cause she lied to bolster her by-line."

"I'm acting like this because you're speaking to me like I'm an idiot and I'm over it. I can handle myself. Also, by the way, she did not lie in that article." Loey had no clue what Tabi might have done, lying or otherwise. "I know what she's after. She told me plain as day. To be honest, I think it's a good idea."

"It ain't a good idea." He resembled a blustering Burl Jinks, the man Matt had idolized before the sheriff's fall from grace, God bless him. "Actually, it might be illegal given all the lawyers Mrs. Rose is parading around town."

"You sound like you've been spending too much time with the lawyers."

Matt squeezed the brim of his ball cap like he was squeezing sense into her instead. "Loey Grace—"

"Why are you here?" she interrupted, feeling none too nice and losing the last of her patience by the second.

"You didn't come by yesterday like I asked."

His text popped into her memory. She pressed the heel of her palm against her forehead. Her anger fizzled out in the face of her blunder. "Shoot. I totally forgot. Yesterday got … busy."

"I came by, but you'd closed the shop early. You never close up early. I'm worried about what you're getting yourself into. I'm assuming you closed early for Dale?"

She stared at him, not giving anything away.

"Sure. Girl pact and all that. Secrets to the grave. Next time you see her, tell her she needs to come by the station. I don't want to have to go by her house and pick her up in a cruiser."

"I'll give her the message."

"There's something else," he said quickly before Loey could return to stacking mugs.

She raised her eyebrows at him.

"This business is embarrassin' for the state, and with Burl's death and how that's shedding uncertainty on his casework … well, the county district attorney is rushing this through." Matt had turned pale. "They have the plea ready for you and Dale to sign. They're trying to get it all taken care of before the media picks it up. That's why you should stay away from Tabi and her paper."

"Matt—"

"And I would never imply you can't handle yourself," he forged on, "but this is bigger than you. This affects a lot of people."

"You think I don't know that?" Her knuckles turned white around the edge of the countertop. "I know all about how this lie has affected people. That's why I want it over with—so it can stop holding so much power over everyone."

Matt took off his hat and ran his hand through his hair. He was due a trim. It curled over the tops of his ears and made him look like a teenage boy again.

"You should have kept this to yourself. Would've saved everyone a lot of trouble."

Her insides flushed cold. In her silence, Matt sensed his error.

"That came out wrong. I meant—"

"I know exactly what you meant. You said it plain enough."

"I'm sorry, Lo."

"Yeah. Aren't we all?"

CHAPTER 15

TODAY WAS THE DAY OF Righteous's Fall Festival. The festivities lasted from early Friday morning until the final event at the rodeo tonight. The event would be all people spoke about. It would soon spill over from the town square and down Main Street like a venereal disease.

Dale had always hated festivals. If not for the traffic they created, then for the fake cheer everyone tucked into so heartedly like they hadn't done this exact same thing every year since they could stuff a caramel apple into their chubby child cheeks.

Normally, she passed the time with a few pills and an endless quest of supplying baked goods, but today she had other plans.

The thought that had stirred at Loey's mention of her grandmother's Tending book had simmered in Dale's reserves all day yesterday while she'd lain in bed like a pathetic excuse for a human. She'd woken this morning to the thought bursting across her mind and remembered what had been nagging her.

Last Saturday, before all Hell broke loose, Grandmother Helene had mentioned finding a book right around the time she'd been close to freeing Barty. In the tractor-trailer load of shock Helene had dealt that day, the innocuous comment about a book had slipped by Dale without much notice.

141

It could be nothing, but Dale didn't believe in coincidences anymore.

She woke early and made coffee. The house was quiet; a quick listen outside Travis's room indicated he'd left sometime in the night again. She hoped he had the good sense not to get behind the wheel if he found himself in the same drunken state as yesterday.

Coffee mug in hand, she started on her first call.

"Good morning," a voice chirped on the other end. "This is Green Hills Luxe. How may I direct your call?"

"Hi!" Dale matched her cheer for cheer by channeling her former pageant days. "I'm calling to speak with my grandmother, Helene Rose. This is Dale Rose-Jinks. I should be on her approved list."

"Let me pull up Mrs. Rose's file." A clattering of keys sounded through the phone. "Ah, yes. I see your name here. I can connect you to Mrs. Rose's on-duty nurse. Would that be okay?"

"Yes, ma'am. Thank you."

"You're welcome. Please hold."

Dale spent the few minutes on hold downing her coffee and pouring another cup from her French press. Leaning a hip against the marble counter, she stared out over her backyard, an expanse of forgotten vegetable patches and rose bushes that grew purely to spite her. Out here, with one foot in the valley, she could almost imagine she didn't live in Righteous. As if she could ever leave; her mother would never stand for it—Roses were only important in Righteous.

"Mrs. Rose-Jinks?"

Dale started at the voice in her ear. "Yes?"

"This is Cathy. I'm your grandmother's nurse. You wanted to speak with her this morning?"

"Yes, ma'am. I wanted to chat with her."

"I'm afraid she's not having a good day. We've given her medicine to keep her calm, but it makes it hard for her to comprehend what people are saying."

"I don't want to agitate her, but I would like to try to speak with her? She might remember me if I told her some stories ..."

She let her voice trail off hopefully, appealing to the good nurse's compassion. Nurses, Dale knew from experience, were pure freaks. She had no idea how God had created such devoted, patient, empathetic creatures, but the world sure as shit got lucky that there were some people breathing on it who were willing to endure, and enjoyed, the job of nursing. Those individuals deserved sainthood. They were better humans than Dale would ever be, and she wasn't ashamed to admit it.

Cathy crumbled under Dale's well-meaning ruse. "Certainly, Mrs. Rose-Jinks. Let me put her on the line."

She felt bad manipulating the nurse's good nature, but she was on a mission.

"Thank you, Cathy."

"Of course, dear."

The phone scratched, and soft wheezing filled the line.

"Grandmother?" Dale asked carefully, wondering who she would get on the other end.

"Who's this?" came Helene's biting reply.

It was the cold matriarch today, the one hiding behind senility and frailty. Dale smiled at her good fortune. It also eased her guilt over tricking the nurse; Grandmother Helene was operating the ruse of all ruses right under their noses. She was a tough old bird, but she was grudgingly earning Dale's respect, aside from nearly getting Dale killed in her own mirror.

"It's your granddaughter, Dale."

"I see," Grandmother Helene gusted, put out. "The pill whore."

"The pill whore you got trapped in a mirror."

143

"Young people these days are so foolish. Especially you. Who did you say you were again?"

"Cut the shit, Helene. Can your nurse hear you?"

"Dale, you say? Isn't that a boy's name? How strange."

"I'll take that as a yes. Now listen here, you old trout. I'm close to getting him out, but I need more than some symbol that'll trap me in a mirror." Given the obvious history between the women of each family, Dale didn't dare tell her grandmother she was working with a Keene.

"Are you coming to take me home? I have bridge at noon today. You best not be late."

"I'm looking for a book, and I think you might have stolen it."

"Dear," Grandmother Helene crooned. "Don't treat me like I'm senile. I've had bridge every Friday at noon for years."

"I know you saw that symbol in it. You were scribbling them in your Bible as you remembered them, which means you don't have the book anymore. So, if it's not with you, where is it?"

"Ask your mother. She knows everything. Or she thinks she does anyway. She'll tell you to come and get me."

Dale sighed. She'd been afraid her search would lead back to her mother. "The storage unit?"

"Tell her I want my brooch back too. The one with the sapphires. I know she took it last month to go to that vulgar dance with the Keene girl's boyfriend. I want it back. You tell her that too."

Grandmother Helene might not be as present as Dale thought. Why had she mentioned Loey's mother? Her boyfriend in high school had gotten her pregnant with Loey. Why the hell had Dale's mother gone to a dance with him?

"The Keene girl?" Dale asked before her grandmother could prattle on in riddles. "You mean Evelyn, right?"

"Who did you say you were again? I can't talk long. My daughter is coming to take me to bridge."

"Wait, but—"

"About that boy you've been seeing," her grandmother interrupted.

"What about him?" Dale challenged. Barty was her mirror man; he belonged to no other Rose women. She didn't care if they'd tried to rescue him before her; she was the one who'd see it through, accomplish the mission, be his hero.

"You listen to me." Grandmother Helene's voice became clear and strong, and Dale regretted ever doubting the old woman's mind. "You listening, girl?"

"Yes, ma'am."

"Men like that, they need women like us. They're good men, but their hearts are soft. It makes them mighty fine to love, like a good chocolate pudding, but it makes it easy for the world to break them. It takes a strong woman to see them through, you hear me? Don't you let him down because you like your pills or your pretty things or the pool boy. Be strong enough for him if you're the one of us who earns him."

No one had ever called Dale a strong woman in her entire life. She'd only ever been pretty, but sometimes too sexy, useful though inconvenient on occasion, and bold bordering on loose. But never strong. She liked the way it sounded.

"Do you understand?" Helene pressed in a softer voice.

"Yes, ma'am."

"Good." Approval almost warmed her grandmother's tone. It was more than Dale had gotten from her own mother in years. "Earn him with your strength, and he'll earn the right to your love every day after that. Strong women, Dale. We Roses are strong women. That's why he comes to us. That's why he found you. Don't ever doubt yourself, young lady."

"Thank you." Dale clutched her phone in both hands, pressing it tight to her ear. "Thank you, Grandmother."

Helene's voice reverted to her fluttery, detached tone.

"What time are you coming again, Darlene? I've been waiting for ages."

Before Dale could gather her scattered wits to respond, another voice came on the line.

"Mrs. Rose-Jinks? This is Cathy. I'm afraid it's time for your grandmother to rest. I'm sure she enjoyed speaking with you this morning, though."

"Thanks, Cathy." Dale tried to conceal the tears in her voice. "Give her a kiss for me."

Cathy laughed. "I don't want to be smacked, thank you, ma'am. But I'll let her know you send the intention."

Dale couldn't help but smile. "Perhaps tell her that next time I visit, I'll bring a bottle of gin and some fresh limes."

"That sounds more like Miss Helene."

Feeling better than she had in days, or years, Dale said, "Have a good day, Cathy. I'll call back soon."

"Bye, ma'am."

Dale hung up the phone. Thoughts tumbled one after the next. Her grandmother had Ellery's Tending book; she'd admitted as much or as much as she could. That success, however, paled in comparison to her grandmother's words about strength and how Dale would be the first Rose woman to earn Barty. That he needed a woman like her to hold him steady. That he *needed* her.

That was all Dale had ever wanted. She just wanted someone to need her.

Feeling giddy, she dialed her next number.

"What, Dale?" her mother answered.

"Good morning to you too." Dale refused to let her mother burst her bubble.

"I'm very busy with this Fall Festival mess. What do you need?"

Dale forced herself to swallow back the words she knew

would trigger a full-blown argument. As entertaining as it would be to send her mother into a tizzy, she stayed on task.

"Grandmother Helene called me. She wants that brooch, the one with the sapphires, from storage."

"Sapphires? What? Why did she call you?" In the background, someone asked her mother a muted question. She covered the phone to answer them. Farther away, children screamed and a truck beeped as it reversed. It sounded like Darlene Rose's version of Hell, and that made Dale very happy to consider.

"Well?" Darlene prompted, returning on the line. "Why did she call you?"

"I guess I was the most recent number in her file from our visit last week. They must have gotten confused," Dale said. Before Darlene could pick apart the explanation and find fault with everyone involved, Dale hurried on. "I know the Fall Festival is today, but do you have time to get it out of storage? She's already called me twice. Or …" She let the word hang. "I could tell her to call you."

"No!" Her mother cleared her throat. "I mean, no, that's not necessary. You're likely not busy today. Why don't you go by storage and pick it up? You can mail it to her."

"You're sure? I don't want to mess up your system."

In addition to Darlene's extreme vehemence toward Helene, Dale also knew her mother's OCD tendencies, especially with organization. She permitted no one, not even Cross, who shared the same proclivity, to rummage through the sprawling two-thousand-square-foot, climate-controlled, triple filtered air system storage unit that cost a small fortune in rent each month.

"Make sure you put everything back the way it was, understand?"

Dale pretended to think on it. "I have a massage this

afternoon …"

"For Heavens' sake, do this one thing for me, will you? I don't have time. Yvette is trying to get Tonya to sing the National Anthem tonight at the rodeo. Can you believe that? *Tonya*. She couldn't carry a tune in a bucket. She has the taste of a two-cent—"

"Fine. I'll go." Dale couldn't act too nice; otherwise, her mother would get suspicious. "Text me the row and bin number. I don't want to be digging around for hours."

"There's an inventory spreadsheet taped at the start of each row," her mother said. "You'll see every item listed on there, organized by type and description. The bin number will be on there."

Dale hadn't realized her mother had gone that far, but it would certainly help her search.

"Great. I'll text you after I mail it."

"Get insurance and a tracking number."

"I'm not stupid. Bye, Mother." Dale pulled the phone away from her ear to hang up.

"Oh, Dale! One more thing."

Cautiously, because this couldn't be good, Dale said, "Yes?"

"I know this is last minute, but can you ask Loey if she'll ride during the National Anthem to kick off the rodeo? Ashley Conley, you know, Terri's niece, the unfortunate looking one, was going to do it, but her horse is lame. Loey is the only other rider I know who's carried the flag before."

"Ah," she fumbled, genuinely at a loss. Had her mother asked something of her in a nice, borderline polite manner? "I mean, you know, after her accident, she hasn't ridden in a rodeo, but her horse, Butters, is a reigning gelding. He can do lots of cool shi—stuff while the song is playing."

"That's why I'm asking, obviously." Her mother returned to her brisk, holier-than-thou tone, and everything was once again right in Dale's world. "Can you talk to her or not? I need an answer within the hour."

"I can text her on my way to storage," Dale offered.

Her mother sighed. It wasn't good enough, never was, but this was familiar territory too. "That'll have to do."

Darlene hung up without a goodbye. In a touch of shock, Dale fired off a text to Loey about the event.

Within ten minutes, she was leaving the house, her bandaged feet coaxed into a pair of Uggs, her hair thrown up into a ponytail that would've appalled her mother, and her skin bare of makeup. There was no time. Every minute spent dawdling was a minute she didn't have her hands on that book. She also couldn't risk her mother calling Grandmother Helene and realizing it was all a lie. Darlene would likely think Dale was stealing heirlooms to sell for pills, and Dale didn't have the patience for that kind of bullshit.

The storage facility was in the next town over, right outside of Maryville. Dale pulled into the parking lot in record time and parked in the closest space available, her body vibrating with excitement as she bounded up to the building's entrance. In the lobby, she signed in and the receptionist escorted her into a wide hall. A man in uniform picked her up in a golf cart. He drove her straight to her mother's unit, the engine whistling beneath them.

He hit the brake outside Unit 1539's red metal door. She waited while he unlocked the door and rolled it up for her.

"Thank you," she said.

He turned on the unit's lights. "You're welcome. Use the buzzer to call the front desk when you're ready for a pickup or if you need assistance with a heavy item. Have a good day, ma'am."

All business, he turned on his heel and zipped away in the speedy cart.

Inside the unit, industrial shelving divided the space into tight rows lined with airtight bins, all numbered and color-coded. Furniture, wrapped in plastic, was stacked against the back wall. The air smelled like plastic and her mother's perfume. Perhaps Darlene spent her free time sitting in here, organizing bins until she felt like her life was perfect enough.

Dale started with the inventory lists at the end of each row. With her phone in hand to take pictures of locations, she read one list after the next. Unfortunately, there was an entire section of books. Most were named on the list and qualified as possible contenders, but there were enough without titles or descriptions that she couldn't eliminate them without seeing them first.

Her phone buzzed with a text message from Loey.

Tell her I can ride. I'll be fine. Right? Right. Where are you btw?

Dale responded: *You'll be great. Breathe. I'm on a mission. Chat later.*

After confirming Loey's involvement with her mother, Dale stuffed her phone in her purse and went to the towering section of books. She sighed. Leave it to her family to be too old-fashioned for a Kindle. Who kept books anymore?

No man had ever been worth this much work in her life, but Grandmother Helene was right: Dale would earn Barty, and her first step was finding this damn book everyone was so worried about.

CHAPTER 16

T HE BRIGHT ARENA LIGHTS DREDGED up a potent mixture of emotions so dizzying Loey couldn't begin to identify them. Even though she rode Butters into the arena that Friday night for the Fall Festival's annual rodeo and not Tempest, fear twinged down her legs, clad in her best Wrangler jeans.

The opening notes of the national anthem played. Everyone stood with their cowboy hats over their hearts, the men's belt buckles polished to a fine shine beneath the day's fading light. The American flag Loey carried waved over Butter's haunches as they loped a circle around the arena.

She sped up with the music, changing directions and circling, throwing in flying lead changes and quick, tight spins. Butters moved smooth as silk beneath her, his black mane streaming upward, his yellow hide flashing like fool's gold. Loey turned at the top of the arena, and Butters sensed her heartbeat rise and her grip tighten on the reins.

He gathered himself and tore off, galloping straight down the center of the arena as the anthem reached a crescendo. It wasn't as fast as Tempest had run—no other horse would ever be as fast as Tempest—but it was fast enough to drop her stomach. She trusted Butters with her life, but she squeezed her eyes shut and prayed the people in the first row couldn't see her shake with fear.

At the middle of the arena, Loey sat back a fraction in the saddle and whispered a soft, "Whoa."

Butters hit the brakes. They slid fifteen feet to a stop, with dirt flying and the crowd cheering and Butters's haunches low to the ground as he executed the sliding stop perfectly.

"Give a round of applause to Righteous's own Loey Grace Keene and her Quarter Horse gelding!" the announcer said over the sound system.

Loey leaned along Butters's neck and took off his bridle. She tipped her hat to more cheers and nudged Butters forward. With the flag in one hand, she waved with the other as she and Butters loped bridleless out of the arena.

At the end of the chute, she slowed Butters to a walk with a simple, "Easy." She handed off the flag to a volunteer and swung down from the saddle, not bothering to replace Butters's bridle. She scratched his favorite spot beneath his jaw and planted a kiss on his velvet-soft nose. He smelled of molasses and apples from the copious amount of treats the kids had given him earlier. He huffed against Loey's shirt.

"What do you feed that thing to make it have an ass like that, and where can I get some?"

Loey rolled her eyes as Dale caught up with her and Butters. "Your butt is already perfect."

Dale's dressy boots kicked up dust, and her toned, tanned legs flashed beneath her too-short jean shorts. She wore an immaculate white lace top.

"You looked good out there," Dale said. "Were you nervous at all?"

They walked out of the arena and into the main gravel parking lot. Trailers and trucks and dusty SUVs were all parked together. Near the arena, a corral of bulls was sectioned off, waiting to be loaded into chutes and prepped for the bull riding event later in the night.

Loey wrinkled her nose in distaste. "Did I look nervous?"

"I didn't think you would agree to do it, to be honest."

"I surprised myself too, but I'm tired of fear ruling me all the time. Although I did close my eyes during that sliding stop."

"If I'd been run into a metal chute at a full gallop, I'd probably close my eyes too."

Loey shot her best friend a droll look. "Thanks for that."

"In all seriousness, though," Dale said, "I'm glad you weren't too nervous. It was good to see you back out in the arena again."

Loey's fingers touched the side of her mouth of their own accord. "It didn't feel right without her."

"Tempest would be happy you have Butters. You should start doing some AQHA shows with him."

"Maybe …"

The overhead spotlights flickered on as the sun began to set. Farther out in the parking lot, they neared Loey's Sundowner horse trailer hitched to her truck. Butters ambled at her side. She didn't know if it was talking about the accident or the ride, but her left leg ached enough to make her back teeth clench.

"Where have you been? I was trying your cell all day," she asked.

"That's what we need to talk about."

Loey stopped. Butters followed suit. Dale continued for a few steps before looking back over her shoulder.

"I'm not moving until you tell me."

Dale glanced around, but the lot was empty this far back. "I found Ellery's book."

"Are you freaking serious?" Her heart battered against her chest. "Where? How? Why didn't you tell me this right away?"

Dale hushed her. "My grandmother mentioned having it, which means she probably stole it, the old bat, but in all the chaos, I didn't remember until this morning. My mother was keeping it in her storage unit."

"Oh my gosh." Relief flooded through Loey so completely she thought she might cry. "Holy crap, Dale. This is huge. This changes everything."

"Let's get this fatty unsaddled so we can go home and talk."

At Loey's trailer, Butters went straight to his hay bag, stuck his pink nose into the sweet grass hay, and pulled out a big bite. Loey eased on his halter as Dale loosened his cinch. They made quick work of unsaddling him and brushing him down until his buckskin coat gleamed.

"What does it look like? Where is it?"

"I haven't looked through it yet." Dale shrugged. "It's your grandmother's book. It didn't seem right to do it without you, but it's at my house. I didn't want to risk bringing it here."

Loey frowned. "Why?"

"You know why. I don't want him to have it, Loey. We can't trust him."

"Jer—"

"Don't say his name out loud. What if he's listening?"

"If he is," Loey said, practicing patience, though all she wanted was to get her hands on that book, "he's already heard enough. If we can't trust him, we're screwed, Dale. I don't know if we can win this fight without him, and I might need his help to figure out that book."

"We can try, and Barty can help with the parts we don't understand."

"You're willing to draw symbols we don't understand and see what happens? What if you get stuck in a mirror again—or worse?"

Dale sucked in her cheeks. "That was one time. Let's get Butters home. Then we can go back to my house. We'll go through it there. It'll be easier to talk too."

"I want to see the book as soon as possible, but there's a reason I was trying to call you all day."

Dale frowned at Loey's change of subject. "What could be more important than this?"

"The book is incredibly important," Loey clarified. "It's the most important thing, but I thought of a way to prove if Knox was on the ridge that night, and we won't have another night like this to look without risking someone spotting us."

Dale's surprise suggested she thought the new topic important enough. "What way?"

"There's only one way to know for sure if Knox was alive or dead by the time the storm hit the ridge."

Dale caught on fast; she only played the dumb-blonde card if it benefited her, but she was alarmingly clever. She knew the dark place Loey's mind had gone. "You're not suggesting what I think you're suggesting."

Loey twisted her mouth into the facial version of a guilty-but-not-sorry shrug.

"You are!" Dale accused. "You're suggesting we dig up your great-great-grandfather!"

"I know it's foul," Loey hissed, shushing her friend, "but we're surrounded by lies. Don't you see that? We're trying to figure out what the hell happened over sixty years ago on that ridge, and the only people who know are Frankie, who's a ghost across the Seam, and the Skinned Man. I doubt he'll be letting us in on those secrets either. Unless you want to sit around and wait on the men to tell us what happened, this is the best idea I've got. Tonight's our best shot. The police will be on a skeleton crew, and Jeronimo has to stay here until the final prayer at the rodeo's award handout. I desperately want to see my grandmother's book, but we need to know who else was up there that night."

Dale's brows arched above her wide blue eyes. She let out a whistled breath. "Shit, Lo. *Shit*."

"Believe me, I know. If Knox isn't in the ground, and if we

can't find any evidence to place the revenuer up there at the same time, he could very well be the Skinned Man. If he is ..." Loey couldn't bring herself to finish her sentence.

"Bad news bears?"

Loey groaned. "Something like that."

"Okay. We do this tonight ..."

"And we'll go through the book first thing tomorrow afternoon after I close up the coffee shop. We can spend all evening with it if we need to. However long it takes, we'll figure out a plan we're both comfortable with."

Dale's shoulders heaved with relief, her worries easing. "I can get behind that. Digging up bodies tonight, old magic books tomorrow—with cake."

"And I'll need wine after—"

Butters snorted right as Loey heard the crunch of gravel behind them.

"Evening, ladies."

They spun around to find a tall dark figure approaching between two trailers. Jeronimo stepped into the moonlight, his cattleman hat tipped back, his jeans low on his hips and too tight, as Ms. Ida May would've tutted. He moved smooth as smoke. Worn boots whispered over the gravel as he came toward them.

Loey and Dale exchanged a look of concern that said, *How much did he hear?*

"Jeronimo." Loey sounded like she'd climbed a set of steep stairs though she'd been standing still. "You scared us."

"Yeah," Dale chimed in, crossing her arms. "You shouldn't sneak around like that. Might get shot."

She stared at Jeronimo like he'd kicked a puppy, and she didn't bother to hide it either.

Jeronimo didn't mind her glare, and that worried Loey more. "Wouldn't be the first time, would it, Loey? You two planning to break into any homes tonight? I heard an awful lot of whisperin' back here."

Preposterously enough, fear spiked through Loey. She had literally argued in favor of *telling* Jeronimo about the book, and the thought of him having overheard them scared her. From the expression on Dale's face, she was worried too, but she covered it better than Loey.

"Breaking into homes? We haven't broken into anything."

"It's just Loey, then. Good to know."

"I'm sorry," Loey said and meant it, but his put-out attitude was getting old, "but it's not like I received countless letters from your grandparents begging for help and ignored them."

"He did that?" Dale's voice rose. "Ellery asked for help and you ignored her?"

Amongst all the heightened emotions, Butters pawed at the ground hard enough to pull on his lead and rock the trailer.

"That's in the past, Dale. I shouldn't have brought it up. He's mad because I broke into the rectory the night I got you out of the mirror. He caught me snooping around."

"Good for you. You beat me to it." Dale clapped for her. "And as for you, Jeronimo James, fuck you for ignoring Ellery Keene. She was a good woman, the best. If I didn't hate you already, that would be reason enough, you hear me?"

Jeronimo cocked his head, blandly digesting Dale's words. "I'm sorry, did I do something to offend you, Dale? Or do you hate me now that my brother has poisoned you against me?"

"Oh, bite me." Dale scowled. To Loey, she said, "We should pack up and get going. I don't want to waste any more time here."

"You're right. I'll start loading—"

"He's not who you think he is," Jeronimo told Dale, cutting off Loey's feeble attempt to dissolve the rising tension.

Inwardly, Loey groaned. They would never get to the cemetery, and she would never get her hands on her grandmother's

Tending book, although she ached for it like this book was the missing piece she needed to feel right again.

"Don't you talk about him like that," Dale fired back at Jeronimo.

"I'm his older brother. I've known him a hell of a lot longer than you have. I can talk about him any way I want."

"Good point! Then you can frame him for another murder you committed while you're at it."

Jeronimo's jaw flexed. Loey didn't like how Dale was winding him up. They were already close to yelling, and the parking lot wasn't completely dead. Anyone could overhear.

"I didn't kill Frankie," Jeronimo growled.

Dale feigned wiping sweat from her brow. "Thanks for clearing that up. For a second there, I thought my best friend might be next on your hit list. Oh, wait, no, I still think that. For your information, Frankie is going insane over there. She feeds off Barty without his permission. Did you know that? That place is evil, and it's turning her mad. She's nothing but an angry, starving ghost of a woman, and it's all your fault. She died that night because of you. Two wonderful souls are condemned to that hellhole while you get to walk the Earth a freeman. It's bullshit, and once I've had my say, you *will* pay for what you've done, to them and Ellery."

Dale was trembling from head to toe by the time she finished. Jeronimo was silent, his face blank and his eyes as dark as the coming night sky. Loey's heart beat in her throat, but before she could step between them or say anything to calm them down, Jeronimo spoke.

"Can I have a moment alone with Loey?" he asked Dale with an alarming amount of politeness given the storm in his eyes and the way his body vibrated with rage.

"Oh, hell no. I'm not leaving you alone with her. I don't relish coming back to find my best friend's throat slit."

"Dale," Loey warned. "It's fine. Give us a minute and we'll go."

"Fine, but if you touch a hair on her head," she snarled at Jeronimo, "I'll feed you bite by bite to every ghost across the Seam who wants a taste. There'll be nothing left of you to hurt anyone else ever again."

Dale strode off across the parking lot toward the bathrooms.

Loey patted Butters, more to reassure herself than him.

"You didn't tell me about Frankie." The spotlights cast his face in long shadows as the sunlight dwindled. "About her feeding off Barty."

"You didn't give me the chance."

His gaze raked to hers, and she found anguish in his eyes. The emotion rippled across his face. His mouth opened and closed, but he shook his head, deciding better than to voice his thoughts.

Giving him space because she couldn't imagine the pain he must be feeling at hearing about Frankie's growing madness, Loey began packing her trailer.

Jeronimo watched her put away her saddle and saddle pad into the trailer's small tack room along with the rest of her tack. She wrapped Butters's legs for the trip home, ensuring the puffy white cotton went smoothly up from his pasterns to right beneath his knees and hocks. With everyone calm again, Butters's tail swished happily as he munched his hay.

By the time she'd loaded everything except Butters, Jeronimo had collected himself.

"I didn't come over here to fight. I wanted to check on you after your ride." He looked as though the ghosts of his past had been feeding on him, not his brother. "I thought you looked …" He scrubbed his hand over his mouth, fighting with himself and his demons. "I thought you looked beautiful out there."

Loey's heart swelled and ached and broke all at the same time. She wanted to go to him and pull him down from his tall

BLESS HIS CURSED SOUL

height for a long hug.

"J," she breathed out. "We need to—"

"Loey, there you are. I've been looking—oh."

Matt came in from between the trailers parked beside Loey's. She had to start paying attention to her surroundings. This was getting ridiculous.

"Hey, Matt." She hoped she didn't sound as annoyed as she felt.

"Loey." Matt tipped his cowboy hat. He gave the preacher a loaded, "Evening."

Jeronimo only lifted his chin in greeting.

Matt turned his narrow-eyed gaze from Jeronimo to Loey. The frown on his mouth and the little furrows between his dark brows deepened. "You headin' home?" he asked her.

"As soon as Dale gets back from the bathroom."

Matt's face fell. "You're not staying for the bull ridin'?"

"You're a bull rider?" Jeronimo's question was carefully laid out, like a bear trap beneath the leaves. Loey heard its metal teeth in the quiet places between words.

Tonight was really, really not the night for this.

Matt caught the challenge plain as day and rose to meet it. "I do. Champ three years runnin'. You ever gone for eight?"

"Never felt the need to."

Gravel crunched beneath Matt's boots as he shifted his weight. It looked, briefly, like he was considering charging at Jeronimo.

"Sorry, I'm not staying," she said in a rush to distract everyone. "With everything going on and all, I need an early night so I can be at the cafe on time. I'm sure you'll do great, though."

Relaxing a fraction, Matt turned away from Jeronimo, excluding him from the conversation. "After our last conversation, I wanted us to talk. Make things right between

162

us. You could come by the station tomorrow morning. I'll be on duty, and we could get lunch after."

Loey groaned. How had her life become so crazy that her lie about Folton was the least of her concerns? "I forgot. I'll be by tomorrow. I don't mean—"

"Why does she need to come by?" Jeronimo interjected.

"Oh, she hasn't told you? I'm sorry. I thought y'all were closer than that. Apologies." He tipped his hat at Loey. "I best get back to the arena before I let anything else slip."

He winked at Loey, and that one little gesture contained all the innuendo of every night they'd spent together.

How could men say so much with so few words?

"Bye, Matt," she said before Jeronimo made this any worse than it already was. "Thanks for coming by, and sorry again for missing your event."

"It's no problem, Lo." His smile returned to the real one she'd known since high school. "You looked good tonight. We're all real proud of you for getting back out there."

"Thanks."

He surprised her with a hug. A lingering one. Over his shoulder, Jeronimo looked ready to rip Matt apart. Loey stepped away before Matt got punched.

"You ready—ew, you're still here?" Dale rounded Loey's truck, her mouth pursing at the sight of Jeronimo. She spotted everyone else. "Oh, hey, Matt. I like those chaps. They make your butt look good. Loey, don't they make his butt look good?"

Matt chuckled. "Thanks, Dale. How you been?"

"Can't complain." She didn't pause to chitchat before untying Butters. Leading Loey's horse to the back of the trailer, she called over her shoulder, "Let's get this cream puff loaded and go home."

CHAPTER 17

TWO DAYS LATER, DALE WAS still feeling the effects of Frankie feeding off her. She hid it well as she and Loey hiked down the hill from the Keene house to the cemetery, and Dale managed not to limp on her cut feet. Her shoulder and chest already ached from the looming promise of all the digging ahead.

Worse than the pain was missing him.

She had her mission out here, on the other side of the Seam. She was doing all she could to free him, but it wasn't enough. He wasn't *here* with her *now*.

"Dale?"

Dale flinched as she crashed back to reality. "Did you say something?"

Loey watched her with concern. Dale shifted her bag onto her other arm, acting like she hadn't completely zoned out on a full-blown Barty daydream and missed her best friend talking right beside her.

"Is your shoulder okay? Do I need to carry that?"

"It's fine. What were you saying?"

"I asked about the book. Tell me more about it."

Dale pictured the stiff wooden book cover bound in worn linen. The pages inside were thick vellum, the old type of paper made from animal skin, but Dale had been able to tell that from holding it. On the cover, in gold foil worn with age and faded into near nonexistence, was not a title but a name. An original author, perhaps.

Given what they were about to do, recalling it gave Dale the shivers.

The gold foil had spelled "Knox Keene" in bold box letters.

Loey was itching to know everything about the book, so as they walked with Dewey bouncing through the grass ahead of them, Dale told her all she could from her short time with the book.

Loey asked question after question, from what the book smelled like to how much it weighed and what its dimensions were. Dale did her best to answer. The evening's chill had her huddling deeper into the old flannel shirt she'd found in the trunk of her car. It had belonged to Travis before she commandeered it for whatever reason, but it still smelled like him, and the scent brought back memories of high school football games spent flaunting his letterman jacket while he dashed around the field, a young god in the glorious body of a teenage boy.

Loey had lent her black jeans to keep her legs warm.

Chattering about all the things the book could contain—most of them Jeronimo's thoughts that Loey spouted as her own, annoying Dale enough that she had to clench her jaw shut and ignore half of Loey's talk to keep from saying something that would lead to a fight—Loey carried a shovel and step stool to help them climb in and out of the grave. She opened the cemetery's squeaky back gate. Still discussing her theories with herself, Loey moved through the graveyard like it was her second home, and perhaps it was, but Dale would never feel as comfortable here beneath the tall hemlocks, the lonely cypresses, and the heaping gardenias. All the flowers lent the air the strange smell of a funeral parlor, and it was all too much death for Dale. But this was the most at ease Dale had seen Loey all week, so she trailed after her best friend as she tiptoed between the graves with light-footed hope.

Loey believed the book would solve all her problems.

But Dale had lied. She had peeked inside the pages, and she'd found them covered in tiny, illegible cursive. Every millimeter of page was utilized with what appeared to Dale— because she certainly couldn't make out the words to read them—random scrawls and half-finished symbols. On some pages, words were written on top of each other.

It was a mess, and Dale doubted how useful it would be to anyone not an expert on Tending. She kept that to herself since they were about to dig up a body.

They hurried to the central part of the cemetery as the coming night had nearly reached full darkness. They didn't have long, and grave digging was time-consuming business, or so all the movies they were basing their endeavor on implied.

Loey stopped beside Knox's grave and propped her shovel against the headstone. With her hands on her hips, she considered the earth in front of the rounded old stone.

"We're not digging out the entire thing, right?" Dale asked, already tired. She'd never been one for manual labor. "We don't have time to move that much dirt. Not unless you brought a tractor down here."

Loey chewed on her lip, lost in thought.

"Probably a hole big enough for us to fit in. We can take turns? We can break the coffin's lid and look inside. After this long in the ground, even treated wood would be soft and easy to break through."

"Just a little look-see for a dead body, no big deal." Dale's stomach churned. She had another thought. "Even putting the dirt back in the hole, it'll look freshly dug up."

"I thought about that earlier," Loey said with a guilty

grimace. "I picked up a bunch of flower arrangements from the store. We can pile them on top until the grass grows back."

"Oh." It unnerved Dale how good Loey was at this. "That's a good idea."

"We better get started. This'll take a while."

They divvied up the work, with Loey insisting on starting first and taking double the turns since a monster had bitten Dale and a ghost had fed off her. Perks of cross-Seam travel, she guessed. She sat on the ground while Loey attacked the earth with gusto.

"This is probably random," Loey said, panting from her efforts, "but do you remember anything strange when you were in Little Cricket?"

"It's Little Cricket. What isn't strange?"

Loey swiped at her forehead with her gloved hand. The dirt she'd piled atop a folded tarp so they could dump it back into the hole was growing at a decent rate—far faster than it would with Dale at the helm.

"I mean, anything to do with the symbols. Someone who might know about them? Or asked about the mirrors?"

She had Dale's attention, though her stomach was growling and she'd been fantasizing about a cheeseburger. "It's all hazy. I was high by the time I got to the Neely's. Why? Do you think someone knows about the symbols over there?"

"The night we got you, I found a symbol on a piece of human skull hanging from a tree outside the trailer you were in."

"What kind of symbol?"

The hole into Loey's great-great-grandfather's final resting place deepened with each shovelful of dirt. "The kind that invites communication."

"With who?"

"Anyone across the Seam."

"Here." Dale stood. Loey was already drenched in sweat in

the balmy night air. "Let's switch."

Loey hesitated for a fraction of a second before handing Dale the shovel and gloves. She took Dale's spot on the ground with a sigh of relief.

"You think someone in Little Cricket is communicating with the Skinned Man?" Dale asked as she dug.

"They're trying, and they know the right symbols."

Dale glanced up in surprise in time to see Loey do a one-shoulder shrug that looked exactly like Jeronimo's hallmark gesture. It roasted Dale's insides to witness. She was losing her best friend to a man, or she had already.

"Why would anyone want to talk to him? Wouldn't he kill them?"

"Jeronimo says they likely don't know what's over there. They have experiences and feelings and, for all they know, it could be the Devil they're talking with. They talk to him like he's a friend and they ask him for things and—"

"Wait." Dale kept her head down as she slung dirt onto the pile. "How do you know they're asking for things?"

Loey frowned. "Jeronimo says—"

"I don't give a shit what Jeronimo says. I want to know how *you* know."

"That's the only way I know anything: if he tells me or if we figure it out together."

"Loey," Dale said, mentally reaching across the void to her best friend—the void *men* had carved between them.

"I know what you're going to say. You've said it a million times already."

"I wouldn't say a million."

"You don't trust him, but I do. He may not remember that night right, but that doesn't mean he killed Frankie."

"If this coffin is empty, that means Barty was right about Knox being there, and that means the part in Barty's story about Jeronimo stabbing her in the heart has to be true too."

"Just because one part might be true doesn't mean the rest is. There could be a million reasons why my great-great-grandfather isn't in his coffin."

"Really?" Dale raised her brows at her friend in between shovel loads. "Name one."

"Maybe our family didn't trust anyone to salt his body properly."

"They would've been the ones doing it!" Dale shot back.

"Someone might have tried to sabotage the salt ring during his first night in the ground," Loey amended. "A lot was going on with Townsend and Obidiah during those days."

"It seems to me that Knox started it all by willing the land to Townsend in the first place."

"I have someone on that."

Dale's mind stuttered as she processed Loey's words. "Who?"

"Tabitha Richart. The editor at *The Daily Righteous*."

"Oh, God, Loey."

"She was going to do a piece on Folton regardless. This way I get something out of it. She's digging into the land deal, and I get to control how the story comes out."

"Jesus Christ."

"It's fine."

"It is *not*."

"Don't be so dramatic."

"She's a Yankee."

"She doesn't seem that horrible."

"She's a *Yankee*."

"Switch."

They changed positions. The grave digging progressed faster than Dale had anticipated. Before digging deeper, Loey tidied up Dale's sloping sides to keep the hole round and orderly.

"My grandmother warned me about this," Dale said to the ground, pulling up bits of grass until her fingers turned green. "She said Ellery thought she was God and kept Barty in there for no good reason. She mentioned that my mother and your grandmother had worked together to get Helene out of Righteous, likely around the time she had Ellery's book, because she said she was getting close to saving him."

Loey stopped shoveling. Dale felt her hot gaze on her skin. It took more courage than it ever had to meet her best friend's stare.

"Come on," Loey said. "You knew my grandmother. She loved you like her own. She wouldn't keep an innocent man over there if she could help it."

Loey's words hurt because they were true. Ellery had been more of a grandmother and mother to her than her own kin. How many nights had she spent at Loey's house? Ellery and Harlan had always welcomed her, even in the middle of the night, when Dale had pounded on the door with a tear-streaked face. Ellery had prepared Dale's favorite drink—a cappuccino with cinnamon sticks.

Loey's words, though, also highlighted one of Dale's growing fears. She knew Ellery wouldn't abandon an innocent man across the Seam, but like Loey, Ellery had needed him to contain the Skinned Man. And, also like Loey, other matters—or people—had taken precedence over a man easily forgotten by those with protected mirrors.

They worked in silence, their minds on overdrive, though neither were willing to speak their peace. A Seam might as well have separated the different worlds Dale and Loey existed in. It was becoming harder to agree on anything.

"It might not mean he's the Skinned Man if he isn't in here," Dale said sometime later, after they'd switched again. They were coated in sweat and dirt, and the hole was deep enough that they had to use the small step stool.

Dale didn't pause in her digging, but she sensed Loey studying her. "It would make more sense if it was the revenuer. Heck, he could have killed Frankie too. Maybe Jeronimo and Barty are both right. Neither of them did it and they're pointing the finger at the wrong person."

"But why would Knox tell Barty he saw Jeronimo kill her?"

Loey absently played with her nose ring. "That part might not be true. Barty said he was pretty out of it that night. He couldn't drive his truck up Devil's Maw. He had to walk. He could have hallucinated Knox?"

Dale laughed.

Loey looked up at the bitter sound that rang across the silent graveyard. The moon was high, and they were running out of time before Jeronimo came back.

"Why are you laughing?"

Dale threw down the shovel and stripped off her gloves. She scrambled out of the hole. "You will twist any story until it keeps Jeronimo's hands clean."

Loey jerked to her feet. She stood on the opposite side of the ruined grave from Dale. All they needed was a wall of lights between them. Possibly two tall brothers picking sides to stand behind each woman as well.

This night had been a horrible idea. They should've gone to Dale's house for the book. The useless freaking book. Dale had to choke down another bitter laugh.

Loey grabbed the shovel and gloves from the ground and resumed digging where Dale had left off. She was over waist-deep in the hole.

Dale almost didn't hear her speak. "Excuse me?"

"I said, 'That's ripe.'"

"And what does that mean?"

"You ripped Jeronimo apart tonight based on Barty's word,

after you accused me of listening to everything Jeronimo has to say like a blind dog—"

"I never call you a blind dog."

"—but you do the same with Barty. You believe whatever he says, especially that Jeronimo killed Frankie. You will stop at nothing to tear Jeronimo down based on Barty's word. Yet, you say nothing about all the people Barty killed. You let that slide because it's far easier for you to accuse Jeronimo of one murder than acknowledge the hundreds Barty committed."

Dale's lips parted. Her breath stole out between them. Loey had a point—Dale did act like a hypocrite at times—but it was for fear of Loey's safety.

She was still choosing her words when Loey released her final punch.

"And," she said, her shovel striking the hard-packed earth with rage-fueled strength, "I didn't want to be mean and say this to your face, but since that's not a concern anymore, I'll say it."

"Go ahead." Dale waved her hand. "Let's let it all hang out, Loey Grace."

Loey stopped shoveling. "I think it's creepy that Barty has watched you from your mirrors since you were a teenager. Not only that, but he's done the same thing to any Rose woman he could find. He's literally stalked your family for generations, and you think it's sweet and sad and—"

"We should stop," Dale said, snapping off each word with cold clips.

Loey lifted her chin and sniffed. "You're right. This isn't doing us any good."

"We're going to say something we'll regret."

"So we stop," Loey agreed icily.

"We stop."

An hour of silent digging later, their shovel struck wood. It took a few minutes longer to remove the last layer of dirt and toss it out of the eight-foot-deep hole.

Dale cleaned out the last bit of dirt. Loey leaned over the hole's opening, her pale face streaked with dirt.

"What do you see?" she asked Dale.

"I think you should be the one to look."

Loey's face twisted up as she considered it. Dale thought she was going to back out, but, surprising her, Loey said, "You're right. Come on up and I'll climb down."

Dale used the wobbly step stool to get within reach of Loey's hand. Working together, they got Dale out, scrambling and kicking and getting themselves filthy.

Before Dale had turned around to situate herself at the mouth of the hole, she heard the wood break.

She peered down as Loey looked inside using her phone's flashlight.

Loey muttered something.

"What did you say?" Dale's voice bounced between the headstones.

Loey stared up at her, her face a pale moon down a dark hole.

"It's empty," she said.

CHAPTER 18

JUNE 19, 2014

DALE CAME BACK TO RIGHTEOUS the summer after her sophomore year of college. It was the first time she'd been back for any real length of time since freshman year's Thanksgiving break.

She wished she could've rolled into town a new woman, like she had at the University of Tennessee. There, she commanded, she swaggered, she owned. She was Dale Rose, untouchable not because of her last name or the dirty things spoken behind her back, but because she was badass. A formidable power unto herself that she had earned. People *cared* if she walked into a room. She *mattered*.

She couldn't be that untouchable version of Dale Rose in Righteous. Here, she couldn't return after well over a year of absence and breeze through the streets like a remade woman.

No one had that luxury in their hometown.

A hometown knew you. Knew you from your days toddling down the street, holding your mother's hand. Knew you from the awkward middle school phase with braces. Knew you from every Sunday at church, where you pretended to listen to the preacher. Knew you from the bad stuff too. Every rumor, every lie, every scandal.

She returned as Dale Rose, untouchable not for her last name—not anymore or ever again—but for last year's unfortunate scandal. Bless her heart, though, it had brought a killer to justice, and he was rotting behind bars like he deserved. Too bad about all those other messy, *distasteful* happenings.

She walked to Deadly Sin Roasters from her family's house. It was only a few blocks away, and it was a beautiful summer day, the likes of which she'd missed up in Knoxville, where the air was mostly car fumes and the mountain views were obscured by tacky buildings too inconsequential to be high-rises but tall enough to hide the Smokies.

Here, in Righteous, Dale almost saw beyond her jaded notions of her hometown and appreciated the beauty of the low-lying brick buildings on Main and the clear sun-kissed air blowing down from Shiner's Ridge and the mountains beyond. American flags flapped from street lights, and cars drove by slowly with their windows down. She caught snippets of conversations from every angle as she walked. A twangy version of a Springsteen song drifted down the block.

A smile pulled at Dale's lips. As she turned her face up to the warm sun and listened to Springsteen croon and experienced the quaint easiness of her hometown deep in her bones, she was completely content for the first time in a very long time.

Dale sighed. She would be okay. They would be okay. This town could heal. It could—

"Dale!" a too-sweet voice called out. "Looky here! You came back from college."

Mrs. Prather came out of the second-hand boutique with a brown paper bag in her arms. She smiled too widely at Dale, her head cocked as she waited for her response. She'd been in the Righteous Garden Club with Dale's mother since before the dawn of time, and Mrs. Prather thought a yearly magazine full of boring plants made her a "friend of the family."

Regardless, Dale had her smile in place. "Hi, Mrs. Prather. How are you?"

"Just fantastic, dear! Don't you look pretty as a petal." Her eyes lingered on Dale's admittedly revealing jean shorts and cropped tank top. Mrs. Prather's eyelashes fluttered as she fought to keep the judgment of the nation's youth from her face. "How's college treating you?"

"It's great." Dale was already over this conversation, one she'd had countless times already. So pointless. She hurried to answer the next question to expedite the tediousness. "I love UT. My roommate is great. She goes to church too. I'm majoring in social work. I want to be a guidance counselor for kids."

"Well! My goodness, isn't that excitin'!" Mrs. Prather faltered beneath the onslaught of information. Dale was already backing away, one small step at a time, her hand ready to wave goodbye. "That's so wonderful to hear, dear."

"Thanks, Mrs. Prather. Have a nice day." Dale waved.

"You too, dear! I'll pray for you."

Dale had already started walking away, but she stopped. The switch flipped in her. "I'm sorry. Why do I need to be prayed for?"

"Oh, sweetie. We heard you joined a *sorority*. We know how those college kids like to drink up in the big city. After what happened with that teacher, well, we worry about you, dear! That's all. But you're going to be a guidance counselor? That's sweet. You can keep other young girls from experiencing ..." Mrs. Prather lowered her voice. "... what you went through."

Dale told herself the middle-aged woman with her sagging jowls and fluff around her middle was *trying* to be sweet in her own well-meaning way, but try as she might, Dale couldn't hold it in. She was out of practice and out of shits to give.

"Oh, you mean my Art History teacher repeatedly raping me?" she said loudly enough so every open door on the block could hear. "Yeah, that was an experience I *deeply* regret having to go through."

Mrs. Prather let out a flustered laugh. She darted a glance around to see who was witnessing the debacle. Hopefully not her church group. That would be downright unsightly.

"But, oh, right," Dale continued, "you're praying for me. Thank you so much. I need it, being such a slut and alcoholic."

Mrs. Prather's beleaguered smile fell straight off her face, her lipstick-stained lips spluttering an indignant response from deep within her well-meaning heart. Dale practically read her thoughts as they moved like a fat sow through mud. *That Dale Rose, she was such a nice girl. She was so sweet. What happened?*

"Have a nice day!" She fluttered her fingers in a wave. "I'll pray for you too."

She forced herself not to run as she walked away. She kept her head up, unblinking beneath the sun's rays that warmed the sidewalk and her legs. Her cheeks burned and her eyes stung and she was so *stupid*.

She wasn't a child. Part of her had known things would change after lying about Folton. She told herself it couldn't hurt that badly because she'd known. She was smarter than to let their words take her aback. To let them sting her so deeply. Darlene Rose had raised her after all.

But Mrs. Prather had taught her elementary Sunday school class. Back then, Dale and Loey had been two giggly little girls who liked to color with big-girl markers while they listened about Jonah and the whale.

Dale was fighting back tears as she pushed open the door to Deadly Sin and the bell rang overhead. Her eyes swimming behind a sheen of tears, she searched for Loey, but it was Ellery standing behind the counter.

"Hello, Dale." Ellery smiled a version of Loey's former smile. "Loey will be right back. She ran to the bank for her pap."

Dale blinked back tears. Ellery caught on, and her smile

dimmed, her head angling to listen to everything Dale wasn't saying.

"Maybe I'll …" Dale couldn't go home, couldn't stand another moment with her mother, but staying here with Ellery didn't feel like much of an option either.

Coming home had been a mistake. She should've known.

"Can I make you a cappuccino like old times?" Ellery didn't put on a fake cheerful voice, and sadness tinged her smile.

The shop was mostly empty, and it would be nice to have a break from all the do-gooders outside in town. She took a stool at the counter. "Extra frothy? I like the milk bubbles."

Ellery had been making Dale cappuccinos since the girls were allowed coffee. "Coming right up."

Dale watched Ellery work, the older woman's slender hands fluttering from machine to grinder to sieve to frother.

"Do you have those cinnamon sticks, too?" Dale asked, her chin in her hand.

Ellery laughed. "We do, and I hadn't forgotten either."

"Thank you."

"Of course. How's college?"

Another lukewarm question. Another stilted conversation. After the one with Mrs. Prather, Dale felt too raw and only barked out a laugh.

"That good, huh?"

Tears again rose in Dale's eyes, but she pulled a sharp smile onto her lips. "It's *so* great," she said, drawing out the sarcasm.

"You don't like the football games and tailgating and drawing orange T's on your friends' cheeks?"

Ellery's sarcasm floored Dale. This time, she laughed for real.

"It feels like four more years of high school."

"Dale," Ellery said, smiling again, "it *is* four more years of high school."

Ellery placed the drink in front of Dale, the milk extra foamy and a cinnamon stick peeking out. Dale wrapped her hands around it tightly.

"Loey misses you." Ellery picked up a rag and wiped down the counter.

"She would've liked UT. Not the sorority stuff," Dale quickly amended, "but there's a lot of vet students there. She would've had a lot of friends."

Ellery's towel swept over the same patch of clean counter, like it wasn't the counter she was trying to make better with each swipe but something else. "You've been a good friend to her, Dale. You're a good girl, and you've been there for Loey when she's needed you most."

"I know the accident was hard." Dale sucked in her cheeks, hating the words. "*Obviously*, it was hard, but I know she's not dealing with the after stuff so great."

Ellery's eyes searched Dale from behind her reading glasses perched low on her thin nose riddled with freckles and age spots, parsing Dale's words for a double meaning or something more. Dale waited, refusing to say anything more. She wasn't accustomed to someone listening so closely and truly wanting to hear the unspoken things between words.

Ellery's focus dropped back to her towel. "She'll be okay."

"She will," Dale added for solidarity.

"She's strong."

"She is."

Ellery looked up again, and her gaze struck Dale with full force. She sat back on her stool.

"You two need to look out for each other," Ellery said. "You'll fight and possibly hate each other sometimes, but best friends are always there for each other in times of need. No matter what. That's real love. The kind that never fades."

Dale's mouth fell open. An adult had never spoken to her

like that, not ever. "I …"

The door chimed open, and Loey limped in, her knee still healing from the never-ending surgeries. Her face, still pink and swollen and not the face Dale remembered, brightened beneath the scars. "Hey! Why didn't you text? I was at the bank."

Dale pushed aside Ellery's words and pulled up a smile for Loey. She hadn't seen her best friend so happy in a long while. Dale wouldn't bring her down by dwelling on the apprehension her conversation with Ellery had left in her, like Ellery had been trying to warn her.

"Come on." Dale drained her cappuccino. "Let's go meet up with Travis and Cross. Thanks, Mrs. Keene!"

"You're welcome, Dale," Ellery called as the girls left. Quieter, so Dale barely caught it, she repeated more to herself, "You're welcome."

CHAPTER 19

SATURDAY MORNING SUCKED.

Loey prided herself in reserving that sentiment for rare occasions, but today certainly qualified.

She'd had three hours of sleep after climbing out of her kin's grave, heaving the dirt back down the hole, covering it with garish flowers, saying a frosty goodbye to Dale, and taking an eons-long shower that hadn't left her feeling clean. She'd woken at 5:00 a.m. and dragged herself out to the barn to feed the animals before driving into town to meet Matt at the police station. The deal proposed by the lawyers had been laid before Loey in stark black print, and she'd pretended to read it as Matt looked on. She'd signed with a shaking hand, and Matt, God love him, had pretended not to see.

He'd taken the thick stack of papers after she'd finished and asked, "Do you want to talk about this? We can go get those fancy waffles you like in Maryville."

"I have to meet Dale, but thank you. I'll be fine."

Those last three words had become a mantra, if mantras were lies people told themselves to feel better.

"He'll be released soon. I'll do my best to keep him away from you if he's foolish enough to come back to town, but there are no restrictions on his release," Matt had explained, knowing Loey hadn't read the deal.

"Thanks, Matt." She'd nearly started crying. What if she'd married Matt? What if she'd picked an easy life with him instead of the path she'd set herself on with grim determination? "You're a good man."

After starting her morning like that, Loey was not in the mood for her cheerful coffee-plying ways. The Saturday lunch brunch rush consisted mainly of the type who liked to take pictures of their coffees and pastries before eating them, their eyes on their phones as they spoke across the table to their spouse or kids. The shop was crowded, but no one was actually talking to each other. Loey felt like she was walking through a dispassionate zombie horde as she collected dishes and took refill orders.

She was happy to see the last customer shuffle out. She flipped the Open sign to Closed. Her nerves jigged. She pulled out her phone to text Dale that she'd come over as soon as she'd finished her afternoon chores, but she already had two texts.

The first was from Dale: *Come to the library after the shop. I found something you'll want to see.*

Given their adventure in the cemetery, which had felt more like a war zone, Loey was nervous to see her best friend. They were on a hair trigger these days. She texted back: *On my way with coffee.*

The next text she had was from an unknown number: *My place at 3.*

The text, which had to be from Tabi, was followed by a kiss-face emoji and a vampire emoji and a girl doing yoga.

"What the heck does that mean?" Loey mumbled, staring at the weird little images.

Whether it meant she was giving blood while doing yoga or something far kinkier than Loey wanted to imagine, she had to get moving. Her afternoon had gotten very busy.

She tidied the shop in a superficial blitz, whipped up two

coffees for her and Dale, and dumped them into thermoses. She picked up her bag, juggling the coffees in her right hand, her phone between her teeth, and her keys in her other hand. At the front door, she checked over the darkened shop one last time as she always did.

Sunlight slanted through the closed blinds. The rays made the worn wooden floor shine. Dust danced through the still air threaded with the scents of leather and books and her grandfather. She could picture him standing at the counter, his head bent over a freshly opened bag of coffee, his nose pressed into the beans as he inhaled. He'd smile and Gran would laugh and child-Loey would run through the room with a book in her hand. Loey didn't love owning a store—the coffee shop didn't fulfill her—but it was a time capsule, the last kiss from the people she loved. She'd hold on to it until the day she turned back at the door and couldn't find her memories in the musty, sun-bright air. She slipped out the chiming door and locked up.

On Main, the town was tasting its first nip of fall, officially still a few weeks away. The September air gusted loose the first orange-crisp leaves from the maples in the town square. They tumbled end over end down the street while the townspeople on their lunch breaks called out *hellos* and *how are yous*. Shop doors were open, and fall displays adorned most of the window fronts. Loey had decorated hers this morning between the morning and brunch crowds, using pine cones and antique mason jars, string lights that reminded her of the Seam, and pumpkins and gourds of all colors from a local farm.

Angela Tilley must have recently pulled out a batch of pumpkin spice cakes from her bakery's ovens, for the scent of cinnamon and cardamom merged with the breeze and swept like the leaves down Main.

Loey jogged across the street with a wave to Mr. Weebly in his mail truck. She kept her head down, her shoulders hunched against the chill, and headed to the library next to the town bank.

Inside, the air was dusty and the blinds were shut to preserve the books from fading in the sunlight. The main desk was empty. A sign read, "Out To Lunch." Loey had timed her arrival perfectly so she wouldn't have to deal with Delilah's nosy questions. She left a note on the desk that said she was downstairs and headed through the basement door.

The lights were already on. The microfiche machine clicked and swiped below.

She rounded the corner of metal shelving containing all the extra books and found Dale sitting on a stool in front of the machine. Her hair was tossed into a messy bun atop her head, and her pale face was bare; Loey had never seen Dale go this many days in a row without makeup. She had a pen between her teeth and a notepad balanced on her knees, and from her slouched posture and glazed eyes, it looked like she'd been there for a while already.

She glanced up as Loey walked in and stopped beside the machine. The first thing Dale did upon recognizing her friend was frown.

"Hey," Dale said.

"I brought coffee." Loey held out Dale's thermos.

Dale closed the top page of her notepad as though she was the good girl in class who didn't want anyone cheating off her test. Loey told herself it didn't bother her. "Thanks."

Dale took a sip. She closed her eyes in appreciation. Loey adjusted her purse on her shoulder, the silence between them filled with all the cutting things they'd said last night, but Loey didn't feel like she should be the first to apologize. Dale was too stubborn, though, and she relished her grudges like she relished being the only woman in town who could make a perfect soufflé.

"About last night," Loey started. She tightened her grip on her coffee. "I went too far. I said a lot of things I shouldn't have."

Dale sat her thermos down on the cheap seventies desk the machine sat atop. From her spot on her stool, she had to peer up at Loey as she said, "We have to stop that."

Loey had hoped for an apology, but it looked like she was getting something else instead.

Dale continued, "We've treated each other like we're made of glass since our senior year in high school. We haven't said a lot of things we should've for years. Folton. Your accident. My marriage."

If there were threads inside Loey as well as all around her—and she liked to think there were—she felt their frantic, snapping ends fall calm at Dale's words as she set things right between them.

"You're right. We have to stop that," Loey said on an exhale.

She pulled up a wobbly chair from another table. Dale scooted her stool back to make room as Loey joined her in front of the machine. She dropped her purse on the floor, sat her thermos on her side of the table, and took Dale's hand. Dale only hesitated a beat before squeezing Loey's fingers.

"Let's say what we mean from now on." Dale's voice was raw, and up close, she looked as exhausted as Loey. "I meant a lot of what I said last night, and I know you did too, so there's no use in apologizing. But we can handle our shit better and take it out on the people who deserve it, not each other."

Not an apology but something else, and it worked. Loey nodded. "I want you to know I don't blindly follow Jeronimo. I know his story about that night is off. I don't think he killed Frankie, but I think something else happened. Whether he's hiding it from me or doesn't remember because it was too awful, I don't know, but I will find out. The hard truth is that I need him right now. This Tending stuff is hard and I love my grandparents but they left me holding this town's threads together without a clue what I'm doing."

"I get that," Dale said. "And while we're clarifying, Barty is not creepy. He's been coming to the women in my family for decades. Your family burden is important, but the Rose women have a secret too, and it's been killing us for a long time. I don't want to be the next Rose to die. And I do like Barty. It's nice to have someone need me. That doesn't negate the fact I have to stop this before another young Rose girl grows up thinking she's crazy."

Loey's stomach curdled around all the coffee she'd drunk today. "That's true? Did Helene tell you that?"

"Helene isn't the crazy old lady my mother would have everyone believe. Turns out there's merit to the Rose family madness after all."

"You're not crazy." Loey thought it a touch awful that Barty had wreaked such havoc, but she kept that to herself. She tried to lighten the mood with a tiny smile. "Although, I don't know if I'll ever get over how he watched you while you were underage."

Dale's mouth quirked. She bumped her shoulder against Loey's. It wasn't their normal, comfortable togetherness, but it was close.

"I think it's kinda hot." Dale winked.

"Ew. I'll pretend I didn't hear that. Where's this article you found?"

"Hang on." Dale picked up her phone and searched for the picture of the article, swiping her thumb across numerous pictures. "Here it is. It's about the revenuer." She handed the slim device to Loey. "Turns out he went missing around April of fifty-six. It lends credibility to Barty's theory that the rev followed Frankie, and it puts another suspect on the ridge of who could be the Skinned Man."

"And he could've killed Frankie."

"I thought that too. Read it."

Loey read. The article was a reprint from a city newspaper in West Virginia. It was brief but named the revenuer—Thomas Wooten—and cited his recent casework involving the notorious James brothers. Loey assumed that was why *The Righteous Daily* had picked up the news article on Wooten's disappearance. The rest of the article recapped the explosion and the brothers' deaths.

Reading it through twice to make sure she hadn't missed anything, Loey handed Dale's phone back and took a long sip of coffee.

"It doesn't make it any easier to identify the Skinned Man, but it's a relief to have another option besides Knox," she said.

"Exactly." Dale sat back in her chair and crossed her arms, satisfied with herself. "And what fun would it be if the answer came too easy?"

They spent the next hour combing through the articles Dale had found about that night, tossing theories back and forth, and scribbling notes. They carefully avoided any mention of either Barty's or Jeronimo's possible involvement in Frankie's death. It was one thing to agree to be more honest, but it was a separate matter altogether to incite another battle like the one from last night.

When it was almost time to meet Tabi, Loey said her goodbyes, and they made plans to meet later that evening at Dale's to go through her grandmother's book.

Tabi's house was everything Loey had expected and more.

She hadn't needed an address. Everyone knew where everyone lived in Righteous, and Tabi's aviary was hard to overlook. Loey parked on Tabi's lane in a neighborhood that dated back to the fifties or sixties. The old row townhouses were settled beneath towering oak trees with trunks as wide as a horse. As Loey got out of her truck, she heard the bird calls right away.

Before she could knock, Tabi swung her front door open with a gap-toothed smile, her eyes sparkling with a vitality that made Loey tired to witness. She wore black yoga pants with mesh paneling in geometric designs and a gauzy white top that set off her rich black skin. Her curls bounced as she waved Loey inside.

"You're early, but that's perfect. I just finished my yoga."

"That's a relief. I was worried you'd make me try it."

"That'll be our second date. Kitchen's this way. Want some lemon cake? I worked up an appetite."

"Ah …" Loey stammered. Second date? Was this a first date? Did Tabi think Loey was a … *lesbian*? "I mean, sure. Lemon cake sounds great. Just the cake, though. Nothing else."

Tabi laughed as Loey followed her. She glanced around the small home. The living room had an old fireplace. The walls were painted a happy robin-egg blue, the trim sparkling white. Photographs of landscapes and striking portraits hung on the walls; they must have been from Tabi's journalism days given the stark realities they portrayed. Vases of bright flowers sat on almost every surface—a hodge-podge collection of salvaged antiques. Past the living room was the dining room—a small table stacked with books, papers, and a MacBook, which Tabi snagged on her way by—and beyond the dining area, a simple half wall separated the kitchen.

Tabi waved Loey to the table as she danced on her toes, collecting teacups and coffee, lemon pound cake, and her good china. She laid it all on the table adorned with freshly cut flowers in a chipped blue mason jar. Loey took a seat. From the table, she could look out into the wild backyard at the aviary.

The domed roof stretched into the oak trees, using the thick branches as support beams. The patched-together windows and doors contained no glass but a soft mesh. Birds of all colors and types flew about. Their back and forth chitter-chatter bounced song-like through the air.

"It's gorgeous," she said in awe.

Tabi looked up from cutting the cake. It oozed a rich-smelling glaze. "Thank you. It all started after I found a pigeon with a broken foot. You can see it escalated quickly."

"No kidding. How many do you have in there?"

"Not as many as it seems. I rehabilitate some, temporarily home others, and work as a sort of foster system for many until they find families to take them. Bit of a passion project that takes up all my free time. It's great. Here."

She deposited a fat slice of cake in front of Loey before sitting in front of her laptop. She put on a pair of pink glasses, turned on a slim voice recorder and placed it on the table between them, and asked, "Ready?"

Loey felt sick in the anticipatory silence, but she nibbled on a bite of cake. Its lemon zestiness burst across her tongue so sharply it stung. "Where ... where should I start?"

"Wherever feels safest. This is your story, Loey. I'm only listening."

Loey had never doubted why Tabitha made such a sharp-nosed journalist, but she now understood why people might freely hand over their secrets to this woman. Here she was, a friend sitting across the table with bird calls slipping in through the open window.

"I guess I'll start at the beginning, on the first day of senior year. My locker was next to Leigh Parker's."

Loey meandered through the tale. Tabi rarely interrupted to ask a question, except when they reached the part about

Leigh's murder.

"A symbol on his chest? That wasn't in the papers." Her fingers flew across the keyboard of her laptop, taking notes like a fiend.

Loey blinked. Her mouth opened but nothing came out.

Tabi's fingers stilled atop the keys. Her voice recorder's light flashed on the table between them, capturing the entire weighty silence that carried the burden of Loey's lies.

"What symbol, Loey?"

"I don't know. I never found out."

Tabi motioned for her to continue, but Loey doubted Tabi had bought her lie. If she had, she would've asked more questions, pressed for more information. She hadn't. Loey reached the end of her story, with the day she'd lain in bed as Dale told her everything she'd done to frame Folton on her Thanksgiving break from college. She took another bite of cake, ravenous now that the words were free.

Tabi closed the laptop. "What about Dale?"

Loey froze with her fork halfway to her mouth. "What about her?"

"She didn't want to be here for this? I thought you two were best friends."

"We are."

Tabi shrugged. "Why isn't she here with you?"

"She's already done too much. It's hurt her, this secret."

"The pills?"

Loey jolted straight, knocking her fork off the table. "Don't put that in your story!"

"I won't. This is off the record. I'm not a monster, Loey. I'm trying to understand."

"Oh, well ..." Loey bit her lip. "Dale's dealt with a lot already. It's hard on her, and I don't want to add to her burden."

"With her husband and brother."

"How do you know about them?"

"I have eyes," Tabi said dryly, arching a brow.

"That's a secret too. We don't talk about that."

"Seems to be a trend in this town, all the things people don't talk about." She was echoing the sentiment Loey and Dale had discussed in the library.

Loey had never dwelled on the custom of keeping feelings and thoughts and issues secret, but she understood the damage they dealt to a person's insides. Eventually, all secrets fought for freedom. Loey's eyes went to the aviary, the birds flying from branch to branch, and she wondered if they ever missed the open sky.

"Are we done?" she asked. "I have chores to do."

"We're done whenever you say."

Loey stood, her chair scraping back. She wanted to be anywhere but here.

Tabi didn't stand. She watched Loey from her chair. "I might have a few follow-up questions. I'll let you know. What about our deal? The journal you 'found'?"

"I nearly forgot. It's lucky I put it in my truck after we talked."

Loey dug around in her bag until she found the thickly padded Ziploc bag she'd put the journal in. Soft tissue paper buffered the book's crumbling edges. She sat it on the table beside the voice recorder. It was still on, catching every word.

"Nothing else happened to it in your truck, did it?"

"Of course not," Loey said, offended.

"Sorry." Tabi pulled the bag toward her, her fingers skimming over the plastic and kneading the book's edges. "But I've seen your truck and the bear that sometimes rides with you, slinging drool out the window like a rain storm."

"Now you're talking crap about my dog too?"

Tabi ignored her. "Obidiah Jinks's journal ... I bet a lot

of people would be interested in this." She looked up at Loey. "You read nothing in this before you washed it?"

"I told you, I forgot about it," Loey said, bristling at the implied stupidity on her part. "It's been a busy time here."

"Right …" Tabi drew out the word. "I'll see what I can dig up and let you know."

"And don't tell anyone else you're working on that for me," Loey added in a rush.

Tabi's mouth quirked. "Sure thing. Your secret is safe with me."

"It's not a secret. Just private."

"Privacy is a journalist's specialty."

Maybe this had been a bad idea after all, but it was too late to take it back.

Much like everything else in her life.

CHAPTER 20

DALE HAD NEVER BEEN ONE for libraries, but she stayed long after Loey had left.

She found one more article from 1956. The storm that night had done record-breaking damage, flooding the sawmills and tearing the roof off the soda factory. Three people died. There was no mention of the ridge or anything she didn't already know. Regardless, she took a picture of the article right as Delilah came down the stairs into the library's basement.

"It's time to close. Are you finishing up down here?"

"Thanks, Delilah. I'm all done. That's a pretty dress. Did you make it?"

Delilah flushed. She glanced down at her dress like she'd forgotten what she was wearing. The floral print looked vintage, perhaps salvaged from another clothing item, but Delilah had always had a knack for design and sewing. The sweetheart neckline accented her ample chest, and the waistline was tucked in high and draped perfectly over her hips.

"I did," Delilah answered, still blushing. "I saw something like it in *Vogue* and thought I could make it too."

"That's amazing. You should sell some pieces at Terri's boutique."

Delilah's eyes widened. "You think?"

Dale gathered up her stuff, dropped it carelessly into her bag, and tossed her empty coffee thermos in the trash. Turning off the machine, she said, "Sure, why not? I can talk to Terri if you want. She's friends with my mother."

"Oh, Dale. That would be great. Thank you so much!"

Her excitement took Dale aback, but she smiled nevertheless. They chatted as Delilah turned off the lights and they headed upstairs. Delilah walked Dale to the front doors. Outside, the sun was setting up on the ridge, the evening shadows chasing away the last dregs of sunlight. It was far later than Dale had thought, her concept of time having warped in the library's basement.

"Is it true?" Delilah asked as Dale stepped onto the sidewalk. Delilah glanced up and down the empty street of closed shops before she added in a whisper, "About the man who killed Leigh? Is he getting out of prison?"

Dale sucked in a sharp breath. "How did you find out?"

"So, it's true? He was innocent?"

"I didn't say that."

"People are saying, well …" Delilah's excited flush waned.

"What are people saying?" Dale demanded.

"That you lied about what he did," she murmured, not quite meeting Dale's eyes, "because you wanted the attention."

"The attention?" Dale laughed, a bitter peal that rang down the darkening street.

Delilah winced. "I'm sorry. I shouldn't have said anything."

"It's fine. Whatever. I've got to go."

Dale started down the street toward her BMW.

Behind her, Delilah called out, "You'll still talk to Terri for me?"

Dale threw up a hand in a gesture of acquiescence. She opened the driver's side door, slid in, and tore off down the street, zooming by Delilah and her worried face.

Dale pulled up to her house and groaned. Travis's truck sat in the driveway. Of course, on the one night she and Loey needed privacy, he wasn't out drinking. She got out, shut her door, and started up the driveway. Her boiling annoyance with her husband kept her from hearing the shouting until she was on the front steps.

She growled. She had to deal with Cross too. Judging by the sounds of their fight, it would take some effort to cool them down and send them on their way to make up.

She locked the front door behind her and stalked toward the kitchen, ready to yell at the men for making such fools of themselves.

The crack of a fist against skin filled the house, followed by a crash.

Dale sprinted the final steps into the kitchen.

Cross was sprawled on the floor with his hand to his face. Travis stood over him. The fury in his eyes and his trembling fists told the story all too well.

Dale reached into her purse for her .38. It looked cute as hell, but it could kill a man, especially since she used hollow-point bullets. She clicked off the safety and pointed it at Travis.

The sound of the gun drew their attention.

"Dale," they said with the same touch of fear they always had in their voices after she'd caught them.

"Get out," she snarled at Travis.

Travis glanced down at Cross, who was bleeding all over her tiles, and back at Dale, confused as to who she meant. His brows spiked in surprise. "Me? I live here. This is my house."

"Whose name is on the deed, you piece of shit? Out."

"Dale, hang on." Cross pushed himself up onto his butt, his face already swelling.

Dale threw a tea towel from the island at him. He caught it cleanly and pressed it against his face.

"Travis," she warned, her aim steady on his chest, "I won't tell you again."

"You're both crazy," he spat. He grabbed his overnight bag, the one he'd been living out of since his father's funeral, and slung it over his shoulder. He stomped by them. He called back, "Everyone is right about the Roses. Y'all are a bunch of greedy psychopaths."

"And don't you forget it!" Dale shouted after him.

The front door slammed hard enough to knock a picture off the wall in the living room.

Dale sat on the floor beside her brother. He wasn't hurt badly enough that she needed to doctor him, and she wasn't in the compassionate nursing spirit anyway. She flipped the gun's safety on and set it beside her in case Travis decided to come back for more.

"I'm calling the cops," she said.

"Hang on." Cross dabbed at the blood gushing down his chin, staining his favorite shirt, the one that made his biceps look so toned. Losing the shirt should have been criminal enough. "Don't call the cops."

"He hit you, Cross."

"I—"

"If you say you deserved it, I swear on all things holy, I will hit you too and knock some sense into you."

That won her the glimmer of a rueful smile. "I wanted to tell the truth. He didn't like that."

Dale raised her brows at her brother's destroyed face. "Yeah, no shit."

"If it was the other way around, I would've hit me too."

Dale threaded her fingers through his. "You're too good for that, and you're too good for him. You deserve a man who loves you."

Cross's eyes were hot coals on her skin. Staring at each other, she thought they were finally going to go *there*, have the talk and hash it out once and for all, but the look in his eyes faded. The moment passed.

Like nothing had happened and he was over to test one of Dale's new recipes, he said, "We should talk about why you smell like a musty old lady. Do you put on makeup anymore? Mother will start harassing you about it."

An ache blossomed inside that she wished she could ignore, but this would always be the crux between them. It was the conversation that would always asterisk their love for each other. If it went away, Dale wouldn't have to doubt her brother's love for her or why he always chose Travis over her. The irony didn't escape her that she'd told Loey they needed to stop hiding their feelings, but this was a feeling Dale couldn't share so easily. She couldn't bear the thought of Cross having to choose between her and Travis.

"What *have* you been doing?" he asked, solidifying their move away from deeper waters of conversation.

She smiled wide enough to show teeth. "Diggin' up graves and chasing monsters."

Cross threw back his head and laughed from deep in his belly. It was infectious. Dale joined in, chuckling. It was pretty funny to think about.

Cross swiped beneath his eyes, his laughter trailing off. He slung an arm around her shoulders. She'd won back his affection, a small victory over Travis, even if it was just for tonight.

CHAPTER 21

"**W**HERE ARE YOU GOING?"

Loey leaped out of her skin. The keys, which she'd been using to lock her back door, fell from her hand and clattered to the porch planks. She whirled around.

Jeronimo stood at the bottom of the steps, leaning against the railing.

"Gosh," she breathed out, bending to pick up her keys, "you have to stop sneaking up on me like that."

He cocked a brow at her. "I've heard that jumpy people have a guilty conscience."

"Or maybe you have me on edge all the time."

His mouth quirked to match the angle of his cocked brow. "Is that so?"

"Don't try that with me," she warned. "I'm still mad at you for the scene you caused at the rodeo with Matt. He didn't deserve that."

"He shouldn't act like he has any right to your time."

Loey charged down the steps and shouldered by Jeronimo. "He's a good man, and he's my friend. He can have my time whenever he wants it." She shot him a cocked brow of her own as she strode to her truck.

Men weren't the only ones who could stuff words full of innuendo.

He followed her, not taking the bait, meaning he was either in an excellent mood, he wasn't mad at her anymore, or he had something else on his mind.

She got in the truck, and Jeronimo climbed into the passenger seat before she could stop him. "Where are we going?"

"Excuse me? *We're* not going anywhere. Get out."

"You found the book."

It wasn't a question; he already knew. His eyes were on her large leather shoulder bag. It contained a stack of stationery, pens, and her laptop—in case she and Dale needed to Google how not to summon the Devil.

She was already worried enough about the Skinned Man showing up.

"That's silly," she blustered after a too-long pause. "You know I would tell you if I had. Why would I hide that from you? That would be stupid."

Jeronimo wasn't buying anything she was selling tonight, innuendos or lies. He leaned over the truck's bench seat until they were nose to nose. His minty breath washed over her lips like a ghostly kiss.

"Don't you lie to me, Loey Grace."

She pressed her back against the door and scrubbed her tingling nose, a blush creeping up her neck. "I ain't lying," she mumbled.

He stared at her, searching for the answers she wasn't saying but he somehow heard in that way of his. He sat back; hurt spread across his face, and any hint of his earlier smirk vanished. It surprised her, that flash of emotion.

"You don't trust me, do you? That's why you didn't tell me."

"I trust you." *Mostly*, she added in her mind. "But Dale found it. Her grandmother stole it from my grandmother long ago, and Dale's mother had it in storage. She's the one who doesn't trust you, I swear. We were going to look at it together tonight."

"And what? Russian-roulette the symbols until something stuck? *That* was your plan?"

"I don't appreciate your tone."

"This isn't the latest issue of some magazine with sex tips. This is important."

"You think I don't know that?"

"Why the hell are you going to Dale's?"

"So Barty can help us!"

He recoiled. She'd done it again, shocked him straight out of the jaded narcissism that came from his immortality. Shaking his head, he asked, "You trust him more than me?"

It was such a normal thing to say. A question rooted deep in brotherly insecurity. That someone would favor one brother over another was an issue as old as time, ask any therapist. It also said she was important to him, that he needed her to side with him. It showed such vulnerability. Realizing how it sounded, he looked like he wanted to tear the words down from the air. His face darkened with shadows as he tucked his head.

Carefully, quietly, she said, "I'm out of options, J. You haven't been around much, and if we'd found this book together, we would need help to understand it. You and Dale keep thinking I'm picking sides, but I'm doing whatever it takes to Tend this Seam and not shame my grandparents' memories by ruining everything they were trying to protect."

If baring her soul to him had softened his heart, it didn't show on his face or in his words as he asked, "Is that why you dug up Knox Keene? To protect your family?"

Sweat spread across Loey's palms. "How did you know about that?"

"I know everything that happens in the cemetery, whether you try to hide it with cheap plastic flowers or not."

Her heart kicked. "Oh."

"You would do well to remember that next time."

207

"I'm done digging up bodies."

"You sure about that? You might need to disprove another part of my story."

He was starting to tick her off. She glared at him. "If you think I'm going to apologize, you're wrong. I'll do whatever it takes to protect this town."

His fight drained away at once. He sank against the truck's seat and stared hollow-eyed out the windshield. "That's what scares me."

"Why?"

"We all want different things. You. Me. Dale. Barty. The Skinned Man. Frankie. Our desires put us all at odds with each other, leaving nothing left for the fight that matters."

"The fight being sealing the Seam."

He didn't respond, but he didn't have to.

Dale opened her back door to find them on her stoop. She crossed her arms. "I thought we were doing this alone."

Loey stepped around Dale, who was doing a good job of blocking the kitchen's back door. The kitchen smelled like cleaner, the floors extra shiny like Dale had just finished cleaning. A full-length mirror leaned against the refrigerator. It took effort for Loey to look away from it and address Dale.

"He knows about Knox and the book."

"Fantastic." Dale stomped to the substantial tumbler of whiskey waiting on the island.

Jeronimo eased the door shut behind him.

Dale hadn't come close to the nuclear meltdown Loey had braced for on the drive over. It was possible the meltdown had already happened, and they were catching Dale on the comedown. Her eyes were red, and she chewed on her manicured nails like she needed the sustenance between sips of whiskey.

"Is everything okay? You look …"

Dale's eyes flashed. "Crazy?"

"Um … is tonight a good time? We could take the book and—"

"No, we're doing this. I'm fine. Everything is fine. We'll look at the book together, at once. That's fair." She flapped a hand at the mirror. Clearly, she meant everyone, Barty included.

"That's fine. I think that's a great plan." It wasn't the time to push Dale, not if they liked breathing; Loey had seen her best friend like this throughout the years. It never ended well. This was a horrible idea, but Loey needed that book.

"I don't like you," Dale told Jeronimo as if she hadn't been clear enough on that already.

"I don't like you none too much either." Jeronimo's lips quirked into a smile. Never a good sign. This smile looked too daring, too devilish, to be a good thing. Apparently, he hadn't understood it wasn't the time to test Dale.

Dale dipped her chin, accepting his sentiment, a fair fight between enemies. She threw back the remainder of her whiskey. Even Jeronimo looked impressed.

"I'll get the book."

Dale didn't go far. She went to her stand mixer and pulled out a small green linen book from the bowl. Loey pinched her lips together before her comment on the poor hiding place could slip out. Thank God Jeronimo did the same.

Dale offered it to Loey like it was a signed check to the electric company during winter.

Loey took it tenderly. Dale spun away to pour another drink while Jeronimo stood at Loey's shoulder. Together, they stared down at Knox Keene's name embossed in gold on the cover. She turned it over and around, back and forth, familiarizing herself with this book that contained her family's history.

Holding her breath, she opened it.

The pages were thick as Dale had described and yellowed with age. Loey paged through them, carefully at first then faster, skipping entire sections toward the end. She reached the back cover, and the book fell closed in her hands. She might have dropped it if Jeronimo hadn't taken it from her.

Loey stared at Dale. "Oh my *gosh*."

"I know," Dale said.

"You looked."

"I looked."

Loey was too stupefied to be angry that Dale had lied about waiting for her. "Is this English?"

"Not all of it," Jeronimo supplied, though she hadn't meant it as a question. "Some of it is Latin. A bit of French, which is interesting. I thought the Keenes were Irish." He flipped through the pages with the reverence Loey wished she felt.

Any glimmer of hope she'd managed to garner over the prospect of the book was crushed. There was no way she could read that book, much less use it. That explained Dale's drinking. Loey had never been one for whiskey, but she wouldn't mind one.

"We're screwed," she told Dale.

Dale lifted her glass in a cheers. "Can you believe we're the ones who have to save the town from a monster? They don't normally show the bumbling idiots in the 'save the world' movies. Typically, the heroes have their shit together."

"This magic doesn't exist in a vacuum here in Righteous. People and cultures have used it for millennia. They use different vessels for the magic," Jeronimo said. "We could cross-reference the symbols and explanations with my research. Some of them look familiar to my work on portals at Savannah's Seam."

"He does have a lot of research," Loey offered in bland support, her mind on the book and the paper bomb that had gone off in the rectory.

"That's truly great for him," Dale said, "but we're also asking Barty. He's been waiting."

Loey's eyes flashed to the mirror. "He's here?"

"Barty," Dale called. She strolled to the mirror, swirling her drink in its glass without spilling a drop.

Barty materialized in the mirror, its reflection darkening behind him. He'd been youthful and solid, tall and beautiful, and strong enough to beat the Skinned Man in the cemetery. Tonight, the change in him startled her. He'd grown wan, and he kept glancing over his shoulder as though someone were sneaking up behind him.

"Can you use that symbol from Little Cricket?" Dale asked beside the mirror, beside Barty. "The one that will let him talk?"

Loey exchanged a look with Jeronimo. He nodded.

She prepared her paper and pens. From memory, she drew the symbol from the piece of skull she'd found. Dale had a piece of tape ready. Loey finished and stuck the symbol to the back of the mirror. Loey leaned the mirror back into place.

"Hello, Jeronimo," Barty said, seeing his brother for the first time since the night Jeronimo had tried to kill him.

Jeronimo gently closed the book in his hands. He walked closer. The three of them formed a loose semicircle in front of the mirror.

What was the right thing to say in this moment? The brothers not only had to cross a divide halved by murder and love, but also by worlds and decades. In the end, Jeronimo asked quietly, "She's really hurting you?"

Barty dipped his chin in answer. The gesture cost him more of himself than he could afford to share. Frankie was like a moon the James brothers kept in their orbit; she dictated their tides toward each other.

"She wouldn't do that. She loved you. Loves you," Jeronimo

amended, and that cost him too. Frankie and Barty, for better or worse, were over there, in part because of him.

"She hasn't loved me for a long time, JJ." Barty lifted his chin to his brother. The fight stirred in his light-colored eyes. "That night on the ridge? She was going after you—to warn you—'cause you were the one she loved. Not me."

"No."

"And you killed her."

"No!" Jeronimo roared.

Loey flinched. Dale dropped her whiskey glass. It shattered across the floor, the whiskey spilling like liquid gold across the tiles, the glass skipping in all directions—jagged shards of tiny truths ready to cut them wherever they stepped.

Neither brother noticed.

"Knox watched you kill her!" Barty shouted loud enough to rattle the mirror.

Jeronimo lunged, ready to peel Barty from the reflection. "He was *not* there that night. He was dead, Barty. Dead!"

Jeronimo's shouting echoed through the house. Silence fell. No one moved.

"No, she was dead," Barty said quietly into the silence, defeated and accepting. "She was, JJ."

Jeronimo withered at Barty's words. The brothers bowed across the mirror, separated by worlds but held together by one terrible night. Their moon was gone, and no amount of shouting would bring her back.

Still bent, Jeronimo murmured, "We're fixing this. Tonight."

"No." Loey whirled on him. "Absolutely not."

"What? How?" Dale managed to stare at Jeronimo without open hatred since he might be on her side, leaving Loey completely alone.

"We let him out. See if distance is enough for us to exist on the same side," he added for Loey's benefit, sensing her argument.

Loey opened her mouth, but Dale cut her off. "Distance? Why would that matter? What happens if you're on the same side?"

Jeronimo's eyes settled on Loey with judgment, and her skin flushed cold. She scowled at him, refusing to let him judge her for doing her best. "Don't give me that look. I was going to tell her."

"Tell me what?" Dale nearly screamed.

"I'm cursed," Jeronimo deadpanned with a one-shoulder shrug. "Something happened in the explosion, and my soul went across the Seam but not me. It's left me ... *unable* to be around Barty if he's near a tatter for long."

"It hurts you?"

Loey did not like how quickly Dale had homed in on that little fact.

"I think it's the only thing that can kill me, actually."

"You think enough distance could be the answer?"

"Possibly."

Here it was, the honesty they'd promised to speak. No more holding back. No more pretending. "I'm the Tender. I'm the only one who can loosen the threads, and I am not letting him out. Not tonight anyway."

"She's right." Barty nodded to Loey. "I'm not weak enough yet that I can't keep him back. With me here, he'll think twice about going near the tatters, and he doesn't know the ghosts have turned on me. Frankie always helped me fight him. She won't no more."

The moon's betrayal, turning on Barty, for another bite of life. Beneath the weight of Frankie's fall, Jeronimo blinked at Loey, his eyes begging her for something he should've known better than to ask.

"I'm not letting him out just to save him from Frankie,"

she told him in a murmur, but everyone heard. "It's done, J. Whatever happened that night, you need to come to terms with it."

He offered her the book. She took it, and he backed up a step, his boots crunching over glass. He was at the kitchen door, and with one final long stare at Barty, he left.

"He's always leavin'," Barty said as the door closed. "He's always going away."

"Barty," Dale tried. "It's okay. You don't need him."

To Loey, he said, "Don't go loving him. It isn't worth the pain. He don't stay and he won't ever. Not even for someone he loves."

A distant cry pierced the quiet in the kitchen. Its faraway quality told Loey it had come from the other side of the mirror, but she still cringed from reflexive fear.

"What was that?" Dale surged closer to the mirror, her bandaged feet skidding over the glass without slowing her down.

Barty stared over his shoulder. He was already turning to leave, saying, "I have to go. That's him."

"Wait! You're too weak." Dale grabbed the mirror.

"Hang on." Loey joined her so their shoulders smashed together. "One more question."

"There's not much time. He's coming."

"Loey," Dale begged and grabbed her arm. She had too much pride to fall to her knees, but Loey imagined she was close as she pleaded, "Let him out. Please. For me. He'll die over there."

Barty watched them. How could one night from over half a century ago interlock so many lives? But they were interlocked, and he knew it and she knew it.

"I can't," she said. "He has to stay and fight. He's all we've got."

"Loey—" Dale tugged on her arm.

Loey didn't budge. She wouldn't. Not on this. Dale sensed her resolve and released her arm with a scoff of disgust. She turned away, her face in her hands, and screamed, the sound of her frustration muffled to keep from alarming the neighbors, if the night's yelling hadn't already.

"What do you need to know?" Barty asked.

"Where were your squirrel holes? Where did Jeronimo hide the moonshine?"

Barty frowned. His surprise added some life and color back to his face. "Why do you needa know that?"

"You said you thought the revenuer was following Frankie to them that night. I want to see where they went."

Another screech echoed across the black plains, closer this time. Barty didn't react.

"Got a piece of paper? Some of these places ain't safe. You'll need to be careful."

Loey quickly grabbed a thick page of stationery and her calligraphy pen. "I'm ready."

"This is bullshit," Dale snarled behind Loey, but neither she nor Barty listened.

Barty described the squirrel holes and the location of the central still in detail, his accent heavy in his rush. As he spoke, the screams drew closer, and a heavy sense of dread leached through the mirror to saturate the air in the kitchen.

Dale tried to interrupt them, but Barty ignored her, and his disregard turned her efforts quieter each time.

At the end of his directions, Loey had eleven spots to check plus the still, and those were the ones Barty could describe with enough confidence that she could find them. The others would remain a mystery unless Jeronimo took her, and she wasn't counting on that.

The sound came again, loud enough to clatter Dale's mirror against the fridge.

Barty paled impossibly further. A shadow pulsed in that hazy darkness behind him, flickering in and out of the reflection's range. Loey was about to warn him, but he noticed its presence with grim resolve. He pulled a fistful of salt from his pocket.

"I have to go," he said, the words detached and directed at no one.

"Wait." Dale returned to the mirror. "Don't go. He'll kill you."

Barty's bloodshot eyes rose to Dale's. He looked pained as he said, "Dale, I—"

The shadow erupted over his side of the mirror. Dale screamed.

The shadow slipped away like a piece of fabric falling to the ground, and the reflection was their own, with the kitchen behind them and the glass on the floor, sticky from the drying liquor.

"Loey."

Her name on Dale's lips was her best friend's last plea.

To leave Barty across the Seam was as good as murder.

To let him out, however, even if he wanted freedom enough to ask her, would unleash an evil onto the town. And it wouldn't just be the Skinned Man who stepped across the torn Seam, but the hungry ghosts led by Frankie too.

It was one man's life or hundreds.

It felt like justifying her lies about Folton all over again.

"I'm sorry." She forced herself to look Dale in the eye. This might be it. This might be the end of them. "I can't. He has to stay."

CHAPTER 22

"**Y**OU WERE NEVER GOING TO do it, were you?
You never had any intention of trying to get him out
after you had the book. Not for some bullshit excuse
of the Skinned Man, but because it would hurt Jeronimo. You
won't risk it. You won't even try."

"It's complicated," was all Loey said.

"He's *dying*, Loey. You're killing him. You're a murderer."

"Your great-aunt's killing him, not me! I'm doing the best I can."

"The best you can?" This felt bad. In Dale's chest, this
felt real bad. Something evil was tearing her apart, and she
wondered if this was what Frankie felt like. Dale had fought
with Loey before, but never like this. Never had she wanted so
badly to cut her best friend down just to inflict the pain. "You're
doing the best you can to protect Jeronimo. That's it. You don't
give a shit about the rest of us."

"That's not true."

"It is! Look at you, Loey Grace! It's Jeronimo said this, and
Jeronimo did that. You don't have a fucking clue what's going
on because you're so far up his ass you can't see he's using you.
He needs a Tender. He can't do this alone. His life is at stake. If
you find out the truth about what he did that night and you let
Barty out, like you should, Jeronimo will die, and he's making
you think he loves you so you won't. He's using you."

Loey's mouth fell open as Dale spoke, and in her eyes, Dale saw the same tearing happening inside her too. They were all hungry ghosts feeding on each other.

"You think that little of me, huh?" Loey said. "You think I'm that stupid?"

"I think you're blinded by his smooth accent and tight ass. I think you hide behind your scars and your nose ring and your self-righteous constant goddamn atonement for a sin you think condemned you to live out your days in suffering. I think you were lonely, but Jeronimo came along and brought you back to life. It probably feels good, but he's a liar and a user and a piece of—"

"Stop."

"Truth hurts, doesn't it?"

"The truth?" Her best friend's eyes were the color of a long-burning fire. "You want to hear the truth? I'll give you the truth, Dale Rose."

The price of having a best friend who was closer than a sister was the type of pain she could inflict. They knew all the secrets. Knew where all the bodies were buried. They knew all your weakest spots because they'd held you at your weakest. That information, turned around and pointed back at your heart—well, it could cut like a razor blade.

Loey cut.

"You sit up there in your sugar-spun perfect house with your frilly aprons and your handsome husband. You smile and laugh and do your hair and buy the nicest outfits. You walk through town like you own Righteous because you're a Rose and Roses think they own us all. But everyone is talking about you. They don't say good things, Dale. They say ugly truths about your lie of a life. We all know it's a lie, don't we? Why do you think you care so much about Barty? Why are you fighting so hard for him?"

"*Don't*," Dale spat, teeth chattering from the rage surging through her, "bring him into this."

"Why not? You did. You inserted yourself into this entire thing. I was trying to protect you by not telling you, yet here you are, against all reason. You talk about me being up Jeronimo's ass? You came back from your mirror in love with Barty. Why do you think that is?"

"He loves me too," Dale choked out, throat tight with unbidden tears that surprised her. She couldn't remember them starting.

"You were the first woman he saw in nearly seventy years who wasn't a ghost. Any man would love you in that situation, but that's not the point, is it? You're so desperate for someone to love you, because your daddy never did and your mommy never did and Travis never did. And Cross is fucking your husband, so that doesn't say much about his love either, does it? So Barty clings to you because maybe"—Loey held up her finger, her lips pulled back—"just maybe, he's using you too. Desperate recognizes Desperate over there across the Seam, and he jumped on a sure thing when he saw one. What about that for truth, Dale?"

Dale stared at her bandaged feet, at the glass on her floor, the mess. All the mess. She told herself not to. She told herself a cut didn't equal a cut, but Loey hadn't simply cut.

She'd slashed Dale's fucking throat, and Dale was pissed.

"That was a good speech, Loey," she said. "Very strong. Very opinionated of you. Looks like you found a backbone after all. Too bad it was after Jeronimo had you on your back that you finally found it. Why do you think I lie about my perfect life? I lie because of that night with Folton and what Cross and I did for you. I'm a pill popper and a desperate wreck of a person, and it's your fault, Loey Grace Keene. You made me this way, and now, after you've met a man, you're tossing me into the trash. A used-up doll, pretty once but not interesting enough anymore. Well, that's too bad." Dale shook as everything came undone. "This doll won't be tossed out. She's coming back for you, and she's got teeth, you bitch."

Dale grabbed a stool from the island and flung it across the kitchen. It smashed against the cabinets with an almighty clatter.

Loey didn't react to the bang or the crash of Dale's anger. She put the book in her purse and settled the strap on her shoulder. It felt like a final thing, like a wave goodbye. She left.

The door snicked closed behind her.

She wasn't original enough to have a different exit than him. She had to leave the way he had. Because she loved him, and because Cross loved Travis, Dale would always be the one left out. The unloved one. The unchosen one.

She stood there, alone, knowing Loey was leaving, and her righteous anger stopped feeling right.

In the comedown of her anger's high, it felt *wrong*.

Dale hadn't heard Loey's truck start—she still had time to stop her—but she imagined him. Imagined his sad eyes and tired face, worn down from decades trapped in a hell full of monsters and ghosts because the Keenes were too comfortable using him as their guard dog.

For him, Dale told herself.

And for you, the voice in her mind whispered back. Her pride, that big awful thing, refused to let her rush out to Loey and make things right. Outside, Loey's truck rumbled. Dale pictured it backing out of her driveway and pulling away.

Her back door opened, and her mouth was already rushing to form the apology, but she froze. It wasn't Loey in her doorway.

"Jeronimo? What the hell?" she asked the tall shadow filling her doorway.

"Is she coming back?" He stepped farther into her kitchen,

and Dale didn't know if she liked that.

He scared her.

"She's gone to the ridge to check your squirrel holes."

"She won't be back soon."

Dale held her breath for a short count, hollowing her cheeks, her belly shrinking toward her ribs. "I don't think she's coming back here for a long time."

Jeronimo stared at her, understanding far too much, and she hated that look in his stupid black eyes. "I knew this would tear us apart. Barty and I have been doing that for years."

Dale didn't want to talk about Barty or that night. She wanted this man out of her house without him seeing her fear. "Whatever, Jeronimo. Why are you here again?"

"I've come to help."

She considered him closely. "Help me do what?"

"Get him out."

That was the last thing she'd expected him to say, and her arms fell to her sides in shock. "But Loey took the book, and she's the only one who can open the threads on this side."

Midnight eyes glittering like the Devil's, he said, "I have a plan."

CHAPTER 23

OEY WAS SICK AND TIRED of everyone thinking she wasn't doing enough. It was relentless. She could only do so much without her family's Tending book. With it, she still couldn't do much. The thing didn't make a lick of sense.

She drove up Devil's Maw without Jeronimo. She had no idea where he'd gone after leaving Dale's, and she didn't care to look for him. He wasn't helping the situation either. He wanted to test his theory of distance protecting him if he and Barty were on the same side. A test that was betting their lives, and the lives of everyone in town, that when the Skinned Man tore through the Seam, they would be strong enough to fight him.

It was a test they'd fail. Jeronimo couldn't get within sneezing distance of Barty without half dying. She didn't need a book to tell her that.

She wanted to go up Shiner's Ridge as soon as she got home, but she wasn't familiar enough with the ridge to follow Barty's directions at night. There were rumors of bears, boars, and cougars out here. Tomorrow's weather called for storms in the evening, but she could spend the morning checking out the ridge. It meant she'd miss church again, but it would be worth it, even knowing Ms. Ida May and her fellow flock of old biddies would chitter away about Loey's descent into sin.

In the meantime, she hauled herself out of her truck, and

dragged her heavy bag onto her shoulder. A bag made heavier by the little book weighed down by secrets she couldn't decipher.

After checking the barn, feeding Dewey and Boltz, and taking a long, hot shower, Loey settled at her breakfast table with a cup of tea and half a leftover carrot cake from the shop. She wasn't proud that she didn't bother with a plate but tucked straight into the cake with nothing but a fork and the strength of will to finish the entire thing.

She opened the book to the first page. A separate notebook for her notes and a magnifying glass from Pap's desk for the more illegible notations sat on the other side of her carrot cake. She didn't dare recopy any of the symbols without knowing what they did, but she traced them with her finger to feel their power.

Page by page, she worked her way through the book, filling up her notebook with scribbles and thoughts. She worked straight through the night. Morning came, and she woke up with her pen in hand, drool on her cheek, and Dewey's head butting against her leg.

He wagged his tail as she lifted her head from the table, notebook paper stuck to her mouth. She peeled it off with a grimace. A check through the back window told her the ridge was still dark, meaning the sun hadn't risen completely from the valley and she hadn't overslept.

She had to keep moving. If she sat here with her thoughts for too long, she might start thinking about last night, and she couldn't. Not yet. She had things to do.

Normally, by the time she finished up in the barn, sunlight would be stretching across her pastures, but today, heavy clouds blocked its rays. A check of her grandmother's watch said it was close to mid-morning. She needed to get a move on if she wanted to beat the storm.

With one last wary glance overhead, she went inside to gear up.

She unearthed Pap's old waterproof pack from the garage first. She checked the shotgun's loaded rounds and stocked extra ammo into the pack. She also added a water thermos, dry gloves, hand warmers, a flashlight, a package of kindling, and a lighter.

Before she swung her pack onto her shoulder, she added her grandparents' Tending book into the bag.

She wanted to take Dewey with her, but she worried the terrain would be too much for him. A smaller part of her didn't know what she would find up there either, and she didn't want him to get hurt or worse. Let whatever might happen happen to her, but she'd see Hell freeze over before she let something happen to her dog. She kissed his wet nose while he stared back at her with droopy eyes.

After bundling up in a Carhartt jacket that had also belonged to Pap and tugging on tall mud boots and a ball cap to keep her hair out of her face, Loey toted her pack and shotgun out to the shed, where the Yamaha four-wheeler waited. It took a few tries, but she got it started. She backed it out and aimed for the trail that led up into Shiner's Ridge from the pasture on the farthest edge of the farm.

Today, the ridge was veiled in fog from the storm rolling down the northern range of the Appalachians. Mist hung near the tree line, and Loey tugged up her jacket's hood as she drove to ward against the fine rain already falling. Up ahead, the pines stood sentinel, guarding the ridge's entrance.

She'd never spent much time in the woods. Though she'd played in the cemetery with Gran, the ridge had been Pap's domain. Despite spending stretches of days up on the ridge, he'd never taken Loey or Gran. Sometimes, late at night, she'd caught him trekking out across the back pastures and disappearing between the pine boughs, his graying head tucked against the mountain chill, his long legs carrying him with a certainty she didn't feel. She'd had no clue what he'd been up to, but now that she knew their secrets, she wondered what had drawn him into the darkness.

She eased off the gas. Back at her house, the lights she'd left on glowed through the gloom. Boltz's silhouette sat in the kitchen window. She imagined his feline eyes on her.

She gave the machine gas. The four-wheeler jostled over the trailhead, and the trees blotted out the sky so just the scant sunlight seeping through the canopy and the vehicle's bouncing headlights illuminated the path ahead.

Loey's first stop was the moonshine still. She hadn't been up here, not since knowing Jeronimo; she hadn't had the time or a reason. With Barty's instructions, she found the path easily enough. On her way, she checked two squirrel holes but found nothing more than a few pieces of trash from hikers and hunters.

However, she knew she was on the right path to the still, because the woods changed.

At first, the brambles and weeds, briars and thickets thinned until only the tall, ancient trees remained. They swept around her, their soot-gray bark peeling away from the trees' hearts underneath. Far overhead, the lowest limbs barely stirred in the soft breeze that blew like a whispered secret.

The air tasted like fire on her tongue, and it burned in her lungs. She clamped her mouth shut to breathe through her nose. Shrugging deeper into her jacket, she drove faster.

The path smoothed out and widened. She accelerated up a turn, the back wheels spinning on loose dirt and spitting it out behind her as she snaked toward the clearing, visible between the trees.

She was so focused on the clearing that she almost missed the trinkets overhead. They dangled on clear fishing line from the branches. Old wooden toys, a shoe, a satin bow with what looked like hair tied through it, and a cheap plastic watch swayed as she drove beneath them.

The bones came next. Small ones, turned white with age, were grouped in clusters and sounded like wind chimes.

Right outside the circle of trees guarding the still's clearing, the mirrors hung.

They caught the dim sunlight from the murky sky and fractured the beams across the forest floor as Loey drove beneath them, her eyes warily on them. The light danced beneath her as if she were caught in her reflection, and she did not like the feeling one bit.

She drove into the clearing with one final burst of speed. On instinct, she hit the brakes. The four-wheeler fishtailed beneath her and rocked to a stop.

She did not kill the engine. She would not be staying here long.

In her gut, this place felt wrong. Bad things had happened here, and those bad things remained.

The obvious focal point was the still, or what was left of it. Where it had stood was a charred gash of earth. Its metal bits were wrapped around tree limbs and trunks, like tissue paper cast out in the wind. Nothing grew from the earth or around the metal blown into the trees. The land was dead. Here, Jeronimo had lain, his body dying, his soul replaced by a curse.

Loey's eyes swept over the burbling creek. On the other side, it appeared as though nothing had happened—the trees unscarred, the earth happy with grass and brambles. That was where Barty had been blasted. His body dead, his soul hanging on, trapped.

And a third person. Where had they stood, dying and living at the same time? The revenuer whose memory she hunted or her great-great-grandfather, who Gran and Pap had spoken of so proudly—which one had burned in the fire and emerged a monster? And what of his soul? Where had it gone?

The clouds rumbled in answer. The wind picked up. Behind Loey, the mirrors and bones and trinkets trilled.

Somewhere higher on the ridge, she heard bells.

The wind fell still, but the bells kept singing a lonesome note, and Loey had the unwavering sensation she wasn't alone.

CHAPTER 24

"**W**HAT ARE YOU DOING HERE?** You shouldn't have come back."

Dale turned around, already smiling. Barty had found her faster than she'd anticipated. He stood behind her, his face solemn, his eyes on a spot over her shoulder. A lock of hair tumbled over his forehead that she itched to sweep back so she could see him clearly.

The silken sky whipped its delicate folds. The mountains soaked up this dark, glittering world and cast its reflection back out, a constant swell of movement. Even the breathing ground beneath her felt less sinister, like an enemy with a name instead of a masked face.

"How did you find me so quickly?"

"The pocket is small, and I felt the Seam change. I thought it was him."

Dale stiffened. "Is he close?"

Barty shook his head. He still wouldn't look at her.

"Barty." Dale stepped toward him, and he stepped back to keep the distance between them. "What's wrong? What happened?"

"Why are you here, Dale?"

"Your brother sent me to get you. It's time to bring you home."

Barty's eyes found hers, unblinking with a younger brother's hope. "He's doing that?"

Dale's heart tugged at the love in his voice. Jeronimo didn't deserve it, but she knew better than to try to turn one brother against the other. She knew, in the end, who Barty would pick, and she didn't dare chance it.

"He is. We just have to wait."

He stomped down that hope like it was salt on a ghost and said, "I can't leave. My job isn't done here. My sins aren't paid."

"You didn't do anything wrong." Dale started toward him, this time refusing to let him escape her. He swayed, and she wrapped an arm around his waist to catch him if needed. "Jeronimo will get us out of here soon."

"All right," Barty said. He leaned over Dale and put his nose into her hair, breathing in her scent. She felt his lips move, her scalp tingling beneath his breath. "All right."

Walking slowly across the plains, gathering salt as they went, they returned to his cove. It was as perfect as Dale remembered. If not for the ghosts and the Skinned Man hunting them, she would have happily lived here with Barty in their own little world.

"We'll be safe here. Everyone is scattered after the last fight." But he still used half his salt to lay down a thick, straight line across the cave's opening.

"What happened?" Dale took his hand after he'd finished and pulled him toward a ledge. They sat, and she pressed herself against his side, craving his touch, and prodded a cut on his cheek.

He glanced at her from the corner of his eye before his gaze skittered to the cave's opening. "The Skinned Man was moving. The ghosts scattered. I thought they were coming for me, but they were running from him."

"What is he doing?"

"I don't know."

"Does he know about Frankie?"

Barty's fingers squeezed hers like he needed her comfort too. It thrilled her. "I haven't seen her around since the last time you were here."

"That's good."

Barty only shrugged, his eyes on his fingers as they brushed over her hand.

"Could the Skinned Man be doing something to the Seam?"

"The lights would tell me if he was."

The words sounded unhinged—lights couldn't speak. His withered appearance, coupled with his paranoid glances like he didn't trust the shadows, made her stomach burn with anxiety. But it was *Barty*, and he knew this place better than she did. If he said it was fine, she believed him. She needed to believe him.

"If we're safe, I know how to pass the time."

"He's really coming?" He looked at her innocently, his face like an angel's. How he'd ever killed anyone, she couldn't guess it. He was so perfect.

"He is. Do you want to pass the time with me or what?"

To help him understand, she eased his back onto the ledge and straddled his hips. Understanding dawned. He marveled up at her like he *loved* her. Perhaps worshiped her. It was all Dale needed. Her heart buoyed and soared. She'd never felt like this before, and she never wanted it to stop.

She tugged her top over her head and tossed it on the ground. He reached for her as she settled herself onto his lap. His hands swept up her ribs, over her back, down and around her backside, and back again. She undid her bra and let it fall aside.

Pressing herself against him, she kissed him like she could slip inside him. She kissed him like he stared at her—like she worshiped him, and perhaps she did. Any man who could make her feel so safe and loved and protected deserved a good woman to worship him. Hadn't her mother always taught her that?

She groaned—not from Barty's mouth on hers or his hands sweeping up to cup her breasts, but because she was thinking about her mother now, of all the times. Dale refocused on the kiss, on Barty's hands and the way he made her feel. She shoved aside the bite of doubt gnawing at her edges, the doubt that had Loey's voice and spoke of Dale's desperation for love.

"You should tell me to stop." He pulled his hands back, his body trembling from the effort. He looked up at her through his lashes. "I want you to tell me to stop."

Dale's thumbs brushed the tops of his cheekbones. If she hadn't been sitting on his hips, he would have removed himself from her. She *hated* the thought. She craved him like she craved Valium during every conversation with her mother.

"I don't ever want you to stop. I'm here for *you*, Barty."

With his hands on her hips, he sat up, their mouths close again. Before she could kiss him, he picked her up. Her legs wrapped tightly around him, and he laid her down on the ledge.

He kissed her mouth and her jaw, undressing her as he went, peeling fabric off her flesh with the reverence reserved for the finest wrapped gifts. He trailed his lips down her neck and placed feather-light nibbles along her collarbone. She arched up against him with her hands on his shoulders.

"It's been so long," he said against the flesh between her breasts.

"For me too."

His chin scraped against her chest as he looked up at her. "But your husband?"

"Isn't interested in my type," she said, running her hand through his hair.

"If you were mine," he told her, "I'd want you every minute

of the day with every drop of my being."

She smiled at him, believing every word and storing them in her heart where she needed them most. "You can have me, Barty."

The corner of his mouth lifted into a crooked smile of self-satisfaction. He went to drop his mouth back to her skin, but a cold sensation swept over her. She put a hand on his shoulder to stop him. Furrows rutted between his brow as he looked up again.

"You should know I've only been with one other man," she said, forcing her voice not to waver. She would not apologize for this. "And it wasn't ..." There. Her voice wavered. She cleared her throat. "He was a bad man, and I haven't wanted to be with anyone until you. I trust you."

Tension coiled up through Barty's body. She felt it roll, like a wave, against her. "He hurt you?"

She nodded.

His eyes deepened, darkened. Darker than even Jeronimo's.

"I'll kill him," Barty vowed.

He went to lower his head, and she let him. His mouth dropped kisses between her breasts, down her belly, past her belly button, and lower. He dipped between her legs and feasted on her until she was a sunbeam bursting across the dreaded silk sky.

CHAPTER 25

IT WASN'T THE SKINNED MAN'S presence Loey sensed.

The threads over the creek were fine, though she couldn't see them. If something had been wrong enough to let the Skinned Man through, she would've seen the threads without needing to draw the symbol of circles within circles.

This was something else.

It came from high up the ridge and trickled like Little Cricket Creek across this dead space of land. It came on the wind, seeped up from the ground, and grew in the gray trees with limbs like fingers pointing toward some dark, breathing evil.

Someone had hung those trinkets and bones and mirrors, and Loey's mind went to the bones in the tree in Little Cricket Trailer Park and the symbol she'd found drawn on the piece of skull.

Someone was up here talking to the dead, and it felt—in the chills prickling Loey's skin—like the dead had answered.

Loey understood why Pap had never brought her up into the woods of Shiner's Ridge. Something was wrong in these woods. Something far more sinister than a hole in the Seam or a monster trapped within lurked here. This felt ancient and old, perhaps as old as the Seam itself. Perhaps as old as the mountain's magic.

Could this evil be the reason Knox had willed the land

to Townsend? Loey shivered at the thought. If that were true, Knox had been cursing Townsend with the land more so than gifting it.

She would check the last few nearby squirrel holes and get the heck off this hill.

She didn't dare drive across the clearing and instead wound her way around through the trees. She wanted to check the squirrel holes closest to the spring that fed the creek, where Frankie had been killed. It meant climbing higher up the ridge, and though every instinct told her to yank the four-wheeler around and race home, she pressed on.

Through the tree leaves, the angry sky glared down at her. Clouds shook with thunder. Occasionally, lightning strobed far away. She did not want a repeat of that night in fifty-six.

Come hell or high water, Loey was *not* losing her soul today.

The undergrowth sprang up thicker the farther she drove from the clearing, obscuring the path. It took longer than she wanted to reach the next squirrel hole, an overgrown and thoroughly rotted log. The next one on Barty's list she never found. The last spot she was willing to check—the storm was close, the thunder loud. Barty had described it as an old bear cave, and it was the most promising one on Loey's list, as long as it was an *empty* bear cave.

It was also the easiest to find; as far as squirrel holes went, it wasn't much of a hidey-hole. It yawned dark and wide between a cropping of rocks that had long ago tumbled from the craggy ridgeline overhead. Kudzu vines twined down from the nearby trees, through the cracks in the rocks, and into the cave. Loey parked the four-wheeler and cut the engine.

Up here, the air was damp and thick. The thunder felt a little closer, a little louder, a little like a warning. She hurried to unwrap her pack's tie and pull out her flashlight. She switched it on. The frail beam could barely cut through the low-lying fog.

She walked to the cave's entrance. It was small enough that her light bounced off the back wall. She bent her head as she went inside. No eyes stared back at her. It smelled but not enough to indicate a bear or animal had used it as a shelter in a long while. Her feet squished over a carpet of vines. As she walked, she broke their stems, and a sharp sappy scent filled the cave.

The heart of the cave was wide enough that her fingertips barely grazed each side. This far inside, she could stand tall and look up at the vines weaving into a canopy an arm's length away. She shone her flashlight back and forth and toed vines out of the way to peek at the floor.

She sighed after a few minutes of pointless searching. Shining her light along the ceiling, she scanned it one last time. Ready to give up and leave, she spotted a slip of faded denim peeking through the vines. She pulled it free, the vines swaying across the cave's arched ceiling, and inspected the torn bit of material.

It was thick, a jacket perhaps. The weathered threads disintegrated in her hands, but it was certainly clothing. She looked up at the vines.

"What are you doing up there?" she murmured to them.

She pushed her hand through the vines overhead and felt around. Her fingertips touched leaves and thick stems, the sap burning her skin.

She bit her lip and stood on her tiptoes. With a grunt, she stretched her hand into the depths. Her fingers brushed something solid. It was just out of reach. On instinct, she jumped and swatted at the hard object overhead.

As she came back down, she grabbed the vines and pulled.

It was a bad idea.

The vines tore free from the ceiling. The hard object was

actually multiple hard objects, and they rained down on Loey, banging into her head and clattering to the ground. Reflexively, she reached to catch the nearest falling item and caught a human skull.

She screamed.

Ashamedly, she threw the skull. It wasn't her best moment of clarity, but she launched the thing across the cave. Luckily, the space was too small for her throw to build much damaging momentum. The skull bounced safely off the wall and rolled onto the mound of vines. It stared back at her with a hollow smile.

A beetle skittered out from an eye socket and disappeared into the leaves.

Loey shuddered, fighting back another scream.

Scattered bones surrounded her. Denim and bits of cloth littered the space between the bones. A glint of light caught her eye among the snarl of vines. She walked over, careful not to step on any bones. She extracted the object, its cool metal familiar in her hand. She twisted around to hold it toward the light of the cave's opening.

It was a revolver.

Loey sat it back down and stood. This wasn't what she'd expected to find in Jeronimo's squirrel holes, but it didn't bode well that she kept finding bodies connected to him. Her stomach growled and twisted with nerves, but she wasn't hungry.

She'd either found Knox Keene's missing body or the revenuer's from West Virginia who'd gone missing while trying to catch the infamous James brothers. Until she knew whose bones she'd scattered around the cave like confetti, she was no closer to knowing the monster she faced.

She went back out to her four-wheeler and checked the sky through the trees.

Heavy clouds churned with rain. A drop splattered on her

cheek. She tugged the bill of her cap lower over her head.

She went to her pack and got her phone.

Her first call was to Dale, but her best friend didn't answer.

"Dale, I know we're not talking right now … or possibly ever again," Loey said to Dale's voicemail, "but we have a problem. Call me back as soon as you get this."

Loey hung up and dialed the second number.

"This is Matt."

"Why do you answer the phone like that? Of course I know it's you. This is your cellphone and I called you."

He let out a long breath. "Good evening to you too, Loey. What's up?"

"I'm on Shiner's Ridge."

"You know a storm's comin', don't you?" His chair squeaked, and she pictured him sitting up straighter, his attention snared.

"That's the least of my worries."

"Not if you're still up there, it ain't."

She walked back to the cave and sighed at the bones. The skull looked like it was watching her from its perch atop the vine-covered ground. "Don't speak down to me from your high horse, Sheriff. You're about to come up here too."

"Why?" he asked carefully.

"Because I found another body."

"Another one?"

As Matt prattled on, Loey toed the edge of a bone. Femur, perhaps.

It was probably a sin to fervently hope her great-great-grandfather had died in this cave of natural, peaceful causes that involved no foul play from either James brother. He would've gone unsalted, his ghost wandering across the Seam, but he wouldn't be the Skinned Man.

She didn't want Knox Keene to be her monster.

CHAPTER 26

MAY 16, 2015

DALE'S HANDS SHOOK ON THE morning of her wedding and didn't stop after she'd downed six mimosas. The Valium took the edge off and more, but she kept nodding off. She took some Adderall. That balanced her out—for the most part.

Didn't stop the hands from shaking, though.

The room cleared out at her mother's request, and Darlene Rose took Dale's shaking hands and clenched them until her fingertips turned blue.

"That'll certainly fix the problem." Dale laughed, staring down at her hands trapped in her mother's. Every bride dreamed of holding hands with her mother on her wedding day. "But you can't hold them at the altar."

"Get it together," her mother hissed, her face so close Dale could smell the wintergreen mints her mother favored to hide the liquor on her breath. "Get it together."

Dale giggled. She might have swayed too. To be honest, she couldn't feel her legs so she didn't know.

Mrs. Rose smacked her.

The blow snapped her back teeth together, and they cut into her cheek. The pain bloomed a breath later, spreading down her neck and up her temples, making her eyes water. Blood from the inside of her cheek pooled atop her tongue, a dirty penny kiss.

Her laughter gone, Dale turned her eyes to her mother.

"You will walk down that aisle today," her mother said, "and you will walk in a straight line. I don't care what you have to swallow or do to yourself, but you will marry Travis and you will smile while you do it. Do you hear me?"

Tears dammed up at the back of Dale's eyes, threatening to ruin her meticulously applied makeup. The key was not to blink and to focus on something far, far away until her eyes dried enough to fall from her sockets and tumble to the floor where ravenous mice could eat them. She pictured that, her pieces being chewed on, until the tears faded.

"I asked you a question, young lady."

"Yes, ma'am," Dale said on reflex.

"Good girl. Now, then. It's time. Your father is waiting."

Dale almost laughed at the thought of her father walking her down the aisle. Her father, the man who disapproved of this marriage but had agreed to it after Darlene Rose had put her Prada-heeled foot down.

"You will allow this," her mother had whisper-hissed.

"I will not! He's a Jinks, for Christ's sake."

"You don't see it."

"See what?"

"The way they look at her here. You don't see it because you're not around."

"Darlene—"

"I've never said nothing about you being gone all the time. Not a word. Not even the year that girl with cheap whore-blonde hair showed up on my *front porch, in* my *town, where* my *neighbors could see and said she was pregnant with your child. I didn't say a word to you about it. So, you will give me these words today. You will tell that boy yes, because the people in this town don't look at Dale right anymore."*

Her father had been quiet for a long time. A very long time. Dale had needed to press her ear against the study's door, where she was eavesdropping, to hear her father's question. *"And how will her marrying a Jinks change the way the people in town look at her?"*

"It'll give them something new to talk about."

They certainly had something new to talk about now. The entire town had shown up for Dale's wedding.

Her mother smoothed her tea-length gown—wine red, elegant cut, and modest. Diamonds pooled between her clavicles, but the largest diamond flashed on her left ring finger.

Mrs. Rose raised her hand to Dale's face again, and Dale flinched.

Her mother paused with a sigh. "Oh, stop being so dramatic. It's not like I'm going to hit you."

Her mother's fingers swiped at her cheek harder than necessary to smooth any creases in Dale's makeup.

That was the thing. There was a difference. A slap from a mother wasn't a punch from a father. Her father could strike Cross, but not her. Her mother could slap both her children and call it discipline on the same breath, and Dale was supposed to smile with her cheek aflame and walk a straight line. Most importantly, she had to look pretty doing it.

A knock at the door and Loey stuck her head in. "People are in their seats. The bridesmaids are ready to walk."

Her eyes lingered on Dale's cheek.

"We're ready." Mrs. Rose sauntered out of the room on a wave of perfume and swishing silk. Loey let her pass with her eyes downcast before she slipped into the room and closed the door.

"Dale …" she started.

Dale held up her hand and smiled. "You said it's time, right? Let's go."

"Maybe we should—"

"Can't have my guests waiting, can I?"

She started by Loey, but her best friend stopped her with a hand on her arm. Loey's touch was gentle; it always was. Loey wouldn't hurt a fly, wouldn't think of it. Her big doe eyes promised warmth and rich coffee and late-night talks over magazines and secrets. Always the promise of secrets. Her makeup almost hid her scars, but not quite. Dale couldn't look at them. Not today.

"Lo," Dale begged, "please don't. I can't fall apart right now."

Loey's scarred mouth twisted in anguish. "Let me say this real quick and I'll shut up and you'll never hear another peep about it. If you need to leave, even if it's during the ceremony, my truck is parked out back."

Dale pulled her friend in for a crushing hug. Against Loey's hair that smelled of Dale's childhood, Dale whispered, "Please don't ever leave me. You're all I have in this dumb world."

"I promise. I love you more than life."

Straightening away from her best friend's comfort, Dale checked her reflection. For the tiniest second, she thought she saw the curl of shadows and the flash of a sad smile. But it was nothing. He wasn't there. She patted her hair and popped her lips. She took a shaky breath. Her smile trembled before she steadied it. She faced Loey, faced the music.

"Let's get this show on the road."

Loey didn't move like she was supposed to. "Your cheek," she murmured, not quite meeting Dale's eyes. "Let's wait for the redness to go down."

CHAPTER 27

FOR THE SECOND SUNDAY IN a row, Matt dropped Loey off at her house in his police cruiser.

She beat him to opening her door for her, unhindered by her battered ribs. Matt waited at the hood of the car.

"You don't have to walk me inside. I know you have work to do. Sorry about that, by the way." She offered him a guilty grimace.

He smiled back at her, his eyes the color of mild coffee with more creamer than Loey preferred. "You do happen across a lot of bodies. It's mildly concernin'."

She laughed, a small miracle after the day she'd had on the ridge and the evening she'd spent surrounded by police up in the woods as they'd picked through the remains. Matt had asked her endless questions she could barely answer. "You will tell me who it is, won't you?"

Matt folded away his smile. "Loey Grace …"

"Matt, come on. I found the body. I have a right to know. It was basically on my property, and I told you who it could be."

He took off his hat and rubbed his head. They'd been on the ridge for hours during the storm, and Matt had worked tirelessly to collect every bit of evidence from the cave, though his deputies wanted to toss the bones in a garbage bag and call it a day.

"No, you told me it could be a missin' revenuer from West Virginia or Knox Keene, who you know isn't buried in his coffin 'cause *you dug it up*."

"Not completely," she emphasized for the countless time. The distinction mattered to her conscience. Matt didn't seem to understand. "It was a tiny hole, and the cemetery is on my property."

"That makes it okay?" he asked like he didn't know her at all.

"I don't want to argue about this again. You'll tell me what you find out? As soon as possible?"

"I'll make some calls tomorrow, and we'll see."

"Thanks, Matt." She hugged him for his sake, not hers.

The back porch light came on. Dewey let out a woof from inside the kitchen.

"You expecting anybody?" He pulled away from Loey with his hand resting on his gun.

Loey wasn't, but she took a wild guess. "It's Jeronimo again."

Matt didn't remove his hand. "You two are getting awfully close if he's coming to your house while you're gone."

"Don't start this. I'm tired, and you won't win."

"Fine, but I don't like it."

"And I don't give a shit."

Matt's hand tumbled off his gun. "Loey Grace, if your gran heard you speakin' like that …"

"She's not here to hear me anymore."

"You didn't speak like that before he came around."

"Goodnight, Matt."

She walked away, and he didn't follow, proving he had some sense left in his head. She climbed the back porch steps as his cruiser's headlights flashed across the yard. A second later, she opened the back door and went inside.

Dewey greeted her with wet slobbers and head butts. She petted him. Her eyes found Jeronimo with a clear view out to the driveway, his hip leaning against her counter. With his hearing, he'd probably heard her entire conversation with Matt too. Body talk included.

"Nosy," she accused.

He shrugged one shoulder, the tiniest rustle of movement from his black and white plaid shirt tucked into worn black jeans. He'd left his boots by the door like he intended to stay, his feet clad in wool socks. A comfortable sight if not for his next words.

"Who's body you find?" he asked without preamble, confirming her suspicion.

"What are you doing here? After yesterday, I didn't think you would be talking to me."

"I understand about Barty ..." His jaw clenched. Whatever he'd been about to say, he thought better of it. "I picked up some of my notes I thought could help and came by for more time with the book, but I can't find it."

"I took it with me," Loey said. "I thought Dale might try something stupid."

Jeronimo simply nodded. They stood for a beat in awkward silence. "Missed you at church this morning," Jeronimo said, perhaps the only thing he could think of to say to break the tension.

The long day had left her depleted, and in the face of Jeronimo's lackluster attempt at conversation, Loey laughed. She dropped her pack by the kitchen table and headed down the hall to the bathroom.

Her shower left steam wafting about the bathroom ceiling. Her skin blazed pink and pruney, and her hair was plastered to her neck. She brushed her teeth. In the bedroom, she dressed in simple pajamas with stars and moons on them like a child's.

After she'd fastened the last button on her cotton top, Jeronimo padded in with Dewey at his heels. The big dog settled contentedly on his pillow. Jeronimo stopped a few feet away from her.

"Where have you been?" he asked.

"The ridge."

His mouth twitched toward a frown. "Why?"

"I wanted to retrace your steps from that night. See what I could find."

"And you came across some old bones," he drawled. He traced the scars on her cheek over and over with his gaze.

"Who is it, J? Who was left up there?"

"It could be anybody. From any time."

"Jeronimo."

His eyes flashed up to meet hers again. They glinted with black flames. "You keep askin', but it don't change nothing. It doesn't make me know. It doesn't make it clearer. I thought I knew what happened, but you keep askin' these questions, and they keep makin' my head all foggy."

His words tumbled over each other, and his accent thickened. It made him sound young, like Barty. His cheeks bloomed with the blood that wouldn't spill if she shot him or stabbed him.

She wrapped her arms around her waist. She couldn't handle another fight, not after last night.

"Lately, I've been wondering if I did," Jeronimo murmured, all defensiveness erased from his voice. "Could I have killed her? I can't remember. That night is all shadows and lightning. But what if I've been the monster all along?"

Loey stared back at him, meeting his pleading eyes.

Five people had been on the ridge during that storm, and only one had come down. It was like a riddle from her childhood, except far more sinister.

"Did I kill her, Loey?" He swallowed thickly, perhaps fighting down tears. "Could I have killed her if I loved her?"

Killed her or loved her. The line between frail as a single thread.

Five people had been on the ridge during the storm, but something else had happened that night. Something no one knew or understood. Jeronimo had never looked more hollow and cursed; of those five souls, she figured none of them had really come back down off the ridge. Not even Jeronimo.

Not in the ways that mattered.

She had to take a side and a stand. She had to plant her feet unwaveringly. No more back and forth. No more sneaking about. No more letting doubt take root inside her head.

"You're not a monster." She stepped into his reach. "You might be soulless and cursed, but I know you. You no more killed Frankie that night than you would kill me. Would you hurt me, J?"

His face blanched. "Of course not. I … I could love you."

"And you loved her too—back then," Loey said, tacking the last bit on. Frankie was long past and far away, but Loey was too insecure in whatever this was between her and Jeronimo to allow the distinction from his past and their present to go unspoken.

"She was with Barty. He loved her. She … she …"

"Loved someone else in the end," Loey said gently. "That doesn't make you a bad brother, and it doesn't make you a killer."

"I can't figure killing her. It doesn't add up."

"Because you didn't."

"Sometimes, I think about that night"—they stood close enough that she heard his shallow breathing, saw the vein beneath his jaw jumping—"and the knife in my hand is already bloody when I put it to Barty's throat, just like he said, but she's not there in my memories. All I know is how much I hate him in that moment by the creek. How much I want to kill him for what he did. What he caused. I want my knife to be clean, but …"

She pulled him to her and wrapped her arms around his neck, until he had to hold her too. She ran a hand between his shoulders, up and down, back and forth, rubbing and consoling and hushing him until any more words died off in his throat.

Any more words that might damn them both.

He straightened an inch away from her, and she let him. She knew she was clinging to him and she should be a stronger woman than that. She released him, but looking at his face again, his expression had changed.

She might not be a strong enough woman, but she was woman enough to know what *that* look on a man's face meant.

She began to tremble. "J?"

"Lo," he said. "I'm sorry."

"For what?"

"I can't resist you."

He kissed her with such force that she had to close her eyes and hang on, a feeling exactly like galloping wild and free on Tempest's back, flying over the ground at speeds so fast it felt like flying. Behind her eyelids, she saw the world's threads as clearly as though she'd drawn the symbol to behold them. His mouth moved on hers, and she parted her lips for him. She was nothing but threads and knots of lights, infinite and untorn.

He pulled away with one last kiss on her lips.

She thought that might be it, thought she had read that look wrong after all, but he reached for the top button of her sleep shirt. He swept it aside, his hands replacing the fabric. Bare before him from the waist up, she still couldn't stop thinking about curses.

"This won't hurt you, will it?"

He paused. "Hurt me?"

Loey bit her lip, drawing his attention to her mouth. Her stomach swooped and dropped in turns. Her fingers clenched tight around his arms to keep from falling over. "Doing this. It won't hurt you since you can't …"

She couldn't bring herself to say the word. It was so crass. So … un-Southern.

Apparently, Jeronimo didn't think so. He grinned devilishly. "Since I can't come?"

Loey wanted to crawl under the bed and never return. "Yes," she mumbled. "*That*."

"You're too sweet for something like me." He dipped his mouth to hers and kissed her again, deeply, memorizing the shape of her lips against his tongue. He pulled back enough to look in her eyes. "It won't hurt me. I promise. If it did, I'd take the pain if it meant I got you."

His hands, rough and calloused, swept over her waist, her bare skin prickling against his touch, his dark eyes watching her lean into him, unable to hold herself upright.

She couldn't, not when he kissed her like the Devil had taught him how, but she was trying to keep up pretenses.

His hands traveled down her hips to cup her bottom. He lifted her onto her tiptoes, her hips flush against his. Her eyes widened at his length pressing against her.

"I'm sorry," he said again.

Instead of talking, she rocked against him. He lowered his head to her neck and nipped her shoulder, encouraging her. She dragged her hands up to his shoulders and moved against his hardness until her vision crossed.

Breathe, she told herself, moving on instinct, body to body. *Do not pass out. Not now.*

"I could love you when you do that."

The words pulled a chirp of laughter from her mouth. He grinned darkly down at her.

"I'm going to make you come over and over again until watching your pleasure gives me all the satisfaction I need. Do you understand?"

She nodded mutely.

"Say it."

She'd never wanted anyone more in her entire life, and she felt that longing deep between her hips like a physical pain only he could heal.

"I understand."

He touched her cheek, right on her scars, tracing them toward her mouth. She pulled back before his fingers could land on the mass of scars at the corner of her mouth, the ones that pulled her lips down and ruined her smile.

"Don't," she said sharply. "I don't like to be touched there."

His hand cupped her jaw to keep her from turning away. "You're beautiful, Lo."

"You don't have to say that because we're about to have sex."

His thumb flicked up from her jaw to skim the underside of her scars. Holding her face steady, he kissed her, right at the corner of her mouth, right on the scars.

The nerve endings there fired too much, too quickly, dead and alive all at once, his kiss sending sparks of lightning through her insides and turning her bones to fire quicker than any moonshine.

"Are you listening?" he asked against her mouth, his lips on her ruined skin.

She again tried to pull back, but his grip tightened. The feeling of being trapped might have sent her into a panic with anyone else, but in Jeronimo's hands, she only felt calm. She trusted him completely.

"Loey." He pressed her name against the worst of her, the ugliest part.

"Yeah," she rasped out, a chill at the base of her neck.

"I like your scars. I like them when you're yelling at me. I like them when you break into my house. I like them even though you call me bad names you have to pray about later.

I like your scars …" Their mouths were separated by a breath Loey held tight in her chest. "I like your scars because you look at a hollow man like you love him sometimes. You're beautiful no matter what, and I love your scars because I could love you, and I'm sorrier for that more than you'll ever know."

His thumb flicked across her mouth, but he didn't linger. His hands went straight to her shorts, and before she could think of a response to the words that had shifted her entire world, he had her on the bed, naked. She could only pull him down onto her, welcoming him inside her body and her heart like he'd always been there.

The hollow man she could love.

She woke the next morning to find Jeronimo gone.

Groggy from the lack of sleep the night before, she sat up in bed and pushed her tangled hair from her face. A pretty thought formed in her mind of him cooking her breakfast or taking a shower; he'd walk in, wrapped in a low-slung towel, and she'd pull it loose and …

She glanced toward the hall, his name on her lips.

Her pack from yesterday sat in the chair by the door. She hadn't left it there last night.

She swung her legs off the bed. Her feet whispered across the floor to her pack. Her hand reached into the open top and rooted through all the supplies she hadn't unpacked. After a minute of searching, she drew her hand out and stepped back, her fingers going to her lips that were still swollen from him.

She knew why he'd apologized so much last night while kissing her.

He'd been planning to steal her grandmother's book.

CHAPTER 28

D ALE WOKE TO A HAND clamped over her mouth.

Her eyes snapped open, and she jerked against the hold on her, but the face above her was familiar, although wide-eyed with fear.

"She's here," was all he had to say.

He dropped his hand from her mouth. Dale scooted upright, her back aching from lying on the ledge. She darted glances around, seeing nothing but darkness and the flashing firefly lights of the Seam outside the cove.

"Do you have salt?" she asked in the barest of whispers.

"Not enough. She brought more ghosts. You should go."

"I can't leave without Jeronimo opening the tatter. That means we leave together or not at all."

"She wants to hurt you."

"She can kiss my ass," she said as she dressed in jerky motions that Barty barely noticed.

A crack like a whip sliced through the air. Barty gnashed his teeth with worry.

"I ain't seen her like this in a long time. She—"

The crack came again, closer to the cove's opening and much louder.

Barty paled by the second. "If she keeps that up, she'll bring the Skinned Man right to us."

Dale scooped up a tiny pile of salt from the ground. It wouldn't so much as hurt the ghost of a fly. "Can you kill her so she doesn't rematerialize?"

Barty reared back. He gaped at her. "Kill her? I can't kill her. I love her."

The salt slipped through her fingers to spill uselessly back across the ground.

Desperate. Desperate. Desperate, the voice in her head yelled. *No one chooses you.*

"She's hurting you," Dale said in her calmest voice, the one that sounded like she wasn't screaming at the top of her lungs to herself in her thoughts. "Why do you still love her?"

And how can you love me if you love her?

"I …" Barty fumbled, realizing he might have misspoken, or he was confused, because he kept blinking as if he couldn't see her clearly. "We have to go."

"Jeronimo isn't ready yet—"

"We need to get to the salt river."

"Is it a good idea to wait out in the open? What about the Skinned—"

A crack snapped right over their heads. Frankie had broken through the salt line.

Barty leaped on top of Dale, crushing her back against the rock. Her head cracked off the gleaming obsidian surface, and all she saw were stars. A ringing filled her ears. Through it, she heard Barty scream.

His weight lifted off her, and he flew backward through the air. His body struck the outcropping hard enough to crumble bits of stone off the rock face. He flopped to the ground and didn't move. His salt tumbled loosely from his pocket.

Dale jerked her gaze to the air between her and Barty.

Frankie landed softly a few steps away from Dale. She was a spectral haze, fluttering in a white top and trousers, her feet bare, her body translucent enough that Dale could see Barty through her body. Long strands of curling hair floated over her slender shoulders.

She was stunning, even as a ghost, and Dale's eye, honed from years of sizing up her competition at pageants, cataloged all of Frankie's perfections against her own flaws. If this had been the Miss Tennessee Teen Pageant, Dale would have lost to her, if not for her one flaw:

Near her hands and feet, eyes and mouth, her veins were solid black. The blood vessels seeped out like a spider's web across her skin until the black faded. She opened her black mouth, the insides thick and oozing like tar, and screamed.

Dale slapped her hands over her ears.

Frankie spun away. Her form blinked in and out of view as she floated toward Barty.

"Stop!" Dale struggled to her feet. "Don't hurt him!"

Frankie snaked around, her black void eyes flashing heat. She blasted toward Dale and slammed straight into her with a force that knocked the air from Dale's lungs. Her back struck the rocky ledge. The rock's lip tore into her. It felt like her kidneys were being shoved out through her belly-button as Frankie kept crushing her.

Dale went limp, and Frankie backed off. She zoomed back to Barty. Hovering over him, she plunged her hands into his chest and fed.

Barty's body arched off the ground. His mouth fell open in an unending scream.

Those black veins stretched up Frankie's arms, thickening and darkening with each gulp of Barty's life. Savoring every drop, Frankie didn't notice Dale move. Or pick up a fist-sized rock from the ground. Frankie took so much life from Barty that the ends of her hair were streaked with black.

Dale slammed the rock into the side of the bitch's head.

The blow landed with a satisfyingly solid crunch. Frankie staggered away from Barty, who slumped back to the ground, his eyes closed and fingers twitching. Dale forced herself not to dwell on his shrunken, ghastly state of hollowed cheeks and sunken eyes. She stepped over him, and as Frankie floundered, she slammed the rock into her skull again.

Frankie went down, and Dale followed, bending over the woman's ghostly body. She raised the rock over her head and bashed it straight into Frankie's face. Dale didn't stop until Frankie wasn't moving and her face was a pit of seeping black sludge, the rock wet with it. Dale threw it aside. She fell off Frankie and crawled to Barty.

He wasn't moving and didn't seem to be breathing much either. She slapped him.

His eyes fluttered open. He moaned.

"Come on," she told him. "We've got to go."

"Leave me." He coughed.

"Not happening." She heaved his arm around her neck and got her legs beneath her. Grunting, she said, "Because you need an intervention. That girl you love is a real piece of shit."

His gusting breath might have been a laugh, or she might have hurt him as she heaved them both upright. Lifting him was easier than it should have been, as though Frankie had made him less substantial as she became more corporeal.

The ghost still hadn't moved from the ground. Dale wondered if she'd killed Frankie; that might be awkward to explain to Barty, but he'd already seen. If Frankie's bashed and bloody body bothered him, he kept his mouth shut.

She moved fast out of the cave he'd so beautifully carved. Dale limped into the open and dragged Barty, stumbling, toward the salt river. The Seam's tatter constituted the brightest spot across the plains, and Dale used it as a guide, remembering how close it was to the river. It looked like it was miles across the plains with no salt in sight between here and there.

The other ghosts had scattered without their leader, but Dale wasn't banking on them staying away if they saw Barty so weak. Their only protection was the salt, but it wouldn't protect them from the Skinned Man if he'd heard the commotion Frankie had caused.

Ahead, against the silk-spun sky, a light flashed, too far away from the river to be the tatter over there. It was close enough that Dale thought more ghosts had come to attack, but the light flashed again, plus a few more near it. The clusters grew, strobing like a racing heartbeat.

Dale swerved toward the lights and nearly fell to the ground beneath Barty's weight.

Barty lifted his head. "Is that Jeronimo?"

"Hope so," Dale panted. Lighter or not, she struggled to carry Barty. She should have baked fewer cakes and worked out more. "If not, we're screwed."

His arm tightened around her shoulders to help her support his weight.

Lightning streaked across the sky, setting the silken folds on fire. Red flames licked out, spreading like wildfire. A winged creature darted out from the silk, wings aflame, smoke trailing in its wake.

"What's happening?" Dale asked.

Barty didn't answer. He was staring behind them, back the way they'd come.

Dale's gaze snapped from Barty's blank expression to the point of his focus.

Her heart dropped.

The Skinned Man leaped down from the overhanging cliff that sheltered Barty's cave. He landed in a crouch, his skin pulling tight and red, raw and roped with scars. His head snapped up, and he snarled. He tore off after them.

"Hurry," Barty said, pulling her now.

They raced toward the lights that had spread into a flapping curtain, like a mourning veil, black and opaque but made of flashing lights.

A hand stuck through the veil, tearing more light free from their threads. Jeronimo's face followed his hand. He spotted them easily in the empty plains, with nothing around them but a monster on their heels.

"He's coming!"

Jeronimo didn't need Dale's warning. He'd already seen the Skinned Man too. He tore the rest of the way through the curtain of lights and stepped over the flickering strands. He swayed dizzily. Blood dripped beneath his nose.

"JJ! Stop!" Barty shouted from her arms, seeing his brother nearly fall to his knees. He picked up speed until he was almost dragging her. "Get out!"

Jeronimo staggered forward, one foot in front of the other in a lurching run away from the curtain and straight toward them.

Not the smartest plan, Dale wanted to advise, but she had bigger problems. Behind them, the Skinned Man was close enough for her to hear his ragged breathing. How he panted with excitement.

She thought it couldn't get worse, but a hunched form moved through the tatter Jeronimo had ripped wide open, and Dale cried out in horror at the person coming through.

Travis.

CHAPTER 29

LOEY HAD WRAPPED UP HER Monday evening chores when her phone chimed with a text message. Thinking it might be Jeronimo, she hurried to check the screen.

But the text was from Tabi: *Come to the office. Super important.*

The message was followed by a series of emojis, each more baffling than the last.

She drove down Devil's Maw for the second time that day after working the morning rush at the coffee shop. The evening was unusually warm this close to fall, and she rolled down her windows. The air smelled scrubbed clean from the storm yesterday. It whipped her air into tangles, but it cleared her mind of the troubled thoughts that had tangled themselves all day around Jeronimo stealing her book.

He had to return at some point. She was the Tender, after all, and he needed her. She'd tried to stay busy to pass the time, but the hours dragged. Matt hadn't called about the cause of death of the revenuer in the cave, but Loey had been mulling over a theory since this morning. Tabi's text was a welcome reprieve.

Loey parked in front of *The Righteous Daily*, and Tabi met her at the office's front door.

"Evening, Tabi. What's so important?"

"I wanted you to see it from me first," Tabi said by way of greeting.

She led Loey through the dimly lit office, the blinds drawn against the last rays of sunshine outside. They went to a cubicle in the back corner of the low-ceilinged room that smelled of stale coffee and paper ink. Computers that hadn't been upgraded since the early 2000s perched like hulking gremlins on each desk. The place was a ghost town, and Loey wondered if Tabi was the editor-in-chief of a one-person newspaper.

"It's releasing already?" she asked.

"News happens fast."

Reaching her cubicle, Tabi slid into her desk chair and swung toward the closed MacBook stacked atop a sheaf of newspapers.

"Goodness, Tabi," Loey said, taking in the cubicle's chaos. If Loey hadn't seen Tabi's house with her own eyes, she would have assumed the older woman lived in her office given the pillow, blanket, and wobbly stack of pizza boxes. "Have you ever heard of cleaning?"

"I like the madness. It helps me think. Here." Tabi offered her a single page.

"I don't want to read it."

Tabi frowned, her hand still extended with the story, all its damnation written in tiny black letters. It reminded Loey of the deal she'd signed at the station. All her lies, in black and white. All her sins, trussed up and tidy.

"Seriously?" Tabi asked, brows raised.

"I trust you."

Tabi lowered her arm. "I want you to know, I told it from your angle—and Dale's. That son of a bitch got no sympathy from *The Righteous Daily* or me."

"Thank you."

"That's not why I wanted you to come down. I mean, it was,

but it wasn't." Tabi tossed the page aside, letting it drift onto the floor beneath the desk, and opened her personal MacBook. She had a multitude of screens and tabs open, her computer a digital representation of her office. It stressed Loey out to see it.

"I dug into that land exchange between Knox and Townsend. At first, I thought it was a bullshit tax-dodging ploy, but I came across a water quality report from the seventies—"

Loey's phone rang. Her heart leaped, thinking it was Jeronimo. She dug around in her purse.

"Loey?" Tabi asked. "Are you listening?"

"Sorry. There's a lot going on and …"

She finally found it. On the screen, Matt's name showed.

"The report showed high levels of—"

"Hang on. I'm sorry, but I have to take this."

"This is important. I think you found—"

Loey held up her hand and answered the phone. "Hey, Matt. Is this about that body on the ridge?"

All annoyance at Loey's disinterest vanished from Tabi's expression at the mention of a body. She licked her lips.

"Hello to you too," Matt said, voice muffled through Loey's phone. "And yes, it is. You'll never believe how I figured this out. Come on, guess."

He sounded like he was in the mood for a woman to fawn over his genius, but Loey wasn't in the mood. "It's not a good time," she snapped. "Did you find out who the revolver belonged to?"

"Is everything okay?" His conversational tone was gone, replaced by his cop voice.

"*Matt.*"

"Fine. But you know, Loey Grace, you shouldn't speak to people like that if they're doing you a favor. It's not polite."

She turned her mouth away from her phone so he wouldn't hear her growl. From Tabi's smirk, the journalist knew exactly what Loey was dealing with.

"They didn't register guns back then like I thought," Matt forged on through her silence. "And serial numbers weren't a thing, so I went to fingerprints. Did you know tax agents filed their fingerprints in the fifties? 'Cause I certainly didn't."

"Tax agent," Loey said. "It was Thomas Wooten in the cave?"

"How did you know it could be him? Where did you get that name? Look, Loey, I don't want you to take this the wrong way, but I need you to come down to the station …"

Loey wasn't listening anymore. Her mind was far, far away, up on Shiner's Ridge, putting the pieces together.

Five people had gone up that ridge. Only one had come down.

The body in the cave wasn't Knox's; it was the revenuer's, and she doubted he'd died of natural causes. Someone had killed him and stuffed him in there to feed the vines.

Five people. Two dead. One trapped beyond the Seam. One a hollow man. The last a monster.

"Oh my gosh," Loey whispered, all her worst fears coming true.

Her great-great-grandfather was the Skinned Man.

As for her theory about what had happened that night, she was one bit closer to being right, though it provided scant solace.

"Are you there?" Matt asked.

"I have to go."

"Loey, wait—"

She hung up the phone. "Oh, *shit*."

The Skinned Man was the greatest Tender Righteous had ever known.

"What's happening? What body on the ridge?" Now that Loey was off the phone, Tabi packed her things with quick, efficient motions. Loey hadn't moved by the time Tabi finished. "Loey, what do we need to do?"

The woman had no clue what was happening, but she was leaping into the fray like any journalist worth her salt.

"We have to find Jeronimo," Loey said numbly. "And Dale. We have to …"

"We'll go to Dale's first. She's closest."

Jeronimo. Dale. The book. It all spun together. She'd been a fool not to guess where he'd taken the book as soon as he'd left this morning. There was only one reason he'd steal from her, and it wasn't for research.

He—*and* Dale—were trying to free Barty.

Loey took off running through the office, Tabi hot on her heels. They stumbled into the open air of Righteous. Loey expected a spray of color from the sunset up on the ridge and the balmy last breath of summer air, but she met something much different. She and Tabi fumbled to a stop on the sidewalk. Across Main, other people were doing the same, their eyes on the sky.

The wind whipped and fell in stops and starts. The air pressure popped her ears. Green skies churned, casting Righteous in a sickly hue. From the red lights, the American flags snapped at full attention in the coming storm.

"You've got to be kidding," Loey said, shocked.

At her dare, the tornado sirens blared and whirred.

"Come on!" Tabi grabbed Loey's arm and hauled her straight to an old Mustang parked in the alley behind them.

The sirens pierced Loey's ears. She yanked open the passenger door as Tabi jumped in the driver's seat. The ignition cranked with a howl. Tabi ripped the gear shifter into reverse and floored it backward, jumping the curb onto the street. She hit the brakes and spun the wheel. The car fishtailed almost perfectly down the street facing Dale's. Tabi shifted gears. The car surged forward, its mighty engine galloping.

"Is it me," Tabi asked as they rocketed down Main, "or is that funnel cloud right over Dale's house?"

Loey craned her neck to look skyward through the windshield. The clouds rotated, and a tiny hook descended, indeed, right over Dale's house.

She was already too late.

"Drive faster," she told Tabi.

CHAPTER 30

ERONIMO CRASHED STRAIGHT INTO DALE and
Barty, and she lost sight of Travis in the curtain.

"Go on! I'll hold him back. Go!"

Jeronimo tried to push them toward the tatter, but Barty
resisted. The Skinned Man was close, his steps pounding across
the plains, the lightning and burning skies following his every
step, yet the brothers still took time to fight.

Dale dragged Barty a few more steps toward the curtain,
ignoring the brothers' shouting. Her focus was on the new
tatter.

Travis reached an arm through and raised his knee to step
across the whipping lights that moved like snakes coiling to
bite him. "Dale! Come here! Get away from them!"

At her shoulder, Barty was screaming at his brother. "…
he's too strong! You can't hold him by yourself!"

With more strength than she would've thought possible
for a man covered in so much blood, Jeronimo shoved them
toward the curtain of lights. Dale stumbled, and Barty was too
weak to resist. He went to a knee, and Dale had to haul him up.

He kept yelling back at Jeronimo, his focus behind them,
and Dale looked forward, to Travis. She closed the distance to
the lights in staggers and lurches.

"Help," she shouted to Travis. "Get his arm!"

277

Travis reached them in two strides. He grabbed Barty without a second thought.

Back the way they'd come, Jeronimo and the Skinned Man collided. The ground contracted in protest. More lightning burst across the sky, setting the clouds on fire.

The ground heaved. The beast breathing beneath them woke, its gentle inhales and exhales forgotten. The wind picked up. Fine grit gusting through the air sliced into them. Bowing their heads against the onslaught and burying their faces against their arms, Travis and Dale hauled Barty to the tatter. Travis pushed Barty through the Seam first, then grabbed Dale's arm. He hefted her up and threw her into the lights.

Dale fell into her kitchen face first. She pushed herself onto her hands and knees in front of the island. Through the sliding glass door, the sky above Righteous glowed green. The tornado sirens wailed. They'd crossed one wild world into another.

A groan drew her attention from the storm building outside her house.

Barty lay a few feet away from her, sprawled on her white tiles.

"Barty!"

She scrambled over to him and felt his pulse. He was alive and breathing, all good signs even if he looked half dead. He groaned, and her shoulders heaved in relief.

"Will someone tell me what the fuck is going on and why we have a scene from *The Exorcist* in our kitchen?"

Dale stood on trembling legs and turned to Travis, who tripped over the last bit of the Seam and swatted at the shadows snaking over his skin. She'd opened her mouth to explain, but then she saw what Jeronimo had done to rescue her and Barty across the Seam.

Symbols were scrawled across her white tiles in black paint that would certainly stain the grout. A candle burned in the middle of three of the larger angular symbols. Above them, behind Travis, the air sparked and flickered with lights, but mainly, she saw a portal to the pocket world.

And the Skinned Man stood right on the other side.

"Travis!" Dale screamed.

The monster's scarred hands reached through the tatter and wrapped around Travis's head, one on his chin and the other splayed across his forehead. His eyes had time to widen at Dale, his mouth opening to scream, before his head jerked to the side.

His neck cracked, and he fell to the floor.

Dale stumbled back. The Skinned Man peeled himself through the tightly torn lights, his body undulating darkness and his stained teeth snapping at her.

Arms grabbed her from behind. Barty pulled her behind him, putting himself between her and the Skinned Man. Dale shook so badly her teeth chattered uncontrollably, her eyes on Travis. He wasn't moving, his neck at an impossible angle, and his eyes stared unblinkingly at the ceiling of the house he'd always hated.

The Skinned Man snarled as he leveraged himself free of the threads. He straightened atop the symbols, eyes locked on her and Barty. The shadows danced across his body, hiding his horrible skin. The scent of rotten meat soured the air in her kitchen.

"Stop!" a familiar voice screamed above the tornado sirens.

Loey ran into the kitchen and skidded to a stop on the other side of the island. A few steps behind her, a woman with black skin and blacker hair in tight curls followed with a semi-automatic assault rifle held tight in the crook of her shoulder, the barrel pointed right at the Skinned Man.

The Skinned Man ignored them both. He lunged toward Barty, who stumbled back, pushing Dale with him.

"Knox!" Loey shouted, waving her arms in the air. "Knox

Keene, look here, you ugly piece of burnt rabbit meat!"

The Skinned Man's head snapped to Loey. His eyes flashed with comprehension. Dale had seen that look during her first trip across the Seam when she'd torn his skin from his back. The tiniest flicker of humanity altered his features, relaxing the muscles of his face such that he looked more man than beast.

His ruined nose flared, drawing in Loey's scent.

"Knox," she said the way she spoke to a spooked horse, "it's me, Loey Keene, Ellery's granddaughter."

His head cocked.

The front door banged open. Through it, the tornado sirens wailed louder, and the wind howled like a train.

"Dale Rose!" another person shouted from the living room.

Dale would've laughed if she could have managed it. Her mother's shout broke the Skinned Man's moment of understanding. Forgetting Loey, he charged straight toward Dale and Barty.

There was nothing they could do. Dale wondered what a broken neck felt like, wondered if she'd look like Travis on her kitchen floor. Barty braced himself directly in front of her with his last bit strength. Even if he'd been at his strongest, nothing would stop the Skinned Man.

But he swerved around them. He charged at the sliding glass door and leaped straight at the glass. It shattered into a million tempered chunks around him as he sailed through the air. He landed in a roll on Dale's back porch and disappeared across her fence, running straight toward the heart of Righteous.

A million things happened at once after that.

Loey shouted for Jeronimo. She ran around the island, slowing marginally to take in the symbols and the strange tatter Jeronimo had conjured. She didn't stop or glance back at Dale before jumping across the tatter.

The stranger with black curls laid her gun on the kitchen

floor to crouch beside Travis. She checked his pulse. Her fingers dropped away from the hollow beneath his neck. The tiny motion told Dale all she needed to know.

Barty slumped beside her, and she let him go. She stumbled over to Travis and kneeled beside him, her shoulder touching the stranger's.

"Oh my god, Travis." She trailed her fingers down his cheek.

"Dale?" her mother asked near the island. Her voice was sharp and full of disapproval even in this moment. "Good Heavens, what is going on here?"

Perhaps worse than her mother's presence was yet another voice from right over Dale's shoulder.

"What did you do? Dale, what did you *do?*"

Cross stood over her and Travis, his face pale, his eyes shattered. His hands fluttering at his side, unable to decide where to reach as he stared down at Travis's broken body.

"Cross," Dale stammered and shot to her feet. "No, it's not—"

Cross's eyes filled with tears. "You *killed* him."

"I can explain," Dale cried, reaching for him.

Cross jerked away from her. Shaking his head, he stepped back, his eyes going between her and Travis. He kept looking at her like it was her hands that had snapped Travis's neck. He reached into his pants pocket and pulled out his phone.

"Cross." Her voice was thick with tears.

Since they'd been kids old enough to totter about, he'd always buckled at the sight of her tears. But this time, his gaze was full of hate. "No, Dale. No more."

"Please," she begged him. "Let me explain. It's not what it looks like."

Cross punched three numbers onto his phone's screen and raised it to his ear.

Dale's world fell to tatters at her feet right as the tornado sirens fell silent outside. In the resounding quiet, she could hear her thoughts all too well.

The one person in this entire world who she knew loved her … didn't love her enough. In the end, like he always had, he'd chosen Travis over her.

Her mother went up to Cross, took his phone, and ended the call.

"Mom—" Cross started, sobbing, swinging his hot glare to Darlene.

But Darlene's eyes were on Dale as she told her son, "That's enough, Cross. We have to help your sister."

Dale clamped her hand over her mouth to hold in her whimpers.

Her mother looked past Dale. Dale turned to follow her gaze. Barty had stood to lean against the island, his clothes covered in black grit, his face cut in a hundred tiny spots. Blood like tears welled up and trickled down his ashen skin.

Darlene said the strangest words Dale had ever heard.

"Hello, Bartholomew."

Barty dipped his head in greeting and mumbled weakly, "Darlene. Good to see you again."

A scream floated to them from across the Seam.

Loey.

CHAPTER 31

JERONIMO LAY DEAD ON THE ground across the Seam. Loey screamed.

A girl in a white top and trousers cupped his face in her hands. Black veins threaded across every inch of her skin not covered by her clothes. She pressed her black-soot mouth to his forehead.

But he couldn't be dead. Not yet. Not ever.

Loey ran to the girl kissing Jeronimo's still body. As Loey closed the short distance between the tear and them, she saw that the girl wasn't a girl. Loey could see the ground straight through her body.

The ghost looked up, her eyes like black coals. With a hiss, she shrank back. Loey fell beside Jeronimo and braced her arms protectively around his body. He wasn't breathing. She pressed her hand to his heart and felt nothing. Her fingers slid up to his neck, searching for a pulse that wasn't there.

"No," Loey whispered.

The ghost let out a soft cry.

On his forehead, shadows swirled out from the ghost's kiss. Like tendrils of smoke, they swept down his face and slipped between his lips.

His chest expanded. Agonizing seconds later, he drew in another breath. The motion faint but there.

Loey's gaze jerked up to the ghost girl. "Frankie?"

"Loey, don't go near her!" Dale shouted behind them, near the tatter. "She'll hurt you!"

With her hands still on Jeronimo, Loey glanced over her shoulder. Dale was across the Seam, her cheeks streaked with tears. She was pointing at Frankie with one hand, her other arm wrapped around her waist like she was holding herself together. At the tatter, Barty tried to cross back over.

Jeronimo groaned. Fresh blood dripped beneath his nose.

Loey threw up her hand toward Barty. "Don't come any closer! You're hurting him!"

Barty froze. Everyone froze.

"We have to get him out of here! Dale, help me!"

"Frankie will help him," Barty said in a wavering voice.

"How can you know that?" Loey snapped back.

His eyes were heart-wrenchingly sad as he answered with the faintest shrug he must have learned from his brother, "Because she always loved him more."

"Lo."

The wheezed word had her bowing back over Jeronimo's body. Hearing him too, Frankie surged closer, her feet hovering above the ground.

Blood seeped between Jeronimo's parted lips. He tried to say her name again but only made blood bubbles.

"Don't think because I keep having to kneel over you and beg you to stay alive," Loey growled, trembling all over, "that I'm not mad at you for stealing my grandmother's book."

Blood poured from his nose into his mouth, and he choked on it. Loey tilted his head up so he could talk.

"You have to go after him," he managed. His voice carried in the silence. "Leave me over here."

What little fight she pretended to have left her in a rush. "I can't."

"Come on, Loey," Dale said from the tatter. "Barty can't come back across the Seam—Frankie is trying to kill him—and Jeronimo can't be in the real world with Barty. Jeronimo has to stay for now."

"Absolutely not. There's no way he's—"

"Barty will die if he stays over here! Is he all you care about? Can you not make this one concession until everyone gets their strength back? We have a monster on the loose in town. We have bigger problems than whether your boyfriend is on the right side of the Seam to kiss you goodnight."

"She's right," Jeronimo breathed out. He looked up at Loey, the effort to move his head taking its toll. The blood from his nose stained his shirt as if he'd been stabbed in the gut.

"J ..."

"I did it."

Loey dipped her chin once. "I thought I had it figured out the morning you left. Matt called that afternoon with the body's identification, and I knew I was right."

Jeronimo's gaze slid to Frankie. She hovered nearby, her hands clutched to her chest. She offered him a small smile.

"I killed you," he told her.

Frankie nodded, but she was still smiling.

"But you were already dying, weren't you?" Loey asked the ghost.

Frankie opened her mouth, and her voice came out like a whisper of bells in the wind, similar to the ones Loey had heard on Shiner's Ridge. "He followed me that day. He caught up to me at the creek. For hours, he ... he hurt me. Tried to make me tell him the still's location. I didn't know I could bleed that much. It hurt so bad."

"You never gave us up," Jeronimo said, his eyes transfixed. He stared at Frankie like it was 1956 and they were the only two people in the world.

Frankie had begun to fade, her body more transparent. Loey had to strain to hear her speak again. "I didn't. I wouldn't. Not ever. Not even at the end when I knew I was dead."

"Jeronimo found you," Loey said. Frankie faded until she was more light than girl. "With the revenuer. He killed Thomas Wooten with his knife and hid the body in the cave. Then he came back for you."

Frankie's face was outlined enough for Loey to see how she smiled down at Jeronimo, her love brightening her eyes to two obsidian gems.

"It hurt so bad," she said, her voice carrying on the tiniest breath of wind. "Jeronimo helped me so I could go on my terms, in a way that didn't belong to no revenuer. You're a good man, Jeronimo James."

As the last of her voice faded into nothing, Jeronimo's face twisted in anguish. Tears leaked from his clenched eyes. He let out a keening sound, long and low and full of such sorrow that Loey stood and stepped away from him, giving him space as he fractured right there on the ground. The memories of that night flooded back, and Loey watched the damage they dealt. He pressed his hands to his face and roared into them.

Only a hovering light remained of Frankie.

To the light, Loey said, "Keep him safe. I'll be back."

The light swept over Jeronimo and stayed.

Loey turned her back to them while she still could. It was Gran's voice in her ear that told her to put one foot in front of the other. Loey walked back to Dale, who held out her hand beside the tatter, her other hand wrapped around the lights, worried they might disappear.

Dale took Loey's hand and climbed back through first. Loey followed, letting Dale haul her across the Seam.

"Knot it back." They stood in her kitchen, shadows streaming over their skin.

288

Dale's kitchen looked like a murder scene. With Cross holding Travis's body to his chest and whispering to him, it was. Darlene and Tabi murmured to each other in quiet conversation at the island. Through it all, Barty watched her, his eyes wide and sorrowful, his sadness matching hers beat for beat from two broken hearts.

"Loey," Dale said to get her friend's attention, "knot it back."

"But if we leave it open—"

"Put it back. Other things will come out."

The Seam's tatter, the one Jeronimo had conjured with symbols and a candle, pulsed with dying light that faded as Frankie had faded. Looking at the threads, their flickering lights blocking the sight of Jeronimo and Frankie across the Seam, Loey wavered.

She'd left her heart across the Seam instead of her soul, and she would trade anything, even this entire town, to have him back. Without him, she was hollow.

Instead, a ghost of a girl he'd once loved was with him.

"They're stronger over there because of Frankie," Dale was telling her. "They'll get out. *Close the damn tear.*"

Loey sniffed. She felt so small, so cold. But Dale was right. The Skinned Man was loose, and as much as it tore every thread in her body, Loey had to leave Jeronimo across the Seam. With shaking hands, she tied the lights back together.

She'd no sooner finished than the tatter's lights blinked out. She turned back to face Dale and everyone else. It was Barty's eyes she found first. He offered her a crooked smile, the sad one, so similar to his brother's.

"He'll be okay," he told her. "Jeronimo's always been good at surviving."

Outside, rain pelted the ground in unrelenting sheets. Beads of shattered glass caught the bits of sunlight peeking through the storm clouds. Her grandmother's book lay on the counter, undisturbed in the chaos, still opened to the page Jeronimo had used. She picked it up and held it to her chest.

One foot in front of the other.

Holding the book and her gran's voice to her chest, Loey faced what awaited her. Her eyes on Travis, she asked those gathered in the room, "What are we going to do about him?"

"What the hell is that supposed to mean?" Cross's arms tightened around the man no one and everyone knew he loved.

"Put him at the base of the back porch stairs," Darlene said in a clear voice that cut through all the chaos wreaked upon such a small space over such a short time. "Everyone knows he's been drinking. The sirens scared him, and he fell through the glass door and down the steps. An accident, that's all. Loey, Dale, Bartholomew, get in Tabi's car. She'll take you to Loey's farm. You three can't be seen around here. I'll stay with Cross. We'll call in Travis's body."

"I won't," Cross murmured, his body curled over Travis's. "I won't."

Dale's face pinched at the sight of her brother holding her husband's body. Loey thought her best friend's heart was breaking, but Loey didn't go to Dale or take her hand or tell her it would be okay. Instead, it was Barty who crossed to her best friend and took her in his arms.

"I won't," Cross repeated, a broken man who'd lost the most among them all today. He lifted his face to his mother. "Please."

"It's time to be a man and own who you are," Darlene said in that clear-cut voice. She turned to Loey, saw her cheeks wet with tears, and commanded, "Get yourself together. You have a monster to catch. Go before it's too late."

CHAPTER 32

SEPTEMBER 23, 2018

DALE FELT LIKE SHE WAS swimming to Little Cricket Trailer Park. Already high on downers, her blood slogged, and time moved in slow motion.

Outside, the world passed her by from Taylor Neely's passenger seat, her forehead pressed against the glass. She didn't care if anyone from town saw her in his truck. He was a gravedigger for the cemetery; disreputable company to associate with based on the job title alone, especially for a Rose. He also ran pills for his mother on the side, which was why he was number two on Dale's speed dial, right beneath Loey's number.

Loey, who'd called her early this morning, before the sun had risen.

We did a bad thing. It's time to make it right. It's killing me, Dale. It has to be killing you too. Doesn't it keep you up at night?

It was killing Dale, and it did keep her up at night.

Loey was going to tell the truth, and there was nothing Dale could do to stop her. Honestly, she didn't know if she cared to try anymore. Right then, there wasn't a thing in this world she could think to care about.

Taylor's truck bounced over Little Cricket Creek's bridge. He turned at a rotted sign that read "Little Cricket Trailer Park" in peeling green paint. Dale was minutes away from

293

salvation, her version of Sunday prayers, and it couldn't come soon enough.

Her thoughts sank away from Loey and Folton and lies. They turned to something darker, something worse.

She hadn't seen him in days, her mirror empty for the first time since she could remember. Dale didn't want to say she missed him because that would make her crazier than she already was for making up a man who lived in her mirror. But she did. He'd been the only thing she could count on since she was seventeen.

Even her imaginary friends left her.

"I need help," she whispered to her reflection in the truck's window.

"Huh?" Taylor asked, chewing tobacco on his breath. He spat a thick brown glob of it into a Mountain Dew bottle.

"Nothing. It's nothing."

"Momma'll get you fixed up. Don't worry about it. You don't have to pay if you don't wanna." His hand went to her thigh and squeezed.

She took his hand, gently, and she heard his breathing hitch with excitement.

"Touch me again," she purred, "and I'll kill you."

He must have believed her. He didn't bother her again. At his mother's trailer, Dale stumbled out of the truck and fell onto the patchy ground. An ugly dog yapped at her from beneath the tree it was chained to.

The front door of the trailer opened, and Ms. Neely appeared. She wore a skirt too short for her coltish legs. Her top hung off one bony shoulder, her gray hair twisted into a thick braid that fell over her breast that the too-large shirt left nearly bare. She smiled down at Dale. She was missing a tooth.

Taylor helped Dale onto the porch and presented her to his mother like she was a prize piece of meat.

Ms. Neely touched Dale's cheek. "We'll get you what you need, Dale Rose. Don't you worry 'bout a thing."

"Thanks," Dale mumbled, her vision slanting.

Ms. Neely held out her hand. On her palm, a symbol was drawn in what looked like soot. Dale took it without thinking, already forgetting about the odd symbol, even as she felt its heat against her palm. Ms. Neely twined her fingers through Dale's like they were two schoolyard girls prancing across the playground.

"Follow me, pretty girl."

Ms. Neely led her to the bathroom. Dale sat on the bathtub as the older woman mashed together pills. With the concoction mixed, she licked her finger and swiped it over the fine powders. She extended it to Dale.

Dale opened her mouth and closed her lips around Ms. Neely's finger. The powder coated her tongue like answered prayers, and Dale closed her eyes in gratitude. She smiled.

"Good girl," Ms. Neely said. "That'll set you right."

The bathroom door closed behind her, and Dale was alone. Her body was liquid, her bones hollow. She slumped onto the floor. Cheek pressed to the cold tiles, she closed her eyes, ready to fade into perfect oblivion.

Right before she went under, vibrations wove through the cramped room.

She opened her eyes.

Above the sink, the mirror knocked once against the wall.

She smiled against the tiled floor. He hadn't left her after all. Her heart soared higher and higher and higher until it couldn't go no higher. Her heart beat against the floor hard enough to make her body jolt. Darkness tugged at her legs, dragging her into an oblivion far more permanent than she desired.

Against the tiles, her cheek turned wet with tears. She was scared. She didn't want to die, but she couldn't move and she couldn't breathe and her heart felt like it might crack out of her chest.

The mirror called down to her again. She cut her eyes upward, unable to lift her head. He was in the reflection, watching her. In his eyes, she saw her fear echoed. His hand pressed against the glass from his side. If she hadn't been busy dying, she would have put her hand against his.

Hold on, his eyes begged.

She'd kept her promise to him for as long as she could. She'd always liked being the hero.

CHAPTER 33

THE SUN SET ON THE worst day of Dale's life.

Everyone else was inside, arguing about what to do next. Mainly, it was Tabi and Barty. Tabi with her constant stream of questions, and Barty with his incessant demand to drag himself up the ridge and fight the Skinned Man even though he couldn't hold himself up without help. Then there was Loey, who sat at her breakfast table, bloody feathers in her hands. When Barty had put his arm around her to comfort her, Dale had had enough. She'd gone outside.

She looked up toward Shiner's Ridge. The hundreds of acres of dense woods could hide all sorts of things. Right now, it held a monster. They knew he'd come this way because he had strewn Loey's precious chickens, the ones her gran had called the Golden Girls, across the back pasture. Dewey whined at Dale's feet, his nose twitching whenever the wind blew, smelling their scattered blood.

The sun gave up and sank behind the ridge. The light turned scarlet in mourning, trickling down the ridge like blood. Far away, down the valley, the storm rumbled with thunder. The air tasted like rain. Up on the ridge, an animal let out a piercing scream that died away into silence.

The screen door opened. High heels clacked across the porch planks. Each step shattered the bit of peace Dale had

Shocking Dale completely, Darlene sat on the stairs beside her without swiping away the dirt.

Dale gave her mother a cautious glance. Darlene didn't yell at her, and Dale asked, "How did it go with Travis?"

"Your brother is a mess, but I think Matt bought the story. There was so much happening with the storm that I don't think he had much time to think it through."

Dale swallowed the lump in her throat. "Cross hates me."

Her mother studied something far off in the pasture. "Your brother loved that man very much."

"You knew this entire time?"

Darlene made a very unladylike snorting sound in the back of her throat. "I'm your mother. Of course I knew."

Dale blinked at her, processing the words. Finally, she shook her head in wonder. "You're a raging hypocrite, you know that?"

"I do." Darlene gazed up at Shiner's Ridge like she was thinking about what was up there too.

Dale couldn't take her eyes off her mother. This woman was a stranger. "Are you okay?"

Unlike the night in the car outside the CVS, Darlene looked at her daughter and asked, "Are you?"

"No," Dale whispered, on the verge of cracking wide apart.

For the first time in so long that Dale couldn't remember the last time it had occurred, her mother took her hand. At first, the touch was gentle, then it turned crushing. Dale whimpered, but this was more familiar territory.

"Listen to me. Are you listening?" Darlene asked with an urgency that unnerved Dale.

"Yes, ma'am," Dale murmured.

"You can hate me, it's fine. You probably should."

That wasn't what Dale had expected. "What—"

"No, now listen. I mean it." Darlene waited until Dale

had nodded before continuing. "I set out on a path to raise you differently from the way my mother raised me. Being my mother's daughter was not easy, as I imagine being my daughter has not been easy for you. To my mother, if you were not gin or that man in her damn mirror, you were a ghost she looked right through. So forgive me if I made you of impenetrable steel, but I did not want you to be raised a ghost. We Rose women are cursed by the man in our mirror. He will haunt us until our violent ends. Most of us welcome him into our hearts with a smile. I did not want that for myself. I did not want that for you. No man, alive or a reflection, should have such easy passage into the good graces of a strong Southern woman. A man should earn his place by our side, and that man in your mirror has earned nothing, but we give him everything. We give and give and give, and we're all ghosts, Dale. These men keep looking through us until we fade into ghosts that follow them around."

Dale cried, but her mother didn't wipe her tears away like a mother should. Instead, she watched Dale's tears spill with hard eyes and a mouth wrinkled from frowning. She was still holding Dale's hand, though, and her grip didn't hurt so much anymore.

"I feel like a ghost," Dale confessed.

"To him," her mother confessed in return, using a quieter voice like Barty might hear them from inside the house, "you always will be."

"But I love him, Mommy."

For a heart-rending moment, her mother looked like she might pull Dale to her side, wrap her arms around her daughter, and comfort her, perhaps rock back and forth with Dale's head on her shoulder. Listening to Dale's crying, her mother would tell her everything would be okay, that Dale was loved, that she was not the reason a scared young man had died today before he could live freely as himself, that her brother did not hate her for her role in crushing that freedom beneath her heel.

Her mother did none of these things.

She sighed, a mighty, tired sound. "I know you love him. We all did at some point. But I can promise you one thing. As a Rose, that love will get you killed."

OTHER BOOKS BY MEG COLLETT

THE RIGHTEOUS SERIES
Bless Her Dead Heart
Bless His Cursed Soul

FEAR UNIVERSITY SERIES
Fear University
The Killing Season
Monster Mine
Paper Tigers
Dead Man's Stitch

CANAAN ISLAND NOVELS
Fakers
Keepers
Hiders

END OF DAYS TRILOGY
The Hunted One
The Lost One
The Only One
Days of New (An End of Days Serial Collection)

WHITEBIRD CHRONICLES
Lux and Lies

ABOUT THE AUTHOR

MEG COLLETT is from the hills of Tennessee where the cell phone service is a blessing and functioning internet is a myth of epic proportions. She's the author of the bestselling Fear University series, the End of Days trilogy, and the Canaan Island novels. Find out more at her website www.megcollett. com.

ENJOYED BLESS HIS CURSED SOUL?
Please consider leaving a review!